Praise for Ellen Hart
and her Jane Lawless series

Hallowed Murder

"Hart's crisp, elegant writing and atmosphere [are] reminiscent of the British detective style, but she has a nicer sense of character, confrontation, and sparsely utilized violence. . . . *Hallowed Murder* is as valuable for its mainstream influences as for its sexual politics."
—*Mystery Scene*

Vital Lies

"This compelling whodunit has the psychological maze of a Barbara Vine mystery and the feel of Agatha Christie. . . . Hart keeps even the most seasoned mystery buff baffled until the end."
—*Publishers Weekly*

Stage Fright

"Hart deftly turns the spotlight on the dusty secrets and shadowy souls of a prominent theatre family. The resulting mystery is worthy of a standing ovation."
—*Alfred Hitchcock Mystery Magazine*

By Ellen Hart
Published by Ballantine Books:

VITAL LIES
HALLOWED MURDER
STAGE FRIGHT
THIS LITTLE PIGGY WENT TO MURDER

THIS LITTLE PIGGY WENT TO MURDER

Ellen Hart

BALLANTINE BOOKS • NEW YORK

Copyright © 1994 by Patricia Boehnhardt

All rights reserved under International and Pan-American Copyright Conventions. Published in the United States of America by Ballantine Books, a division of Random House, Inc., New York, and simultaneously in Canada by Random House of Canada Limited, Toronto.

Library of Congress Catalog Card Number: 94-94417

ISBN 0-345-38189-0

Manufactured in the United States of America

First Edition: December 1994

10 9 8 7 6 5 4

This, too, for Kathy

CAST OF CHARACTERS

SOPHIE GREENWAY: Managing editor of *Squires* magazine; part-time food critic for the *Minneapolis Times Register*; married to Bram Baldric.

AMANDA JORENSEN: Owner of the Gasthaus Rethenau in Duluth; wife of Luther, sister of Jack, mother of Chelsea.

BRAM BALDRIC: Radio talk-show host of WMST in Minneapolis; husband of Sophie Greenway.

LUTHER JORENSEN: Professor of philosophy at University of Minnesota, Duluth; husband of Amanda, father of Chelsea.

LARS OLSON: Ex-chancellor of UMD; business consultant for Grendel Shipping.

HERMAN GRENDEL: Owner of Grendel Shipping; father of Amanda and Jack, grandfather of Chelsea.

JACK GRENDEL: Senatorial candidate for U.S. Congress; brother of Amanda, son of Herman, husband of Nora.

NORA GRENDEL: Wife of Jack Grendel.

CLAIRE VAN DORN: Headmistress at the Tate Academy; assisted Amanda with the renovation of the Gasthaus Rethenau; author of a new book of children's poetry.

CHELSEA JORENSEN: Daughter of Luther and Amanda, niece of Jack; works directly under her grandfather, Herman Grendel, at Grendel Shipping.

RYAN WOODTHORPE: President of North Shore Coalition for a Better Environment; speechwriter for Jack; lives with Jenny.

JENNY TREMLET: Runs a day-care center out of the cottage at Brule's Landing; lives with Ryan.

SYDNEY SHERWIN: Vietnam war buddy of Jack's and Luther's.

JOHN WARDLAW: Detective, Duluth Police Department.

ALICE OAG: The Jorensens' cook and part-time maid.

PART ONE

This Little Piggy Went to Market

There ne'er were such thousands of leaves on a
tree,
Nor of people in church or the Park,
As the crowds of the stars that looked down
upon me,
And that glittered and winked in the
dark.
                    from *A Child's Garden of Verses*
                    Robert Louis Stevenson

1

The gravel against his face woke him. Tiny jagged rocks cut sharply into his soft cheek. As he tried to twist himself into a sitting position, something scratchy grabbed at his neck. My God, he thought, his mind grasping at consciousness: a rope!

He gave himself a minute before rolling over onto his side and looking up at the stars. Where was he? The tape across his mouth pulled at the coarse hairs in his mustache. Lights bobbed and dipped in a strange pattern above him. This must be a nightmare! He closed his eyes, trying to control his growing panic. Behind his back, his arms throbbed. The rope around his hands was beginning to cut off circulation.

What on earth had happened? He dimly remembered a bar somewhere. That was it. He'd waited and waited. Too many gin and tonics. He'd gotten into that car and . . . then what? He shook his head to clear his memory. Sure. He recalled it now. That last drink on the way into town. An open bottle in the car. And then, this strange feeling of weakness came over him. But when was that? His mind struggled to make sense of each new fragment.

Straining to look around, he heard the familiar sound of an ore boat blasting its horn into the late summer night. The Aerial Lift Bridge! Why had someone brought him to Canal Park? The smell of popcorn and newly mowed grass slowly reached his consciousness. Fireworks began to explode in vivid colors across the night sky. The bridgeman, responding to the call from the boat, repeated the same horn pattern. Seconds later, the whir of traffic above him

3

ceased. The bridge was being cleared of cars. How many times had he driven over that same bridge himself out to his home on Park Point? A comforting sense of the familiar calmed him as he lay quietly, looking up at the huge, metal girders. Seconds later, the bridge began to lift. The rough hemp rope around his neck tightened.

Out on the water, the ore boat glided swiftly into the canal as people gathered along the sides of the channel to wave and shout goodbyes. Fireworks cast an eerie staccato brightness on the boatmen standing on deck.

No one noticed the doll-like figure dancing and twisting alone under the bridge. As the figure grew still, the bridge began its descent until the now-slack body came to rest once again on graveled ground. With one last blast of its horn, the immense ship slipped out of the canal and into the vast darkness of Lake Superior. It was the last boat scheduled to leave Duluth before morning.

PART TWO

This Little Piggy Stayed Home

When I am grown to man's estate
I shall be very proud and great.
And tell the other girls and boys
Not to meddle with my toys.
　　　　　　　from *A Child's Garden of Verses*
　　　　　　　Robert Louis Stevenson

2

Sophie stood alone in the dark entrance to the Gasthaus Rethenau. It was nearly noon. The blond wig and false beard she was wearing felt somewhat ridiculous in such familiar surroundings. Still, it was going to be a great joke. Normally, she wore her disguises only in the evenings, but this was too delicious to pass up. Somewhere inside the building she could hear a small orchestra practicing what sounded like a Thirties fox-trot. For a moment, she had the distinct sensation of stepping back in time.

"Can I help you?" asked a young man emerging from the coatroom.

"Indeed you can," said Sophie, in her deepest register. She was glad that, even under normal circumstances, hers was a throaty voice. "I'm looking for Amanda Jorensen."

"She's in the main dining room."

"Ah." Adjusting her silk tie, Sophie glanced at a series of recently acquired antique beer steins displayed on a ledge behind the front counter. Nice. "Where's that music coming from? I feel as if I've just walked into a Fred Astaire movie."

The man laughed. "It's a small orchestra Mrs. Jorensen hired to play at the opening tonight. They're practicing downstairs in one of the banquet rooms."

"Of course. Well, is it all right if I just go in?" She nodded to the wide double doors.

"Sure. I think she's doing some paperwork."

Sophie smiled her thanks and moved across the foyer, past the ornately decorated bar, into a huge oak-paneled room. She'd always found the dining room of the Gasthaus

Rethenau rather daunting, as if the builder had misunderstood the reason for the room, and instead of creating a comfortable space in which to eat a well-prepared meal, he'd built a stage set for a Wagnerian opera. Dark. Germanic. Squarely and a bit too heroically proportioned. Along the far wall, a series of arched windows allowed a magnificent view of Lake Superior. Except for an attractive, casually dressed woman seated at a table in the back, the room was empty.

Amanda looked up from a stack of papers. "Yes? Can I help you?"

"I understand you make wonderful bratwurst sandwiches." Sophie made herself comfortable at a table several feet away. "I've come to try one."

Amanda stood. "Excuse me. Perhaps you didn't see the sign. We aren't open for business right now. We've been doing some rather extensive remodeling. The grand reopening is tonight. Tomorrow," she said, emphasizing the word with great patience, "we would be glad to let you sample some of our famous bratwurst."

Sophie remained implacable. She tugged on her French cuffs and looked grim. "You have *no* bratwurst available?"

"Not today."

"This is outrageous. I've traveled all the way from Minneapolis to have lunch in your establishment."

"I'm terribly sorry. Perhaps tomorrow . . ."

Sophie stroked her beard and appeared to consider the issue. "I'd even be willing to prepare it myself." She stood, narrowing one eye at the kitchen doorway. "After all, Sophie Greenway told me you'd treat me impeccably."

"Sophie? You're a friend of hers?"

"Old pals. We both worked in the circus when we were younger."

Amanda raised an eyebrow. "Sophie never worked in a circus."

"She didn't?"

"No."

"Pity. She's so good with makeup. Disguises. You know." She smoothed an eyebrow. "I'm sure that's what makes her such a successful restaurant reviewer. No one knows when she's coming—and she never looks the same twice. I'm told she rather enjoys her flamboyant reputation."

Amanda's mouth nearly dropped open. "Who?" She moved closer. "Sophie? Is that you?"

"Are you insinuating your old friend has sprouted whiskers?" Sophie pulled off the beard and mustache and grinned.

"You crazy idiot!" Amanda threw her arms around Sophie. "I don't believe it. I thought you weren't going to be able to come!"

"I'm sorry I didn't call," said Sophie, settling herself at Amanda's table and loosening her tie. "Bram just got word late last night that they'd found a replacement for him at the station. We simply got up this morning and jumped in the car—and here we are." She pulled off the wig and shook out her short, strawberry blonde hair.

"I'm absolutely delighted!" beamed Amanda. "I'd made my peace with the fact that you weren't going to make it for the reopening." She glanced curiously at the empty doorway. "Speaking of Bram, where is that lump of a husband of yours?"

Sophie groaned. "He didn't have a chance to get his tux pressed before we left Minneapolis, so he's scouting the area for a while-you-wait dry cleaner."

"Good luck. You know, Luther might have something he can borrow."

"Bram fit into something of Luther's? Amanda, I think restaurant renovation has taken a bigger toll on your psyche than you realize."

Amanda laughed, sitting down and reaching for Sophie's hand. "God, it's good to see you again. What's it been? Four, five months?"

"Since I started as managing editor of *Squires*. I haven't had a minute."

"And you still like the glamorous world of magazine publishing?"

"Forget the glamour—but yes, I absolutely love it. It's what I've been working toward for the last fifteen years."

"I'm curious. They don't mind your strange sideline?" She nodded to Sophie's tweed jacket.

"On the contrary. It's given me a great deal of visibility. Actually, several articles have recently been written about my method of reviewing restaurants. Even though *Squires* deals primarily with the arts, it has an intellectual, almost scholarly reputation. I think they feel my presence adds a certain *joie de vivre*."

Amanda nodded. "You're lucky."

"Listen," continued Sophie, making herself a little more comfortable in the high-backed, wooden chair, "Bram's got a deadline on that book he's writing. You know, the science-fiction thriller for which he intends to win the Pulitzer."

"I can't wait," mumbled Amanda.

"Anyway, we'd love to stay with you and Luther out at Brule House tonight and attend the celebration here in Duluth, but tomorrow we're planning to head farther up the shore. We called about renting a cabin. Bram feels he needs the solitude so he can concentrate on his manuscript."

Amanda wrinkled her nose. "You mean you aren't staying the week?" She slipped her glasses back on and studied Sophie for a moment. "Will you at least consider this: what if Bram worked in Luther's study? He could have all the peace and quiet he wanted. Luther certainly wouldn't mind. And you know how much that husband of yours loves Alice's cooking."

"I don't know," said Sophie, trying not to sound overly confident. Bram was sometimes a bit of a poop when it came to last-minute changes of plan. "I suppose we could discuss it."

"Good. Then it's settled."

Sophie wasn't so positive, but for now, she let the subject drop. As they continued to talk, she let her eyes travel around the newly renovated dining room. Three years ago, Amanda had found a sheaf of publicity photographs taken of the Gasthaus Rethenau in 1923, the year her maternal grandfather first opened the doors. Ever since then, she'd been wanting to get rid of every trace of modernization that had turned the dark Bavarian-inspired den of the Twenties into the trendy mauve-and-gray greenhouse of the Nineties. By the looks of the room, she had done a faithful job. She'd even resurrected the original oak tables and chairs from a downstairs storage room and had them repaired.

Sophie had to admit that the result was amazing. She felt she was sitting in a faithfully preserved nook of pre–World War II Europe. Even the artwork looked authentic. In front of the newly restored floor-to-ceiling mural of the Black Forest, Amanda had found someone to construct a raised platform big enough to accommodate a small orchestra. In front of that, tables had been cleared away for the dance floor.

Amanda had taken over the management of the restaurant in 1978, the year her mother died. There had never been any question of selling. The restaurant was too much a part of her family history.

"By the way," said Sophie, "how is Luther? Your last report hinted that he wasn't feeling so well."

Amanda tugged on her hoop earrings. Her quiet brown eyes looked tired. "He's on some pretty nasty medication right now. It's playing havoc with his digestion. As you'll soon see, he's lost weight. Listen, do me a favor. Luther doesn't like to discuss it, so don't—"

"Did you see the Duluth paper this morning?" The inquiry emanated from the kitchen doorway. In the now uncarpeted hall, the deep voice almost created echoes. "You should call your father right away." A thin, impeccably dressed bearded man entered, a newspaper tucked under one arm. "Sophie! I don't believe it." Walking briskly across the room, Luther bent down and gave her a kiss. With an inquisitive twist of his head, he pulled back and eyed her clothing. "Is that what women are wearing these days in the big city?" He felt the expensive material and smirked.

"If you're a good boy, I may let you borrow it." Sophie was glad Amanda had warned her about her husband's ap-

pearance. She'd always considered Luther Jorensen an extremely elegant man. Tall. Professorial. With a dark, beautifully somber face. Yet never before had she seen him so
gaunt. Even his beard couldn't hide the hollowness in his
cheeks. She gazed up into his intense blue eyes, glad, at
least, that they bore no trace of illness. "Besides, I couldn't
miss the reopening, dear one. I have to keep an eye on you
two, you know." She winked at Amanda.

Luther smiled warmly and sat down across from her. As
always he moved with the grace of a dancer.

"Why should I call my father?" asked Amanda, resuming
the conversation.

Sophie pulled the newspaper across the table and read
the headline out loud. "Ex-Chancellor of UMD Found
Dead Under Aerial Lift Bridge."

"How awful!" cried Amanda. "Read the rest of it. How
did it happen?"

"I'll save you the trouble," said Luther. He reached inside his coat pocket for a cigarette. "Lars Olson was
hanged from the lift bridge last night around midnight.
Someone tied him up, gagged him, and then tied a rope to
the bridge. When it lifted—" He paused to light up. "You
get the picture."

Amanda stared at the files in front of her, her face a
mask of confusion. "That's hideous. I wonder if Jack
knows."

"Jack?" repeated Luther. "What would your brother
care? It's your father who needs to know."

"What does Olson's death have to do with your dad?"
asked Sophie. She'd known Amanda's father for over forty
years. He and her own father had been fast friends since
college.

"Herman hired him as a consultant for his shipping company last year," answered Luther. "Olson had just resigned
from the university. I must say, there was no weeping or
gnashing of teeth in the philosophy department over his departure. Actually, we had a celebration." He grabbed an
empty ashtray off another table. "It was the least we could
do."

Sophie continued with the article. "It says here the man who found the body also found a note in his shirt pocket. The police aren't certain it had anything to do with his murder."

"I see," said Amanda, her voice oddly expressionless. "Does it mention what the note said?"

"This little piggy went to market," quoted Luther. "Kind of an apt little phrase, don't you think? After all, Lars resigned from the university to go make his fortune as a business consultant for Grendel Shipping. And, from personal experience, I can assure you he *was* a pig."

"Don't be a ghoul!" Amanda played nervously with the fine blonde tuft that had escaped from her braided bun. "The man is dead. Leave it alone."

A loud crash drew their attention to the dining room entrance where an elderly man in an electric wheelchair careened into the room. He'd somehow managed to knock over a porcelain statue next to the front door. Several shards were resting precariously in his lap. He came to a stop just inside the room, mutely glaring at them.

"Father!" said Amanda, clearly surprised.

"To what do we owe this unannounced visitation?" asked Luther.

Herman Grendel surveyed the room suspiciously, his gaze coming to rest on Sophie. "Sophia," he mumbled. "Didn't know you were in town." He didn't seem to notice her bizarre fashion statement.

After all these years, Sophie was accustomed to Herman's inexplicable mispronunciation of her given name. "Bram and I came up for the reopening," she explained. "I intend to do an article on it for the *Minneapolis Times Register*. And how are you, Herman? You look well."

"I'm old, Sophia. Tell that father of yours to get on the horn and give me a call. He's still alive, isn't he?"

"Last mother checked, he still had a pulse. I'll give him your message."

Herman harrumphed. "A man his age should retire."

"But you haven't." Sophie tried hard not to grit her teeth.

From her point of view, Herman Grendel had always been opinionated, supercritical, and arrogant.

"Father?" said Amanda, her voice soothing. "Are you coming to the celebration tonight?"

"No. I'm here now." He glanced quickly around the room. "Seems okay."

Amanda shot Sophie an amused look. So much for honeyed compliments.

"I've never had much interest in this place," grumped Herman. "You know that. Your mother brought it with her into the marriage. If it'd been up to me, we would've sold it for scrap long ago."

"Cut to the chase," said Luther under his breath.

Amanda threw her husband a cautionary look. She stood and made a move toward a coffeepot that nestled on a warming plate next to the table.

"Sit down," ordered Herman. "I've come to talk to you and I want your undivided attention."

Amanda stiffened, but caught herself and said, "Of course, Father." She cleared her throat. "Both Luther and I were so sorry to hear about Lars Olson's death last night."

Herman appeared momentarily confused. The expression swiftly turned to anger. "You think I don't know what you and your weasel brother have been up to? I wouldn't be at all surprised to find that one of you was behind Olson's death."

"That's a horrible thing to say!"

"Daddy, please." Luther's voice dripped sweetness. "We have a guest."

"Sophia's no guest!" Herman glared at Luther, then tugged at the top button of his wool sweater. He'd lost weight in the last year. Nothing fit him properly anymore. "There's something funny going on around here. I can smell it. You tell Jack that all deals are off. You got that? Tell him he'd better tread carefully. It's tit for tat, as far as I can see, and you both know what I mean by *that*." He rolled his wheelchair menacingly in front of her. "And add one thing. Tell him I'm withdrawing my financial support from his senatorial campaign as of this minute."

Luther began to laugh. "It's always some pathetic play for control, isn't it, Herm? You're not happy unless everyone else *isn't*. Well"—he leaned over and put his arm protectively around Amanda's shoulder—"if you came here to threaten Jack with that, it suggests your stroke affected your mind after all. I must say, I always suspected it."

Herman narrowed one eye and backed up the wheelchair slightly. "For a man who prides himself on having a quick intellect, you're a remarkable dunce, Luther. You may not be interested in my money, but look at your wife. If a drooling old man can see the flicker of fear in her eyes, why can't you?"

For a split second, Luther registered surprise.

"Father," said Amanda, her voice perfectly calm, "I think we should talk about this . . . privately."

"No more talk. As far as I'm concerned, Jack better watch his step. Give him that message when you see him." He snapped his slack lips together and ran a shaky hand over his bald head. "I suppose I don't need to remind you that I'm leaving everything to Chelsea when I die. She's the net worth of your hopeless and nearly fruitless union." He raised an eyebrow at Luther. "Are you sure she's really yours, my boy? She doesn't resemble you one iota." He glanced back at Amanda. "Chelsea has been at my side for nearly four years now and I've taught her well. I probably don't need to mention that she loathes both of you."

Sophie noticed a small shudder pass through Amanda's body. She felt terribly sorry for her old friend. Herman was a master at probing the most delicate, carefully protected nerve. She wanted to tell him to knock it off, to take his bitter opinions and leave, but knew it wasn't her place. Besides, there was obviously more going on here than simple family strife.

"Chelsea's going to make something of herself," continued Herman. He yanked at the lever of his wheelchair and nearly backed over a potted plant. He seemed oblivious to his comically erratic inability to control the machine. "She's a fighter. Lucky for her she never bought any of your empty liberal values. You're out of date, Amanda dear. The youth of this country see right through that feminist crap. How I could have raised two children so unlike me, I'll never know. You and your women's libber yammering and your brother's high-toned environmentalist claptrap have finally convinced me that neither of you is worth a bowl of warm spit. Let Jack's conservation cronies support him. If they're lucky, they might cough up enough money to buy him a bus ticket back to the statehouse." His last statement struck him as particularly funny, and he began to giggle.

Luther held on tightly to Amanda as Herman bumped his way out of the dining room.

Sophie watched from her own corner of the table, glad that the wooden chairs were already antiques. A few more nicks here and there would hardly be noticed.

"I'm sorry you had to hear that," Luther said with more than a hint of disgust in his voice. "Since his stroke last year, his characteristic bombast has gotten even worse." He glanced at Amanda. "One might almost say he's become a distillation of his former self."

"Oh, shut up," said Amanda, breaking free of his grip. She rose and moved over to the windows, silently watching an ore boat drift toward the horizon. "I have to call Jack."

"Jack will find out soon enough," said Luther. "He and Nora will be here tonight. And besides, I don't give a good goddamn about that old man's money. Neither does your brother. And neither should you. Come on, Amanda—we're hardly candidates for the poorhouse."

"You're a fool."

He studied her profile. "What is it? What's got you so damned upset?"

Amanda turned, forcing herself to smile. "I just need to make a short phone call. If you'll both excuse me, I'll be right back." She crossed to the entrance and headed down the hall to her office.

Sophie found herself shuddering at the entire interaction. So much for marital bliss.

Luther stared at the empty doorway for a moment and then took out another cigarette, lighting it absently from a lighter on the table. He seemed annoyed by his wife's abrupt exit. Remembering Sophie, he turned to her and shrugged. "Sorry. Not a very festive beginning to your vacation with us."

"Luther," she began in a whisper, not wanting to upset him any further, but not wanting him to remain ignorant of her plans either. "Bram and I were hoping to stay with you and Amanda tonight, but tomorrow we'd planned to drive farther up the shore. Bram's writing a book. He needs a quiet place to work."

Luther studied the burning tip of his cigarette. "Doesn't sound like much fun for you."

"I've brought some work, too. And you know me: I'm easily amused. Last week I got this incredible new toy." She reached into her pocket and drew out a small electronic gadget.

"What is it?" he asked, picking it up.

"It's a tiny computer. With it, I can play four-handed bridge all by myself."

"You and your games. I suppose you're loaded down with them." He handed back the computer without much interest.

Sophie watched his eyebrows tighten. She interpreted his expression as disappointment. "Luther, Amanda suggested that I talk to Bram. She thought *you* might be persuaded to let him use your study. I don't want to put you out, but if Bram could work at Brule House, we might be able to stay a bit longer."

Luther tipped some ashes into the ashtray. "Of course he can use my study. If it means keeping you around here for a few extra days, I'd camp out on the shore if I had to." His expression softened. "I'm not complaining, Sophie, but Amanda has been so busy lately. It's been—" He stopped.

"What?" she prompted.

He crushed out the cigarette. "Come on. You didn't come to listen to my troubles."

There was a strange desolation in his voice. Luther was a man who often appeared to be amused by some terribly funny joke no one else had caught. Today, that joke seemed to have escaped him as well.

"You were there for me once when I needed someone pretty desperately," said Sophie. She squeezed his hand. "Come on. What were you going to say?"

He scratched his dark beard and looked down. "Just that . . . I don't know. It's been kind of lonely out at the house. Maybe if you stayed long enough, you could teach me to appreciate crossword puzzles." He looked up and grinned.

She could tell he was embarrassed. He'd always had difficulty talking about himself. Sophie was a bit like that herself sometimes. "I doubt it," she sighed. "A professor of philosophy simply does not have the brainpower to master the necessary nonsense words."

"Ah!" He nodded.

"Lunch!" called Amanda. Her slender, Nordic frame emerged from the doorway waving a menu. "Enough of this doom and gloom. Sophie's here, and it's time to celebrate! I don't know about you two, but I'm starved."

3

"Look at these creases," grumbled Bram, tugging on his badly pressed lapels. "Someone should have warned me about that cleaner. I look like I'm part of an exhibit on Japanese paper folding." He straightened his tie and smoothed back his dark brown hair.

"You look fine," Sophie assured him.

He grunted, eyeing her bare shoulders. "You look pretty fine yourself. I'm glad you decided not to come in disguise tonight. I like the real you much better." His gaze took in her latest purchase: a black, sequined evening dress that worked in perfect contrast to her creamy skin and the short, reddish gold hair that feathered softly around her ears.

Sophie smiled, her eyes carefully examining the now crowded dining room. At least a dozen chandeliers glowed above their heads, bathing the guests in a deep amber light. Against the side wall, a long, linen-covered buffet table was laden with the evening's culinary offerings. Chafing dish after chafing dish was filled with succulent German-style meats and vegetables. The salads and home-baked breads were in the center; and the renowned pastries and tarts were being served from the far end. Everything and everyone in the hall looked so positively grand that Sophie almost imagined that royalty was in attendance. "Do you want to dance? I love this idea of having Thirties-era jazz tonight. It seems sort of . . . decadent. I can almost imagine what it must have felt like to be in Berlin on the eve of World War II."

"Dance?" repeated Bram. "I can barely *walk* in this tux. They must have shrunk it, too."

"Face it, darling. We've both put on a few pounds in the last couple of years."

Bram looked down at his thickening stomach, patting it approvingly. "I'm not getting older. I'm getting better."

"Oh, come on. Except for those sideways creases, you look perfectly spiffy."

"Yeah, well." He closed his eyes and thrust his chin in the air. "What can I say? You married yourself a pistol."

Sophie snorted. "Is that what you are?"

From their first casual meeting eight years earlier, Sophie had found Bram Baldric a thoroughly appealing man. He had a strong, highly expressive face, hair the color of bittersweet chocolate, and an amazing pair of deep green eyes. Most importantly, Bram possessed a restless intelligence. He rarely accepted simple answers or facile solutions. Because of her own somewhat philosophically convoluted past, it was a quality she greatly admired. And then, of course, there was his playfulness and sense of humor. Her parents often remarked that he should have been an actor. Actually, he did bear a striking resemblance to the middle-aged Cary Grant. She couldn't watch *An Affair to Remember* these days and not see her husband. Even the gorgeous voice was remarkably similar. A radio talk show was the perfect job for him. He could be as opinionated and outrageous as he pleased. The public ate it up.

He smiled at her, his eyes twinkling. "I like your new haircut. Short hair suits you." He leaned back and studied her for a moment. "You know, you look a little like my ninth-grade civics teacher."

Sophie tapped her nails impatiently on the tablecloth.

"Don't misunderstand. She was the subject of more than one adolescent fantasy. A sort of sexy Peter Pan."

"Peter Pan? You'll make me swoon with such extravagant compliments."

Bram sipped his Scotch and water. "I suppose I could drag myself over to the dance floor for one little spin. Are you wearing your stilts tonight?"

"Careful, buster. You're treading on dangerous ground." Sophie knew he was referring to her platform shoes. Bram hit the mark at just over six feet two. Sophie was barely five-three. "Look over there," she said, snatching an olive off his plate. "Jack Grendel just arrived. I wonder where Nora is."

"Try looking ten feet above his head. She's usually aloft, pulling the strings."

"Shhh," said Sophie. "Be nice."

"I'm not paid to be nice. I'm paid to be *incisive*." He slapped her hand as she reached for another olive. "When I interviewed Jack last winter—just after the governor appointed him head of the State Environment Board—Nora insisted I go over my questions with her first. Don't you find that a wee bit controlling?"

"No, I don't. So what if his wife wants to take an active part in his career? Admit it. You just don't like her."

"She's like a fingernail being dragged across a blackboard." He tugged at his tight collar.

Jack Grendel floated through the packed room, his blond curls towering over the sea of guests. When he spied Sophie, he made his way straight for her.

Sophie had known Jack and Amanda ever since childhood. Over the years, their two families had spent many summer holidays and vacations together. Sophie liked Jack, though she'd been closer to Amanda. Jack had been a quiet child. Thoughtful, yet not overly sensitive. His insistence on privacy created a certain mystique about him, which, for Sophie, had never entirely faded. Adults had confidence in Jack Grendel. He rarely disappointed anyone. Yet, no one had been more surprised than she when he'd embarked on a political career.

"Ah, if it isn't *Senator* Grendel." Bram smiled. He stood and pumped Jack's hand.

"Hold that thought." Jack grinned, bending over to give Sophie a kiss. He pulled a chair away from another table and sat down.

"So how goes the image wars?" asked Sophie. She was struck by how handsome he looked tonight. He seemed healthy, tanned, even rested.

"Good. But what was it Abraham Lincoln said? If the United States was ever going to be destroyed, it would be by the not-so-noble hordes who sought to live at government expense as officeholders. When I first read that, I thought it extremely cynical. I now know he was speaking the truth." He motioned to a young woman carrying a tray of champagne. "Thanks." He nodded, lifting the slender flute to his lips.

"I understand the polls have you ahead," said Bram.

"I couldn't believe my luck when I heard Heaton had pulled out. Not having to run against a Republican incumbent is going to make all the difference."

"We heard the bad news about your father withdrawing his financial support," said Sophie. "Will that hurt?"

Jack sipped his champagne. "To tell the truth, I've expected it for weeks. Yes, it will hurt, but not as much as he'd like to think. Minnesota leads the country in political sensitivity to environmental issues. If my father wants to remain a dinosaur till the day he dies, that's up to him. My financial backing is solid. It's really the least of my worries." Seeing Sophie's eyebrow arch ever so slightly, he added, "Elections aren't about issues, anyway. They're about personalities. What I *think* is of concern to a very few. Since I happen to be both good-looking and charming"—he winked at Bram—"I have the edge. My opponent resembles an aging, somewhat disheveled Chicago mob boss. It's a pity. But I assure you, as Richard Nixon so eloquently put it, winning is the *thing*. I do have an agenda—perhaps even a revolutionary one—but first I have to win. And I will win."

"Do you give unannounced political speeches at the breakfast table, too?" asked Bram. He popped a meatball into his mouth.

Jack winced. "Touché. I'm even doing it in my sleep. This should be Amanda's night to shine. She's worked awfully hard on the renovation. By the way, where is she? I didn't see her when I came in."

"Bram and I got here about six-thirty. She was back in the kitchen then, talking to the head chef."

"Uhm." Jack took a quick look around. "Will I see you two tomorrow? You're staying at Brule's Landing this trip, right?"

"We are," said Sophie. "Bram's brought some important work with him. I have, too, but I may just take a few days to relax. We thought we might rent a cabin farther up the shore, but Luther's offered his study and Bram's going to give it a try."

Jack nodded his approval. "Good. And you *have* to stay for the big Labor Day picnic on Monday. It's going to be the social and political event of the year!" He grinned broadly. "I'm only a little biased, of course. We're even going to have a pig roast. You have no idea how much I'm looking forward to that. I guarantee it will be a picnic like no other picnic you've ever attended."

"You people really know how to twist arms," said Bram. Sophie was well-acquainted with her husband's subtle sarcasm.

"It's a political asset, I'm told." He finished his champagne in one gulp. "Nora and I will be out for breakfast tomorrow. And I promise: no political speeches until after lunch." He glanced at his watch, his expression registering concern. "I wonder where my wife is? She said she'd meet me here at seven." Several men standing near an ice sculpture caught his eye. "Alas, duty calls. Even if you don't start out a hustler, you quickly become one. See you two tomorrow." He pushed away from the table and was swallowed by the crowd.

Sophie leaned back a little more comfortably and continued to sip her vodka and lime. "He's grown into a very handsome man, hasn't he?"

"Definitely one of the beautiful people," mumbled Bram, stifling a burp.

"Oh, come on. After all, you just compared me to Peter Pan."

Bram tried to hide his amused smile with little success.

The dining room was growing more congested with each passing minute. Sophie spied Luther standing alone near the bar entrance. In the dim, smoky light, his face looked haggard, his eyes hooded and dark. As she watched him, she noticed something in his manner that seemed strangely aloof. It was almost as if he exuded a palpable distaste for the mass of bodies pressed together around him. "Can you amuse yourself for a few minutes while I talk to Luther?"

"I may take another stroll over by the buffet table."

Sophie squeezed his hand. "Save me a meatball." She got up and began to weave through the crowd. Pushing through a wall of people near the front of the room, she emerged a few feet from the bar.

"You look like you need a friend," she called to Luther.

He motioned her over. "It's like an ant farm. I shouldn't have come." He shivered, reaching inside his dinner jacket for a cigarette. His black hair and beard, generally impeccably clipped, looked almost ragged this evening. Yet, interestingly, his mussed hair made his face all the more appealing. There was a certain vulnerability—almost a sweetness—in the way it curled around his ears. "Oh no!" he whispered, moving closer to Sophie. "Why do *I* have all the luck. Here comes Duluth's answer to Susan B. Anthony. I suppose it's too late to find a hole and crawl in."

A woman Sophie had never seen before walked up and stood next to them, acknowledging Luther by touching him lightly on his arm.

"Claire." He forced his thin lips into a smile. "How nice to see you this evening. Allow me to introduce you two. Claire Van Dorn, this is my dear old friend, Sophie Greenway."

Claire extended a heavily ringed hand. "Of course. You're Amanda's friend from Minneapolis. The editor of that arts magazine. And you do something else, don't you? Something sort of outrageous."

Sophie pulled absently at the short wisps of hair around her neck. Sourly, she thought of Peter Pan. "I write an occasional restaurant review for the *Minneapolis Times Register*."

"That's it. And you dress up. Lots of disguises. I remember now."

"Claire is headmistress at the Tate Academy," continued Luther. "It's an all-girls school near Two Harbors. She and Amanda have recently become very good friends."

Sophie knew Luther sufficiently to sense that he had uttered the last word with distaste. "It's nice to meet you."

"Amanda and I met last year at a meeting of the North Shore Feminist Association. I'm the current president."

"Ah," said Sophie. "I've heard of your group. You're very active in the community here."

"We are."

"Amanda found Claire quite useful when she started the renovation," added Luther. "She often says she couldn't have made it through the last few months without her assistance."

Claire accepted the compliment gracefully. "My doctorate is in European art history, with an emphasis on the architecture and painting of the Twenties and Thirties. It's a fascinating period. More recently, I've indulged in another one of my interests. I've just published a book of children's verses."

Luther's nod telegraphed his boredom. "A local celebrity." He smiled.

"Much to my delight, I found that Amanda and I both love children's poetry. It's so rich. Children have such unspoiled, unrepentant imaginations. It doesn't matter one bit if something falls within the realm of the possible. I admire that, don't you?"

Luther nodded. "Deeply."

As Claire and Luther continued their conversational parry and thrust, Sophie took a moment to study Amanda's new friend. Claire Van Dorn's taste in clothing seemed to run from stylishly tailored to slightly arty. Her thick salt and pepper hair was worn fashionably short, emphasizing her high cheekbones and finely proportioned, although somewhat large nose. Indeed, there was something quite pleasing about the broad, open Germanic face. It looked comfortable, lived in. And there was a distinct gentleness about the large, gray eyes. Sophie wondered why Luther so disliked this woman.

"Are we keeping you from something?" asked Luther, leaning over and grabbing an ashtray off one of the side tables.

"What?" Claire appeared startled by the question.

"You keep looking at your watch."

"Oh. Yes. I suppose I do. Well, the truth is I must leave for a few minutes. I have to run some food over to a sick friend."

"You aren't staying for the festivities?" He made a pretend pout.

Claire seemed unaware of the insincerity. "Oh, I'll be back," she assured him. "Amanda knows I'm going."

"I'm sure she does. Don't let us detain you."

With a brisk snap, Claire let go of her long, pearl necklace and turned to Sophie. "I hope we have a chance to talk more sometime soon. How long will you be staying?"

"I'm not sure. A few days. Perhaps longer."

"Well, I look forward to seeing you again."

Luther put a finger to his lips as she walked away. "Come on," he whispered. "I need some air."

Arm in arm, they left the restaurant and strolled down through the parking lot to the edge of the vast lake. Sophie found that she, too, was glad for the respite from the noisy crowd. She had no doubt that Bram was deeply engaged in some intense political or philosophical discussion. He loved to talk. It was one of the qualities she liked most about him.

Outside, it was a lovely evening with a gentle breeze drifting off the water.

"I can feel autumn in the air," said Luther, sitting down on a weathered wooden bench. He draped both arms casually across the back.

Sophie stood for a moment, watching the smooth, dark water lap lazily against the tiny red and gray rocks embedded in the sand. The sky was a cloudless canvas of pinks and grays.

He sighed. "I can hardly believe Labor Day is this Monday. How can the summer be over?"

The dejection in his voice made her turn around. "What is it, Luther? What's going on? Something's wrong."

He shook his head. Stretching his long legs, he pulled off his tie and unbuttoned the top button of his shirt. "This party. That's what's wrong. I can't stand these freak shows any more. I feel like I'm being strangled."

Sophie could tell this wasn't the entirety of the matter. She sat down next to him. "What about Claire? She seems nice enough. Why don't you like her?"

He brushed the question away. "Claire is an annoying gnat who buzzes incessantly around Amanda."

"That's it? You don't like her because she reminds you of an insect?"

Luther began to laugh. "I forget how literal you can be sometimes. You know, I've missed you. No one else around here asks so many damnably prying questions." He tipped his head up and took in the full immensity of the evening sky. "What I mean is, she isn't important. She's simply a pest."

A car roared into the parking lot, screeching to a halt directly behind them.

"Ah, the missing Nora," said Luther, turning to watch.

A tall, redheaded woman emerged from a dark Chrysler New Yorker and flew up the broad steps toward the entrance, her green satin evening dress clinging tightly to her slender body as she ran.

"I need to get out of here," he said, rubbing the back of his neck. "We can talk later. Listen, will you do me a big favor? Tell Amanda I wasn't feeling well and decided to leave. She'll understand."

"And will that be the truth?" Sophie wanted to ask about his loss of weight, the hollowness in his cheeks, but she remembered Amanda's warning. Besides, she felt a certain righteous indignation at his comment about her penchant for prying questions. She was not someone who pried. Well, not much at least.

"Amanda's probably told you about the medication I'm on. It affects my nerves. And I get tired very easily. I'm afraid I'm no longer the suave, dashing, hopelessly sexy man you used to know. Well, maybe I should take that last part back."

"Don't be a ninny. And don't worry. I'll give her your message. Are you driving directly back to Brule House?"

"Probably. Really, I'll be fine." He got up and reached for her hand. "You stay and have a great time for both of us. You can regale me with the highlights tomorrow."

Sophie stood and, putting her arm around his waist, walked him to his car. As he drove away, she favored him with one of her most obnoxious prom-queen waves. Even though she'd never actually been a prom queen, she had the moves down pat. The vapidity of it drove Bram nuts. She hoped it would have the same effect on Luther.

Standing alone now in the growing dusk, she listened to the buzz of traffic along London Road. One thing was certain. No matter how much Luther tried to suggest otherwise, he wasn't leveling with her. Sophie prided herself on her intuition. She listened carefully to the stillness around people, letting the quiet collect so that she could observe the tiny, almost imperceptible characteristics that could so easily be overlooked.

She knew there were more than a few demons inside Luther Jorensen which were far from being exorcised. His relationship with Amanda had never been easy. For nearly twenty-three years, she'd watched the two of them dance jigs around each other. They were obviously attached, yet she was confident that attachment didn't exclude a certain kind of hate. Strange that she should be so close to both husband and wife, and yet they were so different.

Realizing she wasn't going to solve anything by remaining outside and allowing the mosquitoes to eat her alive, Sophie decided to return to the party and find her husband. As she was about to start up the steps, she noticed a piece of paper sticking out from under the windshield wiper of their car. At first she thought it was an advertising flier, but all the other windshields were empty. Walking closer, she saw that it was an envelope. That was odd. If someone wanted to get in touch with her or Bram, why didn't they just come inside? Quickly, she pulled the envelope free and opened it. Inside was a sheet of paper on which someone had typed the words:

> If you want to help those you love, ask the woman with the poodle at the Mudlark Bar what she saw on Thursday night.

Sophie looked up at the huge, two-sided neon sign that sat high atop the restaurant, boldly blinking the words GASTHAUS RETHENAU to cars on London Road. Thursday night, last night—that was when Lars Olson had been murdered. Was there a connection? If so, what possible business could that be of hers?

She read the note again.

The Mudlark Bar. Sure. She'd been there many times. It was midway between Brule's Landing and the outskirts of Duluth. Probably five miles or so from Amanda and Luther's home. But come on. A woman with a poodle? This had to be a joke. Yet she knew she couldn't ignore the possible implications. The first part of the sentence was what stuck in her throat. *If you want to help those you love. . . .* Of course she did! What a question.

Sophie looked around, wondering if she was being watched. This was too strange. Slipping the note into her evening bag, she crossed quickly to the steps. Perhaps someone was trying to confide in her. That was possible. There was, however, one simple way to confront this intrigue. Tomorrow she would take a little drive. It would sure beat playing four-handed bridge with a computer.

4

Herman Grendel sat at a computer terminal in the study of his home on London Road. For the last thirty years, Friday evenings had been spent going over the weekly averages on the various worldwide exchanges. Taking periodic stock of his investments had always been part of his overall plan. At first, his assets hadn't amounted to much. Yet, as the years passed and Duluth became a major inland port for the shipping of ore and grain, Herman saw his fortunes begin to grow. He had somehow stumbled onto the kind of success he'd once considered beyond his reach. It had been a roller-coaster ride; his blood pressure was living proof.

Herman's scowl deepened as the screen registered an unexpected three point drop in one of his most reliable investments. Damn. Why hadn't his broker let him know? You couldn't trust anyone these days.

As he switched the computer's library screen over to commodity futures, the sound of the front doorbell broke his concentration. Annoyed at the interruption, he yelled for Carla to answer the goddamn door. The bell continued to chime. Of course, thought Herman. What was he thinking? It was after seven. Carla had left hours ago. She wanted to attend the reopening of the restaurant tonight just like everyone else, and she needed extra time to get ready.

When he worked at his computer, time often escaped

him. After the stroke he'd suffered, Carla, his personal secretary for over twenty years, had turned one of the downstairs rooms into an office. It was the first new furniture
he'd bought in many years. Herman hated wasting money
on interior furnishings. He'd changed virtually nothing in
the house since his wife's death thirteen years earlier. Carla
now split her time between the corporate offices downtown
and Herman's residence.

Occasionally, real estate agents would knock on his door
to ask if he was interested in selling the place. They promised ridiculously high profits. It wasn't that the house was
so magnificent; it was simply that along with the property
came several hundred feet of Superior lakeshore. To live
that close to the water was an expensive proposition in Duluth. People paid dearly for the privilege. Herman laughed
to himself. They were fools. He'd bought the house in 1947
for next to nothing. The place was cold and drafty, with a
roof that leaked no matter what he did to prevent it. To be
honest, he would have been just as happy to live in one of
those modern condos like his granddaughter, Chelsea. But
this had been home too long.

The doorbell sounded again. Christ! It was cook's night
off, too. And the night nurse wouldn't be along until eight-
thirty. If the door was going to get answered, he would simply have to do it himself. Pushing away from the terminal,
he steered his electric wheelchair out of the room and down
the long corridor to the front door.

"Why am I not surprised to see you standing there?" he
asked wearily, backing up and allowing his visitor to enter.
"I suppose you might as well come in and join me for a
drink. Come back into the study." He wheeled around and
headed down the hall. "Close and lock that door behind
you. You can't be too careful these days. One of my neighbors was burglarized last week." Bumping to a stop directly
in front of a long table filled with crystal decanters, he
reached a shaky hand to lift the top off the ice bucket.
"God almighty, Milda forgot to fill this before she left.
That's the third time this week." He turned around. "You
know where to get more ice. And while you're at it, bring

that cold dinner tray she left for me on the counter. I hate to eat alone. You might as well join me."

"I can't stay. I just stopped by for a moment."

"Hmph," said Herman. "You came for a reason, didn't you? Get that ice and my dinner and then you can make your pitch. I assume that's why you're here."

"All right. I'll be right back."

Herman rolled to the terminal. He no longer had any interest in commodity futures. It was much more important to prepare himself mentally for the attenuated speech to which he was about to be subjected. Why did everything have to be such a pathetic struggle? He knew what was best. He'd always known. "Just set the tray over there," he growled, pointing to a low table next to the couch. "And pour me a drink. Make it a rye and a little dry vermouth. Why don't you have one yourself? You look like you could use something strong."

"No, thanks," said the visitor, slowly mixing Herman's nightcap.

"I insist. And take off those goddamn gloves. You're making me nervous. I've never seen you look so grim."

"Do I look grim? That's funny. It's not how I feel."

Herman grabbed the drink. "You came to talk about money, isn't that right? Don't bother answering. I was sure someone would come crawling out of the woodwork after my announcement this morning."

"Money is apparently your only motivation in life. I feel sorry for you."

"Screw your pity. I don't need it. And anyway, by this time tomorrow, my accountant will have taken care of everything."

"Yes, you're right. It will all be over."

Herman studied the drink in his hand. "I know what you're going to say, so you can save your breath. My mind is made up." He took a sip. "Why are you smiling?"

"Am I smiling?"

"Yes," said Herman. "You are. What's wrong with you tonight?"

"I guess I must think this is all rather amusing."

"I don't know what's so damn funny about it. Hand me that plate of lefse and herring. I need to eat something."

"Did I ever tell you how much I hate being ordered around? Why don't you get it yourself?"

Herman watched with growing nervousness as his visitor stood. "What are you doing?"

"What do you think I'm doing? I'm getting up. You look worried. I wonder why."

"I . . . I'm not worried. It's just that you're so damn strange tonight. What's that? Why do you have a gun?"

"I like guns. I've always liked guns. Didn't you know that?"

"But . . . put it down! Put it away!"

The impact of the bullet caused Herman to arch back. He grabbed at his chest, momentarily amazed at the amount of blood filling his hand. Holding on tightly to the sides of his wheelchair, he had the terrifying sensation of falling from a great height. The last sound Herman Grendel was ever to hear was the clinking of his computer keyboard as the words THIS LITTLE PIGGY STAYED HOME were typed onto the screen.

5

"Christ, it's the middle of the night," groaned Jack, jamming a pillow over his face.

Nora reached over and picked up the alarm clock. "It's nearly two A.M."

She dropped the clock to the carpeted floor.

The front doorbell continued to chime.

"You better go find out who it is," she mumbled, pulling the covers over her head. "It might be important."

"Damn." Jack rolled onto his side and sat up, feeling for his robe at the bottom of the bed. "Whoever it is, I'll get rid of them. Don't get up."

"Do I look like I'm moving?"

He made his way down the stairway and switched on the front hall light. He hated being awakened in the middle of the night, hated having his privacy invaded. Sleepily, he wondered if, after he won the election, he would ever have any real privacy again. "Can I help you?" he asked, yanking open the door.

Two men stood there quietly. The taller of the two was dressed in a police uniform. The other was older, with a mild, forgettable face and thinning gray hair. He was wearing a dark raincoat over a pair of green sweatpants and a UMD T-shirt.

"Jack Grendel?" asked the older man. He peered curiously over his bifocals.

"Yes?"

"My name is John Wardlaw. I'm a detective with the Duluth Police Department. This is Sergeant Severson. I'm sorry to bother you at such a late hour, but it's important. May we come in?"

Jack ran a hand through his rumpled blond hair. "Of course. Please." He stepped back, allowing the two men to enter. "We can sit in here." He switched on several lights in the living room. "What's all this about?"

"I'm afraid I have some bad news, Mr. Grendel. There's no easy way to say this. Your father's body was found earlier tonight at his home. He'd been shot in the chest at close range."

Silently, Jack sat down on the couch.

"It happened sometime between six and eight-fifteen. The cook left at six. She said good-bye to him personally and confirmed that he was alone. The night nurse arrived early—around eight-fifteen—and found the body. There was no sign of a forced entry. Quite the contrary. It appears the person had been invited into the house by your father and the two were having a drink together. Well, actually, that's not quite accurate. Your father was drinking. The other person never touched his . . . or hers. But it does suggest he knew his murderer and wasn't the least bit concerned for his safety."

Jack felt a numbness overtake his mind. "I . . . don't know what to say. I can't believe this. It's . . . senseless."

"I know it comes as a shock, but I'm sure it will make perfect sense when we find out who did it—and why." Wardlaw and the sergeant exchanged glances. "There seems to be a connection between your father's death and that of his business associate, Lars Olson. Were you aware of Mr. Olson's death last night on the lift bridge?"

Jack looked up. "What's the connection?"

"I'm sorry. That's not something I'm at liberty to discuss right now. Please understand, I can't state this for a fact, but it is possible someone may be planning another murder. I know you grew up here in Duluth and most likely you think of it as a quiet town. Generally it is. But this situation is very different from anything we've ever dealt with before. Both of these murders were well-planned, intentional acts. Since your family is involved, I recommend that you take precautions. No one can predict what's in the mind of a murderer, Mr. Grendel. For all we know, you might be in some danger."

Jack's tongue felt thick and dry as he tried to speak. "Have you told my sister any of this?"

"No. We have her address—"

"I want to tell her. I don't want her to hear this from strangers."

Wardlaw nodded. "All right. That's understandable. I'll give you until eight A.M. If you haven't spoken to her by then, I'll have to."

Annoyed at being issued an order, Jack glanced angrily at the other policeman. "Fine."

"Now, Mr. Grendel, I have a few questions I need to ask."

"Questions?"

The detective pushed his glasses back up on the bridge of his nose and flipped open his notebook. "Where were you and your wife earlier this evening, between the hours of six and eight-fifteen?"

Jack could feel his jaw tighten. "I see. I'm not only a potential victim. I'm now a suspect."

"At this point, we can't rule anyone out. Especially family members. If you wouldn't mind answering my question?"

Slowly, he rubbed his temples, giving himself a moment to reflect. He had to exercise caution. "Detective Wardlaw, I don't know if you realize this, but I'm a candidate for one of the highest political offices in the state."

"I know you're running for the U.S. Senate, Mr. Grendel. I have no interest in seeing your reputation or your campaign damaged. I might even say I'm a fan of your environmental policies. Of course, you have the right to consult an attorney before answering any of my questions, but, to be frank, your cooperation right now would be appreciated."

Jack got up and moved to the bar at the end of the room, pouring himself a glass of bottled water. Upstairs, he could hear the floor creak. So Nora had finally become curious enough to get out of bed. He looked at the detective. Nothing suggested that the man had heard the noise from above. "All right," he said, taking a quick sip. "I've got nothing to hide. I'll make this brief. Yesterday afternoon I spoke at a fund-raiser in Clouquet. It was at Hellermann Auditorium. I left shortly before five. My wife had a hair appointment downtown, so she took the car. An associate brought me back here."

"Who was the associate?" asked Wardlaw.

"Ryan Woodthorpe."

"President of the North Shore Coalition for a Better Environment?"

Jack nodded.

"Please. Continue."

"Well, Ryan and I worked here for about an hour. Recently, he's been doing some speech writing for me. While I was taking a shower, Nora called and said she was running late. We were supposed to be at the Gasthaus Rethenau by seven for the grand reopening."

"I understand the restaurant has been in your family for many years."

"Since 1923. Anyway, Ryan offered to drop me off there and Nora was going to meet me when she was done. I arrived around seven. I think she got there about seventhirty."

"Did she say why she was late?"

"No. And I never asked."

"Are there any witnesses who can verify her whereabouts between six and the time she arrived at the party?"

"I don't know," said Jack, taking a deep breath as he looked up at a portrait recently done of his wife. The artist had caught a feature in that beautiful Irish face that he'd never noticed before, yet he had to admit it was clearly there—a certain hardness about the jaw, just a bit of ruthlessness in the eyes. "I'm sure she didn't think she needed any."

"Is she here, Mr. Grendel? It might be helpful if—"

"She's not feeling well, John. May I call you John? I'd prefer we didn't wake her."

"Of course." The detective's eyes traveled slowly to the top of the stairs. "I can speak to her later. Do you own a gun?"

"A gun?" Jack seemed surprised by the question. "No."

"All right. Do you have any idea why someone might want to murder your father?"

Jack finished his water before answering. "He wasn't well loved. I'm sure you'll have no problem dredging up a fairly extensive list of enemies."

"I was told he withdrew his financial support from your campaign yesterday morning."

"Yes. That's right. But I would hardly slink around killing people simply because they don't support my political aspirations. I loved my father, Detective Wardlaw."

"Yes. I'm sure you did." Stiffly, Wardlaw rose from his chair, rubbing the small of his back. "Thank you for your time."

"A running injury?" asked Jack.

"Running? Me?" He smiled. "No. Just old age. What do they say? After fifty, if it doesn't hurt, it doesn't work."

They returned to the front hall.

"One other thing," said Jack, stopping before he opened the door. "Have you told Chelsea yet?"

Wardlaw looked questioningly at the uniformed policeman.

"Chelsea Jorensen," repeated the sergeant, paging through his notes. "Daughter of Luther and Amanda Jorensen. Granddaughter of the deceased."

"Chelsea is my niece. She was very close to her grandfather. I believe she stands to inherit his shipping business."

"Is that right? Well, we'll make a note of it."

"This is going to come as a terrible shock to her. To the entire family."

"Perhaps not to everyone, Mr. Grendel. Good night."

6

Luther carried a tea tray into the living room and set it on a low, antique table. Sitting down opposite Sophie, he placed a bone china cup in front of her and began pouring the steaming Earl Grey.

"Where is Amanda now?" asked Sophie. She reached for a slice of poppy seed bread from a plateful of pastries.

"Up in her room. She wanted to be alone." He leaned back in his chair and looked glum. "I don't know why I feel like this. I didn't even like the old guy. As a matter of fact, I loathed him."

"He wasn't one of my favorite people either," admitted Sophie, "but I wouldn't wish that kind of death on anyone."

Sophie had been awakened shortly after eight A.M. by the sound of loud sobbing. Slipping on her robe, she'd discovered Amanda and Jack in the second floor library, Jack with his arm around his sister, holding her tightly as she wept uncontrollably.

"I'm almost too stunned to speak," she admitted.

"Just drink your tea."

Sophie picked up the cup, her eyes taking in the familiar surroundings of the home's dark, Dickensian interior. For some unknown reason, Amanda had decided to furnish the dank stone structure with furniture befitting a small, turn-of-the-century cottage. It was totally out of character at Brule House. More than out of character, really. The frail, delicate antique furnishings seemed the wrong scale for the rooms. The sensation was like sitting amidst doll house furniture scattered inside a cave. A shame, too. The antiques were lovely, elegant, and beautifully cared for. They were simply all wrong.

Brule House had been built to withstand the harsh winter weather along the North Shore. The original architect, Ezra Holtman Brule, had been a man obsessed with ships. He'd built the stone sanctuary near the sight of an old boat landing as a retreat for himself and his wife in 1903. It was nestled on a bluff, less than a quarter mile from the famous lighthouse that eventually took his name. Over the years, the historic Brule's Landing lighthouse had fallen into complete disrepair. On a whim, Luther and Amanda had purchased it from the county four years before. Since it bordered their property, officials were only too happy to get rid of what they considered a white elephant.

A stout, white-haired woman appeared under the rounded living room archway, wiping her hands on a blue gingham apron. "Mr. Jorensen? There's another call for your wife. One of the women from the feminist association wanting to express her sympathy."

Luther set his cup down with a crack. "Tell them she's indisposed. She can't come to the phone. Oh, and Alice, if they want to talk to me, say I'm taking a bubble bath."

"Mr. Jorensen!"

"All right. Say I'm lying prone on the floor, kicking my feet and shrieking. Anything you want. Only I don't want to talk to anybody, okay?"

Alice shuffled away shaking her head.

"Luther, for pete's sake," said Sophie, reaching for another slice of bread.

"Well, what am I supposed to do? If it weren't for Amanda, I'd break out the champagne. I mean really! You're the last person for whom I should have to feign sorrow. You know how I despised that old goat."

"Luther!"

"All right. I'll stop." He studied her for a moment. "Not to change the subject too abruptly, but that's an unusual sweater."

"Do you think so?" Sophie looked down at her orange-and-black rag wool cardigan. It was her favorite. "Bram picked it out."

"His tastes do run to the bizarre."

"I beg your pardon?"

"Sometimes I wonder where you found him."

"I hardly think a national radio personality was ever lost."

"You know what I mean. Even you have to admit he's a little eccentric. How long have you two been married now?"

"Five years in November."

"Indeed." He grunted.

Sophie decided to change the subject. "I guess Jack and Nora didn't stay for breakfast."

"Nora never came."

"Oh. I assumed she had."

"Jack gave Amanda the news and then left immediately. He had an early meeting with several of his political advisers to discuss the possible negative fallout."

Sophie felt a shiver of disgust. "He's not even allowed to mourn like a normal human being." She nibbled on her bread. "Aren't you eating anything?"

"Not right now."

"What time do you have to be at the university?"

Luther seemed puzzled by the question. "Didn't Amanda tell you? I'm sorry, Sophie, I thought she had. I'm on a leave of absence right now. Have been since midsummer. It's truly amazing how the philosophy department trudges along without me."

Was that a hint of anger in his voice? Sophie wondered why Amanda hadn't mentioned it. "Is it because of your health?"

The question seemed to make Luther uncomfortable. Setting down his cup, he turned to fluff the pillow behind him. "Oh, I suppose. It's all become so tedious." He punched the lumpy annoyance into place. "The truth is, I was getting stale. Each new group of students was beginning to feel like just one more tired horror. Part of my problem stems from the fact that I'm not much of a fan of youth—an unfortunate malady for a teacher. I find that the young romanticize everything. It's a posture I've grown to abominate. I think, as a teacher, I'm pretty much a failure. Students today want a mirror. All I could offer was a window."

The brass knocker on the front door sounded, echoing through the chilly stone interior like a shot.

"I'll get it," he said, rising lethargically. He crossed into the foyer and opened the front door.

"Mr. Jorensen?"

"Yes?" Luther blinked at the strange man standing before him.

"I'm Detective John Wardlaw with the Duluth Police Department. May I come in?"

"I wondered when the police would arrive." He held the door open for him. "If you'll excuse me, I'll have someone call my wife." He disappeared into the dining room and reappeared a moment later. "She'll be down in a minute. Please. Why don't you have a seat in here?" He led the way into the living room.

"John Wardlaw," said the detective, introducing himself to Sophie.

"This is Sophie Greenway," said Luther. "She and her husband are visiting from Minneapolis. Old friends."

Wardlaw nodded pleasantly.

Sophie offered him the plate of pastries and waited while he selected a piece of pear bread. Where were they finding policemen these days? This man looked like he should be reading nursery rhymes to his grandchildren. Or puttering in the garden. She knew the police would, no doubt, be investigating Herman Grendel's death; it simply hadn't occurred to her they would show up quite so quickly. She wondered if Bram would want to be alerted to their presence, but decided to let him keep working. He'd been up since the crack of dawn. She could fill him in on everything later. As she chewed on her own slice of fruit bread, she wondered about the matter of the note she'd found on their car. Should she say something to the police? This would be the perfect opportunity. Her gut reaction told her to keep it to herself—at least for now.

Wardlaw bit into the bread, smiling amiably. "Very good." He nodded. "Homemade, I can always tell."

Amanda appeared in the archway looking composed but puffy, as if through sheer strength of will she had stopped crying. As she entered the room, she dabbed lightly at her nose with a tissue. Unsteadily, she perched on the edge of a wing chair next to Luther.

Sophie's heart went out to her old friend. Yet, wasn't it just like Amanda that even in this damaged state, her fragile beauty seemed completely untouched. For a fleeting second, Sophie felt the same jealousy she had so often felt in the presence of Amanda and Jack Grendel. Even as children, their handsomeness had been completely effortless. Painfully, she recalled her own childhood image. A freckle-faced, insecure little tomboy, with hopelessly unruly hair and overly large, waiflike eyes. Only in the last few years had she ceased looking like an orphan from a Victorian novel.

"This is Detective Wardlaw," said Luther, gently placing his hand on Amanda's shoulder.

Instantly, Amanda started to shred the tissue in her lap. "I don't know what I can say to help you. Jack seems to think you feel one of us—" She bit her lower lip and looked down.

Wardlaw gave her a moment to compose herself. He too seemed touched by her presence. "Please understand, Mrs. Jorensen, we have to start somewhere. Families are often involved in matters like this. Or sometimes they know something they don't realize is important."

She shook her head. "No one in my family had anything to do with my father's death. I can't imagine who might want to hurt him."

Wardlaw glanced at Luther. "Perhaps we should begin with you, Mr. Jorensen." He patted his coat pockets, feeling for a notebook. "Can you tell me where you were between six and eight-fifteen last evening?"

Nervously, Luther cleared his throat. "Well, let's see. I guess I arrived at the Gasthaus about five forty-five. I thought I might be able to help my wife with last-minute details. I left around seven-thirty."

"But you went directly home," said Sophie, coming to his defense.

"No, actually I didn't. I went for a drive along the shore. I doubt I got home much before ten. You can ask Alice— she's our cook and part-time housekeeper. She'd probably know the exact moment I walked in the door. Very little that happens in this house gets past her."

"Did you stop anywhere?" asked Wardlaw. "Did anyone see you?"

Luther shook his head. "No one. I suppose that means I don't have much of an alibi."

"This is ridiculous," protested Amanda. A raw color appeared on her cheeks.

Wardlaw turned to her. "Mrs. Jorensen, I understand your restaurant reopened last night after a lengthy renovation. Did you leave the premises at any point during the evening?"

"Of course not!"

"What time did you arrive there?"

"Around five. Luther and I each have our own car. And I didn't leave until well after midnight. I'm sure I can find a great many people to verify that fact."

"I'm sure you can." Wardlaw's voice was soothing. "Do

either of you own a firearm? We're looking for a .45 caliber handgun."

Luther raised a finger. "I believe I own one like that. All our guns are kept in my study."

"I wonder if you'd mind if I had a look."

"Please," said Luther. He touched Amanda's hand and gave Sophie a nod as he stood, leading the detective out of the living room and into a dark, rear hallway, which ran the length of the first floor. At the second to the last door, he stopped, knocking softly.

"Go away!" came a deep, brusque voice. "The muse is upon me."

Pushing it open, Luther allowed Wardlaw to enter first.

Bram was sitting with his feet propped up on a large, intricately carved mahogany desk, about to launch a paper airplane into the stratosphere.

Luther breezed past the detective, gesturing with his thumb over his shoulder. "Sorry, Bram old boy, but you're going to have to leave. Can't be helped."

Bram yanked a Popsicle out of his mouth. "Yeah? And who might you be?" He glared at Wardlaw.

"The coppers," said Luther, grabbing his arm. "Come on now, be a good boy and go play by the shore for a few minutes."

Bram whipped a paper out of the typewriter. "He's no policeman. My agent sent him to make sure I was *working*."

"That's a good fellow," Luther cooed, dragging him to the door. "Catch you later. Well now," he said, turning to the detective. "There it is." He pointed to a cabinet against the side wall.

As Wardlaw opened the case and began his search, Luther stood in front of a mullioned window and watched the gulls swoop near the water. The lighthouse was visible out on the point. He'd picked this room for his study because of the view, and also because it was the only room on the first floor—other than the living room—with a working fireplace. Patiently, he waited as the detective took a pen and lifted a handgun from the bottom shelf.

"This looks like a government issue," he said, sniffing the barrel. He dropped it into a small plastic bag. "It's been fired recently."

Luther sat down on the edge of the couch, feeling the back of his neck prickle with a cold anticipation.

"When was the last time you remember using it?"

"A few days ago. I often take one with me when I go for a walk. It's the rabbits. They're all anarchists around here. They have no sense of property rights. Also, both my wife and I use the Knife River Shooting Range on occasion. As a matter of fact, we were there yesterday morning. And, of course, the rifles I use for hunting. At least I used to." He slipped his hand under his corduroy jacket, feeling the thinness around his ribs. "A few of the pistols are from Vietnam. One or two might even belong to Jack. I'd have to check. We were in the same company during the war— excuse me, I mean the *conflict*. That's how we met and became friends."

"You've known Jack Grendel for a long time then?"

Luther nodded.

"And his wife?"

"Jack married Nora about three years ago. It's his first marriage, her third."

"Can I assume you and Jack are still close friends and that you're an active supporter of his campaign?"

Luther brushed a piece of lint off his slacks. "We're friends, yes. I can't say I care very much whether he wins or loses. I don't think he's the messiah come to save the state from the wicked businessmen, if that's what you mean. But he's intelligent. That's more than I'd say for his esteemed rivals."

"You're not much for politics, Mr. Jorensen?"

Luther laughed. "Don't you find something inherently repulsive about a person hustling his own integrity?"

"Interesting observation."

Luther shrugged. "The person who gets the brass ring is merely the best actor, the rawest hustler."

"You think that describes Jack Grendel?"

"I think it's a perfect description of his wife."

Wardlaw hesitated, closing the door of the gun case. "You have some strongly held opinions."

"I do. Last I heard, it wasn't against the law. Now can we get on with this?"

"Of course. I'll need to take this gun down to the lab for examination. It's the right caliber. It may or may not be the right gun. I assume you have licenses for all of these?"

"Would you care to see them?"

"In due time. There's no lock on the case, Mr. Jorensen. Don't you think that's a little foolish? Anybody could come in here."

"Why? What would be the need?"

"It seems there may have been a need last night." Wardlaw sat down behind the desk. "I suppose you don't keep the door to your study locked, either."

"Only Amanda and I live here now. Jack and Nora visit occasionally, but you aren't suggesting they had anything to do with the old man's death? And Ryan Woodthorpe and Jenny Tremlet live in the lighthouse-keeper's cottage. It's about half a mile away. It's part of our property, and we rent it out. They may visit here a good deal, but they'd never take something without asking. Ryan especially."

"Why is that?"

"Why? You mean you haven't heard of Ryan Woodthorpe? Jack's new speechwriter? He's the moral lightning rod of our age! It's his mission in life to single-handedly protect the flora and fauna of the entire universe. He wouldn't hurt a flea. I don't believe he'd even eat a flea. It's meat, God save us all. Only slavering carnivores like myself are still eating flesh these days."

The edge of Wardlaw's lip curled in a slight smile. "I'm curious, Mr. Jorensen. Did you and your father-in-law get along?"

Luther stiffened. "No."

"Would you care to elaborate?"

"Elaborate? All right. Let's see, how can I put this delicately? Herman Grendel and I mutually nauseated one another. Does that admission in conjunction with my lack of alibi mean I now need to call my lawyer?"

"I think we may want you to come downtown for a short visit. It's just routine, since the gun belongs to you. And don't worry. You can call your lawyer anytime you like."

Luther smiled. "Your kindness overwhelms."

7

Bram and Sophie strolled hand in hand along a deserted part of the shore. Both seemed to be consciously avoiding the subject of what could possibly be happening in Luther's study. Out on the water, a large pleasure craft was making its way slowly toward the Duluth harbor, fishing poles attached to the back.

"You look like someone in a sleazy French perfume commercial," said Sophie, squinting up into Bram's face. "Did you forget to shave this morning?"

Bram was intrigued. "Really?"

"No, I take that back. You look more like one of those poor guys who sleep under the Third Avenue Bridge."

"Very funny. If you must know, I've decided to grow a winter beard. A man's face gets cold in this intemperate climate. Besides, this is supposed to be a vacation of sorts. Shaving isn't relaxing. And if I ever do finish that book, I'll look incredibly distinguished on the book jacket."

They had reached the base of a newly fallen tree, its leaves weeping silently into the water. Bram picked up a flat rock and walked a few yards away, skipping it far out into the lake. "The operative word here is *if*. I'm not so sure this is the greatest site for my labors."

Gently, Sophie took hold of his arm and eased him over to a driftwood log, waiting patiently while he made himself comfortable. "Listen to me for a minute. I simply can't leave right now. Amanda needs me too much. Perhaps you should consider finding yourself a different place to build your paper airplanes."

Bram raised an eyebrow. "How do you know about the paper airplanes?"

"The engine noise."

"Cute." He harrumphed. "Well, I guess I could try it a couple more days. Maybe I'll move into that cook's room on the second floor. It may not have quite the same ambience as Luther's study, but it might do. As long as"—he narrowed one eye at her—"it's quiet. By the way, have they set a time yet for the funeral?"

"There won't be a funeral. Herman didn't want one. His body is going to be cremated later today. When I talked to Amanda this morning she said Jack was going to organize a memorial service tomorrow at Lakeside Chapel. I said we'd be there."

"Of course." He took hold of her arm and drew her down next to him. "Are you all right? I mean, I know you weren't very close to the old guy, but you've known him all your life."

"I called my parents just after I finished talking to Amanda. Dad took it pretty hard."

"Are they driving up for the service?"

She shook her head. "Dad would have come if he'd been asked to be a pallbearer, but since it's just going to be a memorial, he said he'd rather not. You know how he is about things like that. Mom thought it was best if she stayed home, too. Dad always acts like he can handle anything, but she knows better."

Bram smiled. "I like your mother. She's a lot like you. Strong, yet essentially very kind." He put his arm around her shoulders and fell silent. He knew she needed time for contemplation.

Sophie snuggled close and let her thoughts wander to the soothing sound of the water lapping lazily against the small rocks. Instead of Amanda and poor old Herman Grendel, for some reason her mind conjured up an image of her son, Rudy. He'd been living with his father in Montana since he was seven years old. She hadn't heard from him since his last letter, three years ago. At the time, he'd asked—no, *demanded*—that she stop trying to contact him. He wanted her out of his life. He couldn't be *unequally yoked together with an unbeliever*. Sophie had been disfellowshipped by the World Order Christian Church many years before. Marked as a heretic. Even thinking about those archaic, King James words now felt like something from another life. Yet, just as *she* once had, she knew Rudy believed in the insane doctrines of Howell A. Purdis with his entire heart and soul. Nothing she had ever said could change his mind.

Twenty-four years earlier, when Sophie had been a young, naive seventeen-year-old, she had joined a fundamentalist Christian church near her home in St. Paul. Against her parents' wishes, she attended Sabbath services every Saturday and Bible study every Thursday night. When she graduated from high school, she applied to Purdis Bible College in Los Angeles and was accepted within three weeks. During her four years there, she met and fell in love with Norman Greenway. As with most of the young men at the college, Norman wanted to be a minister. Shortly after their marriage, Norm was sent to a small town in Montana to be the pastor of his own church. Less than a year later, Rudy was born.

Thinking back on it now, Sophie couldn't believe she had been so blindly acquiescent. Those years felt like a terribly remote, yet infinitely depressing dream. Still, in her gut, she knew how passionately the doctrines had held her imagination. After all, she was part of God's *elite*. The rest of the world was filled with lies and religious error, but she was one of the chosen few who knew the truth. She must never turn her back on the Holy Spirit. There *were* unpardonable sins. The lake of fire waited for those who were weak, who yielded to Satan's temptations. Even now the unrelenting litany of spiritual terror could be summoned at a moment's notice. Back then, every part of her life was dictated by either church doctrine or her husband's demands. It was a modern woman's nightmare. Yet, believing in the righteousness of her decisions, she stuck it out until just after Rudy's sixth birthday. She remembered the turning point vividly.

One cold November afternoon, Rudy had come home from school with a fever. Norman sent for one of the church deacons and together they prayed over the boy, anointing him with oil and asking God to heal. Howell Purdis, the founder of the church and God's apostle to a godless nation, didn't believe in doctors. The Bible's way was clear. Call the elders of the church for an anointing and have faith. By evening, Rudy's temperature had risen to one hundred four degrees. Sophie was becoming hysterical. She begged Norman to take him to the clinic in town. Instead, he left in his truck to go fetch a churchwoman known for her natural healing methods. While he was gone, Rudy lost consciousness. Sophie called a neighbor, a non-church member, and asked if she would take them into town. The woman readily agreed, pulling up to the house in her rusted Chevy van a few minutes later. She explained that the local clinic was closed, but she knew one of the doctors personally and offered to drive them to his house. Sophie was so grateful she cried.

Dr. Eli Bradly was having a late supper when they arrived. He checked Rudy over and suggested that he be admitted to the local hospital in Lewiston. Sophie knew Norman would never agree to it. But before she'd left the house, she'd packed a small bag and had taken all the cash she'd saved from her household allowance for the last four years. Over five hundred dollars. An hour later, Rudy was tucked into a hospital bed, a nurse checking the IV that had been hooked up to provide him with both fluid and antibiotics.

During the night, Sophie had called Norman. She told him what she'd done. For some reason, she felt Norman was relieved. Perhaps, in his heart, he wanted his son to get medical attention, but couldn't let the members of his flock know his faith had faltered. The fact that Sophie had done it against his will conveniently let him off the hook. She said she'd call him later and let him know how Rudy was doing.

The next morning, Rudy was well enough to leave. Sophie phoned the same neighbor who had helped her the night before, and offered to pay her for a ride to the closest airport. The woman, sensing Sophie's desperation, agreed. Once there, Sophie booked a flight to Minneapolis. For the next few weeks, she and Rudy lived with her parents. Rudy continued to need medical care, and Sophie needed time to figure out what to do next. One thing she knew for sure, the truths of Howell A. Purdis had ceased to hold any meaning for her. The moral foundation of her life had, amazingly, begun to look like the pathetic whims of a sick, twisted, pompous old man.

Now it was Norman's turn to be hysterical. He might have forgiven her for taking their son to a doctor, but he would never forgive her for the divorce papers he received two months after they left the state. On the advice of his lawyer, a loyal church member, he began a custody battle that ended in a tiny courtroom in New Prairie, Montana. With the entire church to back him, financially as well as emotionally, he produced witness after witness to attest to Sophie's unstable, godless character. It had never really been a fight at all. Sophie knew she would lose as soon as she stepped into the courtroom packed with local church members. Norman was awarded custody, with visitation to be entirely at his discretion. Finally, he'd won.

Sophie had returned to her parents' home in Minneapolis, dead tired and broken. Her parents tried to help, but it seemed that everything they said she mistook as veiled criticism. It was becoming almost intolerable, yet she had no money and nowhere else she could go. That's when, out of the blue, Amanda had called. She'd learned through a mutual friend that Sophie was back in Minnesota. Why didn't she just hop a bus and come up to Duluth? The invitation felt like a gift. Sophie knew she was making her parents' lives miserable, and that only depressed her all the more. Luther and Amanda had bought the house at Brule's Landing the year before and Amanda suggested that she might like to come up and help them whip it into shape—that is, if she had the time. My God, thought Sophie; time was all she had left. Without her son, every day seemed like a pointless eternity. Intuitively, she knew Amanda wanted to give her a quiet space in which to recover.

Gratefully, she'd accepted. She hadn't really understood how deeply depressed she was until she saw herself reflected in her friends' eyes. Amanda and Luther didn't say anything, but their tenderness and generosity became her lifeline.

Even so, three weeks after arriving, Sophie hit bottom with such a crash that she knew she'd never recover. One afternoon she found herself at Enger Tower, her eyes mesmerized by the sight of the ground three stories below. She was certain she would never see Rudy again, and equally certain that a stiff upper lip meant nothing in the face of such hopelessness. As she looked up at the sky one last time, the sound of footsteps caused her to turn around. There, at the top of the stairs, stood Luther. The silent, undisguised fear in his eyes stopped her cold. Slowly, he began to talk. She couldn't remember now what he'd said. It wasn't important. But, somehow, he'd convinced her to take a drive with him. He never actually said he knew what she was about to do, but strangely, he didn't need to. That shared secret had instantly formed a deep, unbreakable bond between them. All these years and he'd never told anyone.

After that day, Sophie had felt as close to him as she had to Amanda. In a strange way, they had become her saviors. Their continuing kindness and willingness to let her talk it out—after the attempted suicide the words burst forth like an August thunderstorm—helped her to heal, if healing was ever really possible.

And now, after ten years of brainwashing, Rudy would not even speak to her. The child whose life she'd fought to save believed his mother to be teetering on the verge of damnation. Norman had convinced Rudy that Satan literally lived in his mother. He was to have nothing to do with her. Yes, thought Sophie with a grim smile, thanks to Luther and Amanda I've still got my life, but Rudy's never going to be a part of it. I can wish all I want, but my child will never know me, and I'm never going to know him.

"Let's head up to the house," she said, climbing to her feet.

"On one condition." Gently, Bram rose and took her in his arms. A slow smile pulled at the corners of his mouth.

Sophie watched the sunlight play with the soft, wind-blown curls around his forehead. "And what would that be?"

"I know what you're thinking. It's still bothering you, isn't it? I can see it in your eyes. Why don't you try calling Rudy again?"

Sophie shook her head. "I can't do that."

"Why? Because you're afraid of rejection? Look, when was the last time you talked to him?"

"Three years ago. You know what it's like. Norm won't even let him come to the phone. It's useless, Bram. I don't know if you can ever understand what that church is like— the hold it has over your mind."

"It didn't hold your mind very well, did it? Rudy is your son. I assume he has your intelligence."

"It has nothing to do with intelligence."

"No? All right, perhaps not. But how old is Rudy now?"

"Eighteen. Last month."

"An eighteen-year-old is a very different animal from a fifteen-year-old. I think you owe it to yourself—and him—to try again."

"But I write all the time. There's never an answer. Some of the letters even come back unopened. I've got to face reality or I'll go crazy. I know you have a good relationship with your daughter, Bram, and I'm happy for you, but don't you see? I've lost Rudy. I lost him the day he was born, and there isn't a damn thing I can do about it."

He squeezed her shoulder. "Do it for me, then."

Sophie looked up into his tanned face, loving his serious demeanor, the deep cleft in his strong chin, his widely spaced, comfortable eyes. His concern warmed her like a winter fire. It was heartening to be loved so intelligently.

"All right," she said, finding it a relief to acquiesce for once.

"Good. You're making the right decision."

"You mean I'm doing it your way."

"Exactly." He kissed her, touching her face lightly with the tips of his fingers. "I kind of like you, you know."

"Good thing for you. I know all your secrets, and I work periodically for a large metropolitan newspaper."

He laughed, spinning them around until they almost fell down.

"Come on, you lunatic! I want to take a little drive. Remember that note I showed you?"

"Yeah, the poodle at the Mudlark Bar. Sounds to me like someone's been grazing in the mushroom patch too long."

She grimaced. "Maybe. But I'm going to check it out anyway. If it's a joke, I'll simply have wasted an hour or two of my precious time."

Arm in arm they climbed up the sandy hill to the woods. As they approached the rear parking lot, Sophie noticed a car turning into the drive.

Bram whistled. "Pretty fancy wheels. Cadillac Coupe De Ville. Cherry red." He squinted to get a better look.

As they came nearer, Sophie could see a balding, rather rotund man lean over in the front seat and search for something on the floor. A second later his head popped out of the open window. "Hi there, folks!" he bellowed. He opened the door and slid out, his eyes traveling up Sophie's body until they came to rest on her face. For a moment, he seemed puzzled. Then he broke into a grin. "You don't recognize me, do you?"

"No," she said, cocking her head. "Should I?"

"Sydney! Sydney Sherwin." With a shove from his meaty hand, he slammed the car door. His light tan suit looked stained and rumpled, as if he'd been sleeping in it for days.

"Of course." She still couldn't quite place either the name or the face.

"Luther and Jack's old buddy."

That was it. She remembered him now. Except this overweight, middle-aged mound looked nothing like the baby-faced young man she had known many years before. Without thinking, Sophie found herself staring at the top of his head.

Following her eyes, Sydney rubbed his balding crown and replied, "Lost my hair years ago. Yup. Sure did. But I gained this." He patted his belly. "Not a fair trade, but then life isn't. You've grown up a little since the last time I saw you, too." He smirked. "But you're still short."

"Thanks." Under her breath she whispered, "And you're still a charmer."

He walked around behind the car and opened the trunk, lifting out a torn leather suitcase held together by a piece of thick, hemp rope. He let it drop to the ground with a thunk.

"This is my husband," she said, realizing she was staring again. "Bram Baldric."

"Glad to meet you, Bram." Sydney thrust out his hand.

Bram grabbed it, nearly getting his arm ripped from its socket.

"Luther didn't tell us you were coming," said Sophie.

Sydney smiled with perfect insincerity and leaned back against the fender. "That's 'cause he didn't know. This is a surprise." He almost giggled. "It's been a lot of years since I last set foot in that cave. I thought it was about time old Sydney livened things up a bit. Besides," he added, arching a serious eyebrow, "I've got some unfinished business I need to take care of. It shouldn't take me long and I'll be on my way." He glanced at Bram. "Luther and Jack and I are old buddies from Nam. Old war amigos never die. Sort of like ex-wives." He snorted at his own joke.

Sophie poked Bram in the ribs to stop him from rolling his eyes.

"Well, so." He stroked the hood of the car. "She's a beaut, ain't she? Bought her the day before I left Fort Wayne."

"Did you just get into town today?"

"Barely minutes ago. I thought, hell, why waste time? I gotta get out there and see my old buddies. Are they here?"

"Luther is," answered Sophie. "Jack was here earlier but had to go back to town."

"No matter." His voice was creamy. "I'll get to him, sooner or later." He noticed Bram eyeing the car. "Wanna see inside?"

"That's all right," said Bram. "Another time."

"Nah, it's okay. Maybe the little lady should go first." He opened the door and stepped away, giving a bow. "Come on, don't be shy. Look at those gorgeous plush seats."

He was like a car salesman from hell. Sophie peeked inside. The interior reeked of rancid smoke and sour sweat, all mixed together with the unmistakable aroma of a brand-new car. The floor and seat were littered with empty bags of potato chips and crushed cans of pop. Under a soiled shirt, she noticed a Duluth newspaper. That was interesting. She recognized it immediately as yesterday's front page, the one announcing the death of Lars Olson. How did Sydney get hold of a day-old paper? The *Duluth Daily News* wasn't generally sold outside of Minnesota. Unless? Had he been in town longer than he was letting on? Why would he lie? She pulled her head out. "Very nice."

Sydney beamed. "Yeah. Well, I gotta clean up some of the crap from the drive, but she's a winner, all right." He stroked the fender lovingly. "Your turn now," he said, turning to Bram.

Bram poked his head inside. "A lovely car," he pronounced, using his deep, resonant, radio voice.

Smiling boyishly, Sydney slammed the door and picked up his luggage. "I see Amanda's still quite the gardener." He shot a patronizing glance at the luxurious flower beds that circled the house. "Things never change. Silly hobby, if you ask me. Well, I suppose it's time I go knock on the front door. Sends chills up your spine, don't it? Old friends reuniting." He roared with laughter. Whistling the navy anthem, he charged up the slope and disappeared around the front of the house.

8

The Mudlark Bar was in a strange building that stood several hundred feet back from the road. The original structure was made of brick. Somewhere along the line, someone had added a stucco addition off the rear. When it was turned into a public bar and eatery back in the late Seventies, another section was built haphazardly onto the front, with a deck encircling three sides. To complete the mishmash, two picture windows had been installed to provide a lake view. They did not match. Since it was so close to town, the weekend business was fairly brisk. White plastic tables and chairs had been set up outside for those who enjoyed sitting in the fresh air to sip their brew. And since it was lunchtime, most of the tables were currently filled with customers eating the simple fare the bar offered.

Sophie swung her car into the parking lot and pulled up next to a pine tree. As she slid out, the stiff breeze off the water kicked up a heavy cloud of dust around her boots. She liked being out in the country. The lack of tar and concrete was a welcome change. Not that downtown St. Paul, where she worked every day, wasn't an unusually beautiful city. It was just nice to get away from it all for a while.

Once inside the building, Sophie moved through the crowded room up to a long, paneled counter. Since her last visit, the walls had been completely recovered in multicolored carpeting squares, with hideous plaster fish dangling from a series of nylon nets strung up behind the bar. Shuddering, she caught the eye of a young woman who was cutting up fresh pineapple near the swinging kitchen door. The woman set down the knife and wiped her hands on a damp towel, sauntering slowly over to where Sophie was standing.

"Can I help you?" she asked lethargically.

Sophie ran a hand through her windblown hair and attempted her most winning smile. "Yes, I hope so. I know this may sound kind of strange, but is there a regular customer who comes in here with a poodle?" She let the question hang in the air. After all, there wasn't much else she could add.

The young woman took her time answering. "You mean Dolores Benz?"

"I hope so," said Sophie. "Does she have a poodle?"

The woman nodded. "A tiny one. She carries it in her purse sometimes. It likes it here. It just sort of sits and growls to itself. Kind of antisocial, if you know what I mean. That is, unless someone offers it food. Then it's friendly enough. If you ask me, it's getting fat. Dolores should put it on a diet."

Sophie tried to look knowing. "I don't suppose she's here right now?"

"Nope. Haven't seen her today."

"By any chance, do you know where she lives?"

The woman studied her for a moment, leaning over the bar and looking down at her feet. The cowboy boots seemed to turn the tide of indecision. "Sure. Why not? She lives up the road about three miles. In Knife River. You know where that is?"

Sophie nodded.

"She rents the small apartment above Elmer's Market. You can't miss it. It's on the shore side of the highway, just as you come into town."

Sophie thanked her and headed immediately back out to her car. If this was going to be a waste of time, she might as well get it over with quickly. As she turned left onto the highway, she realized she hadn't really rehearsed what she would say to the poodle woman—that is, if she could find her. Asking her what she saw on Thursday night seemed a bit broad.

Before she knew it, Elmer's Market appeared on her

right. The young woman had been correct. You couldn't
miss it. It was as if every sign known to modern man had
been affixed to the weathered, perhaps rotting, wood exterior. Some of the advertised products weren't even sold
anymore.

Trudging up the side steps to the second floor, Sophie
knocked softly on the door. She felt suddenly ridiculous,
standing all alone, about to ask a total stranger a completely
inane question. She knew she was losing her nerve.

A voice from inside yelled "Hang on!" A few moments
later Sophie found herself staring at a plump, middle-aged
woman with mounds of curly brown hair and a tight rhine-
stone necklace (collar?) around her neck. What was it they
said about people coming to resemble their pets? She
couldn't wait to see the poodle.

"Yes?" asked the woman, tugging at the waist of her
wrinkled corduroy slacks. She'd apparently not been completely dressed when Sophie had knocked.

"Hi," said Sophie, grinning stupidly. "Yes. Well. I suppose you're wondering who I am. My name is Sophie
Greenway. You don't know me, but I wonder if I could ask
you a couple of questions?"

"You're not selling anything are you?" The woman
looked wary.

"No. Absolutely not." She squared her shoulders and
tried to appear respectable.

"Come on in then," said the woman, kicking a bunch of
dirty cloths out of their path. "Saturday is cleaning day. As
you can see, I haven't started yet." She leaned down and
removed a stack of magazines from a chair. "Have a seat."

"Thanks." Sophie perched uncomfortably on the edge of
a bright, orange recliner rocker and looked around the
small, cluttered room. Bram would have felt right at home.

The woman fell onto the threadbare sofa opposite her.
"Do I know you? You look kinda familiar."

"I don't think so." Sophie hesitated. She didn't know
how to begin. "Actually, I mean, I know this may sound
strange, but . . . what I wanted to ask was—"

"Let me guess." The woman tugged at her tight tank top. "You want to know what I saw last Thursday night."

Sophie's eyes widened.

"I'm right, aren't I? You're not the first person to ask, you know. Don't look so surprised. I'll tell you the same as I told him."

"I don't understand. Who else has been around asking you about this?"

"No one's been around. I got a phone call. Yesterday afternoon. At first I thought it was one of those obscene things. I just hate it when they start that heavy breathing crap. But the guy just wanted some information."

A tiny white poodle crawled out from under the sofa and sat down, batting at its sleepy eyes with furry paws. It looked up at Sophie and whined.

"This is Ducky Darling. She's very old."

"Why is she whining?"

"She wants you to feed her."

Sophie raised an eyebrow. Normally, she liked dogs. She and Bram had one of their own at home: a large black and brown mutt named Ethel. This poodle was the smallest she'd ever seen. And the most rotund.

The dog's manner changed abruptly when she saw that Sophie was not getting up. She glared as if Sophie were an imbecile.

"Nice Ducky Darling," said Sophie, reaching down to pat Ducky Darling's head.

Ducky Darling growled.

"Be a sweet Ducky and give mummy a minute to talk to the lady." Dolores grabbed the dog and dropped her somewhat absently into her lap. Ducky Darling began to lick her paws. Unlike the rest of her fur, the mouth and feet were a distinct orange color, undoubtedly a result of the brand of canned dog food she ate.

"What were we saying?" asked Dolores. "Oh, yeah. About Thursday night. Well, to be honest, I don't remember much. I'm a little embarrassed to admit that I'd had too much to drink." She fluffed her curls. "I work—or I should say, I did work—at the university. I was fired shortly after lunch on Thursday. We won't go into the details, but suffice it to say that I was completely innocent of any wrongdoing. Anyway"—she sniffed, closing her eyes and leaning her head against the back of the couch—"I got to the Mudlark about two. And I proceeded to get smashed. It seemed the appropriate thing to do."

"Did you see anything unusual?"

She pulled on the dog's ears. "Depends on what you mean by unusual. It *is* a bar, after all."

"Well, then, anything out of the ordinary."

She laughed. "Funny, you know there was a guy there I wouldn't have expected to see in a place like that. He was talking kinda intense to some woman at a table in the back."

"Do you know his name?"

"Sure do. It was Lars Olson. You know him? He used to be chancellor at the university. I was a secretary in the administration department. Before he left to go work for that shipping company, I saw him just about every day. A real jerk."

"Why do you say that?"

She snorted. "Ask any woman under the age of sixty who ever worked with him. That randy asshole hit on everyone with a pulse. He was just about to get around to me when he quit. Lucky for him. I'm not the silent type. The powers that be would have gotten an earful. And such a scrawny little bastard, too."

"Who was he talking to?"

"Beats me."

"Can you describe her?"

Dolores thought for a moment. "I don't know. Slim. She had something around her head so I didn't get a very good look at her. Sorry. They talked for a while and then they both left together."

The dog began to snore.

"I suppose you know that Lars Olson was murdered on Thursday night."

She nodded. "Saw it in the Duluth paper. Can't say that

I found it a tragic loss. It is kinda funny though. I mean, I saw him twice that day."

"Really? When was the other time?"

"Later the same night. Yup. Just like I told the guy on the phone. I went home for dinner about six, but I was still so depressed about being canned that I grabbed Ducky Darling and headed back to the Mudlark. By the time Olson came in it must have been close to ten. I was pretty blitzed by then, but I couldn't help notice that he seemed to be waiting for someone. He stood at the bar and ordered several drinks, but he kept looking at his watch and then over at the door. By eleven I'd decided to call it a night. Since it was apparent to everyone there that I was in no shape to drive, Jerry, the owner's son, offered me a lift back here. I do seem to remember seeing Olson get into a car about the same time I was leaving."

"Was it his own?"

"I don't think so. His car was still in the parking lot the next morning. And anyway, someone else was driving."

"Can you describe that person? Or the make of car?"

She shook her head. "Sorry I can't be more helpful. My mind was a little too foggy."

"Do you think the young man who took you home might have seen anything?"

Ducky Darling flipped over on her back and continued to snore, her nose twitching sporadically.

"He couldn't have. I was standing on the deck when Lars came past. He bumped into me and never even excused himself. I remember that much. God, he was an arrogant asshole. With that thin little mustache and his slicked-back, greasy black hair, he looked like a silent movie villain. He said it was natural too—the hair color. Just like Ronald Reagan." She snorted at the comparison. "Anyway, getting back to Thursday night, it's all pretty blurry. Jerry was around the side getting his car. He couldn't have seen anything." Dolores began rubbing the dog's tummy. "I suppose the police are going to want to talk to me."

Sophie nodded. "I would think so. You may have seen

Olson get into the car with the same person who later murdered him."

Dolores's hand stopped its rubbing motion. Ducky Darling's eyes glazed over with pleasure.

Sophie glanced up at Dolores just as her last words seemed to sink in. Hadn't she already come to the same conclusion? By her reaction, it would appear not. But was that it? The note Sophie had found on her car last night apparently did have something to do with Olson's death. But why had someone tipped her off about this woman? The police would find out about her soon enough, so what was the point? It didn't make sense.

"I think I should get going," said Sophie, standing up. "I'm sure you've got things you want to do."

"You know, it's too bad Ducky can't talk," said Dolores. "She probably saw everything." She set the dog down on the floor and gave her a little pat.

The dog shook herself for a moment and then, on cue, she began to whine.

9

He told her he would stop by about seven-thirty. Checking his watch as he entered the impressively marbled foyer of Chelsea Jorensen's luxury condo (her top floor suite overlooked the Duluth harbor), Ryan Woodthorpe stopped in front of a mirror to check himself out. Everything had to be just right. His rich brown hair, short on the top but long in the back, emphasized the strong bones of a classically Roman face. His well-muscled body fit perfectly into the working-class jeans and denim jacket.

Ryan knew he was a chameleon. He could easily be

many things to many different people. Yet the image he felt most comfortable with was a man of the people. Just one of the guys. It was something he had aspired to all his life, even though he rarely fit anywhere, especially with the young jocks he envied in high school and later in college. Ryan was a natural athlete, but since he was too small for most team sports, he was never admitted to the easy camaraderie of The Giants, as he came to call them. Even though he detested cheap pop psychology, he often wondered if his nearly obsessive desire to win hadn't come in some way from his diminutive size. It struck him that perhaps the real battle in life was not between the rich and the poor, the strong and the weak, but between the tall and the short. Time had yet to disabuse him of that notion.

Standing a second longer in front of the mirror, Ryan adjusted his chambray shirt. He knew he was a vain man, but didn't care. He was young, almost twenty-eight, and he'd already written two extremely popular books on the nation's eroding environment. Just recently he'd begun work on a third. And last year he'd been elected president of one of the largest environmental lobby groups in the country. Life radiated with purpose. His future looked bright. And he was about to reel in one of the most fascinating, sexiest women he had ever met. Even though marriage had never interested him, Chelsea Jorensen might just change his mind. He pushed the elevator button and waited, thumbs hooked around his belt, for the door to open.

Chelsea would be expecting him. She'd probably prepared some of those little cheese and spinach appetizers she knew he loved so much. After she'd gotten over her initial curiosity about his vegetarianism—"I've never met a *vegetarian* before"—she began taking an interest in finding him foods he liked. She was almost as obsessive about her life as he was about his own. That made her special, set her apart, and at the same time drew Ryan to her. The fact that she was heir to her grandfather's shipping company only sweetened the pie. Ryan knew he was not an avaricious man. Money was only a means. One day he intended to attain something far more important than wealth. Simply put, Ryan wanted power.

Chelsea's uncle, Jack Grendel, was just another means to that end. Unfortunately, Ryan knew he had one glaring flaw in his own, rather perfectly balanced makeup. It was something he had to watch carefully. The problem was, he truly believed in the righteousness of his cause. The environment had to be saved—at almost any cost. He was intelligent enough to know that single-minded zealots had created just about all the chaos the world had ever known. He didn't want to be a fanatic. He tried to cover the depth of his feeling with reason and methodology, citing a study here, an expert there. He'd worked hard to become a good wordsmith, and for the most part he'd succeeded at eliminating his more radical statements. Right now the biggest problem was his age. He was too young for elected office. That was why he'd begun speech writing for Jack Grendel. Grendel presented the perfect opportunity to learn the ropes. He believed firmly in the importance of a safe environment. The only problem was, Jack was a pragmatist. Down the line somewhere, Ryan knew that would present a problem. But he had a plan. If he played his hand very carefully, he might be able to apply just the right pressure at the right moment. Only time would tell.

The elevator door opened and Ryan got on. A moment later, he stepped out into the expensively decorated yet intentionally sparse living room of Chelsea's suite. A large Navajo rug sprawled across the natural wood floor. The furniture was leather. Cold and yet unmistakably sensual. It never occurred to him before, but the interior was a lot like Chelsea herself. A huge, round, salt-glazed pot sat on top of a simple glass table, a spray of dried weeds erupting from the top. Two highly dramatic air-brushed canvases swept from floor to ceiling, dominating the empty white plaster walls. From the kitchen doorway he could hear the sound of a radio playing softly. It was a news station. The announcer was talking about Herman Grendel's murder last evening.

Ryan found Chelsea standing on the balcony overlooking

the lights of the distant harbor. Her back was to him. In her right hand she held a wineglass. Her soft, honey-gold hair fell around her shoulders. She was wearing a thin, cream-colored robe. And she was barefoot.

"I'm sorry about your grandfather," he said, his deep voice a soothing whisper above the radio's hiss.

Chelsea turned around. Her features were so like her mother's. Yet the piercing, almost unnerving blue eyes were the distinct legacy of her father. Ryan knew Herman Grendel liked to suggest Chelsea was the progeny of some other man, but to know Luther, his quirkiness, his restless inability to ever feel satisfied, was to know Chelsea.

"Ryan," she said, acknowledging him with a half smile, "come over here."

He picked up a clean glass and the half-empty bottle of zinfandel and joined her.

"Grandfather's left me everything." Her voice was steady, but the hand holding the glass trembled.

"I know."

She slipped her arm around his waist.

"Are you all right?"

"Yes. I'm fine."

He could feel the warmth of her body through the thin silk. She was standing with her hip pressed tightly against his.

"Did you get it?"

Ryan shook his head. "I looked through all the files. Nothing."

"Was he . . . ?"

"Yes. He was already dead by the time I got there."

"You didn't see anyone, did you?"

"No. Whoever did it had already gone. The night nurse arrived while I was going through the files. I had to climb out a back window."

Chelsea moved away from him. He could tell she wasn't sure she believed him. "But Olson said the information was still in grandfather's files!"

"I know." Ryan followed her with his eyes as she moved into the living room and sat down catlike on the sofa.

"What do we do now?"

"Either Olson was lying or someone got there first."

Chelsea leaned back into the soft couch cushions and lit a cigarette.

"I thought you were going to give those up."

She ignored the annoyed tone and stared at him, blowing smoke high into the air.

"You still have the copy he sent you?"

Chelsea nodded.

"Somewhere, someone out there has the original." Ryan could tell she wasn't buying his act. And why should she? She was smart. Intuitively, she knew he *was* lying.

"Even without the original, if word got out that Grendel Shipping had engaged in the illegal dumping of industrial waste in Lake Superior during the years Uncle Jack was executive vice president, the rumor alone could kill his senatorial campaign. You and I both know that." She was smoking now in quick puffs.

"And we both know it would break Grendel Shipping financially if the company had to single-handedly clean up the potential disaster it created out there in that lake. I don't think anyone wants that information to go public."

Chelsea picked up her wineglass, holding it to her lips. "For now. I'm not so sure how long I can count on your discretion."

"It's not my discretion you need to worry about. If Olson told other people about it before he came to you, we may be in big trouble."

"Why do you suppose he tried to blackmail me instead of Jack?"

"I think you were only the first target. He knew you had a special interest in the future of the company since you were going to inherit. But believe me, he would have gotten around to Jack in short order. Who knows? Maybe he already had."

Chelsea tapped her cigarette against the side of the ashtray. "I never liked him."

"No. He was an opportunist. He got what he deserved."

Chelsea looked up. "Did he?"

"You know what I mean."

"I'm not so sure I do."

"Look. I had nothing to do with Lars Olson's death, if that's what you're implying. All I'm saying is that I never trusted the man. He found some information he thought he could use for financial gain, and he didn't care who he hurt. Speaking of Jack, you're positive he had no knowledge of the dumping?"

"Grandfather was the only one who ever worked with Weissman Industries. It was very lucrative territory. No one had a clue what he was really up to."

Ryan sat down. "You and I both know the stakes here."

"Why don't I trust you?"

He smiled. "The same reason I don't trust you."

"I doubt that."

"You think that for me everything is expendable."

"Exactly. In the name of your holy cause."

"It's not."

"No?" She got up and climbed the stairs to her bedroom loft.

Ryan followed.

"Where's little Jenny this evening?" She picked up a brush and began brushing her hair.

"At home. And give me a break. You know my relationship with her isn't serious."

"That's what you say. Does she share the same opinion? After all, you're still living together."

He pulled off his jacket and tossed it over a Bauhaus-inspired chair only Walter Gropius himself would have been comfortable sitting in. "She's in good company tonight. I picked up your father at the police station earlier this afternoon, just after they released him. He's home this evening with family and friends—and Jenny. I begged off, saying I had some research to do at the library. By the way, the police are pretty sure it was your dad's gun that killed your grandfather. Did you know that?"

Chelsea turned her face away. "I was questioned by the police several hours ago. No one mentioned it."

"Well, whatever. It doesn't mean he did it. And anyway,

he's all preoccupied with some new houseguest. An old war buddy of his and Jack's—from Vietnam."

Chelsea's head turned very slowly until she was looking directly at him. "Do you recall a name?"

"Sydney. Sydney Sherman—something like that."

"Sydney Sherwin," she repeated, her voice almost a whisper.

"Yeah, that's it. Do you know him?"

Chelsea dropped the brush on the dresser. "Yes. I know him. The vermin are crawling out of the closets."

"What?"

"Nothing." She unhooked her robe and let it fall to the floor. Underneath, she was completely naked. "Make love to me, Ryan." There was a strange hardness in her voice.

Unbuttoning his shirt, he walked across the thick, wool carpet and pulled her thin body toward him. "Chelsea, you're shivering."

"Don't talk."

10

After the memorial service on Sunday morning, Sophie drove with Amanda to her father's home. It was something that had to be done, and Amanda needed the emotional support Sophie was only too glad to offer.

"Thanks for coming with me." With a shaky hand, Amanda unlocked the front door. "I just couldn't do this alone. I suppose this house has some memories for you, too."

Sophie paused directly behind her friend and gazed up at the long, carved flower box bursting with red and white petunias. It ran under the second floor windows and looked like it could use a fresh coat of paint. As a young girl, Sophie had spent many nights in this house. It had always reminded her of a Swiss chalet. The architecture was sturdy and yet, somehow, slightly whimsical. "I'm happy to come along, you know that. I wish there was more I could do to help."

The door creaked open. "It's been awhile since I've been here myself," said Amanda. "I imagine Chelsea will put it up for sale right away." She brushed a tear away from her cheek.

"You're sure of that?"

"She hates it. She always refers to it as *the antique*."

"Is that bad?"

"I'm afraid so. She hates antiques on general principles."

Reverently, they stepped into the front hall.

"I just had to see it one more time," said Amanda, her voice just above a whisper. "You understand. It's where I grew up. It's the place that always comes to mind when I hear the word *home*. Not that all the memories are good, but still. I can't stand the thought of being here when the lawyers and real estate agents descend. It would feel too much like vultures picking at a rotting carcass."

They entered a spacious, although somewhat dark, living room. The deep windows, which could have let in the bright morning sun, were completely blocked by trees and shrubs that had been allowed to grow wild. The effect of the light was much like an old photograph. Everything was bathed in sepia. The furniture was old, yet beautifully preserved. The house seemed virtually unchanged from the time Sophie was a child. Apparently, Herman Grendel had never suffered from the need to modernize. She peeked into a dark side room that had once been the playroom. "What's in here now?"

"Since Dad's stroke last year, he's lived almost exclusively on the first floor. He insisted this room be made into an office. Kind of a shame, isn't it? The walls used to be covered with all our artwork. For some reason he wanted it paneled. All our zebras and elephants . . ."

"Don't forget the dragons."

"Right. And dragons. They're all gone." She sighed. "Just like our innocence."

Sophie turned. The comment seemed unusually self-pitying. "What do you mean by that?"

"Oh, I don't know." Sadly, her eyes surveyed the orderly, yet strangely empty room. "Maybe I'm just feeling old. I simply never thought . . . I'm not sure you'd understand."

"Try me," prompted Sophie. "I *will* say I've never been much of a fan of the concept of childhood innocence. Simple sweetness or lack of experience is hardly the same."

"What do you think innocence means then?"

"Well, without getting too philosophical, I'd say it's the absence of the *need* for illusion. Or, put another way, truly innocent people never need to create elaborate philosophical or religious structures simply to justify their own ideas or desires."

"But that's not simple, Sophie."

She nodded. "I know."

Amanda stood motionless in the silent house, listening to the faint hum of traffic from outside. "Who knows? Maybe I am talking about illusions. I've always had this romanticized idea of what it was to be a good adult. Except that, when I look at my life now, I'm nothing like my ideal. Not that I'm bad, or wrong, or evil. Just that I'm *less*. I don't have the kind of certainty I thought all grownups innately possessed." She forced her eyes away from a framed photograph of herself that her father had kept all these years on his desk. "You always did listen to my rantings with such patience."

"That's me. Patient to a fault."

"And you always beat me at checkers."

"You always found the best hiding places."

"I still do," said Amanda, giving Sophie's hand a squeeze. "But unlike you, I was never very good at games when I was young."

"You've improved?" Sophie's thoughts had become distracted by the crush of memories the room was beginning to evoke.

"I believe you'd find me a worthy opponent today. Listen, will you give me a few minutes? I want to go upstairs to my old bedroom. I won't be long."

"No problem." Sophie ran her hand along the edge of one of the dark oak bookcases. Years ago, it had been packed with children's books, stuffed animals, toys, and her favorite games, the ones her own parents simply could not afford. It now held files, business papers, and stacks of trade magazines. Sad. "I'll wait as long as you like."

Silently, Amanda left the room. Sophie could hear her footsteps ascend the uncarpeted stairs. It was a funny feeling, being back in this house after so many years. The last time she'd been here was the day Amanda and Luther were married, twenty-three years ago. Could it really be that long? After that day, Herman had never again invited her back. He'd never approved of Luther. Perhaps he felt Sophie was a traitor to his wishes, just like Amanda.

Noticing several scrapbooks piled in one corner of the room, Sophie sat down on a tired leather chair and pulled out the bottom album. It was stuck to the one above it by a mixture of dust and the gum of age. Making herself a bit more comfortable, she opened the gilded cover. A black and white photograph of Amanda and her father greeted her. Under it someone had written: THANKSGIVING, 1954. Amanda was about eight. Herman was glaring, with his usual scowl, at the person taking the picture. Such a thoroughly unpleasant man. The past was simply a precursor of the future.

She turned the page. Another picture. This time one of Jack taken shortly after his return from Vietnam. The hair was shorter and the face thinner, but it was still handsome Jack. In the picture he wore his navy uniform. She held the album closer to the window to get a better look. As she did, a yellowed newspaper clipping slipped out from between the picture and the album paper, falling lightly to the floor. Sophie reached for it, carefully unfolding the fragile newsprint. The headline read: DULUTH'S MOST DECORATED SOLDIER DONATES TIME AT DAMASCUS GATE. It was a small article stating that Jack Grendel, son of Herman Grendel, the founder of Grendel Shipping, was going to donate all of next year, 1969, to a halfway house for returning GI's injured in battle. It was located just outside Madison, in Green Dells, Wisconsin.

Sophie checked the date of the paper. December 29, 1968. That was funny. She didn't remember anything about Jack donating time anywhere. As far as she knew, in 1969 he was attending Stanford.

"What's got you so engrossed?"

Sophie looked up. "Chelsea! I didn't hear you come in."

"That's quite apparent." Chelsea Jorensen entered the room, quickly making herself comfortable behind her grandfather's desk. Her beautifully tailored, white linen suit fit her slim body like an expensive glove.

Sophie had only seen her briefly at the memorial service. Chelsea had arrived late and left early, thus eliminating the need to speak to anyone.

"What brings you and my mother here this morning?" Chelsea leaned back in the chair as if she owned it. Which, of course, she did. "I saw her Saab in the drive."

Sophie felt like the proverbial child caught with her hand in the cookie jar. She started to get up.

"No, please." Chelsea motioned for her to remain seated. "I assume Mother is upstairs looting. You might as well keep me company until she comes down."

As far back as Sophie could remember, Chelsea's manner had seemed entirely too sophisticated and world-weary for someone her age. It felt like a pose.

"Don't worry," added Chelsea, searching through the top desk drawer. "I figured Mother would be over sometime today. After all, it's part of the family treasure trove. I'm not going to be unreasonable." Her frown deepened as she yanked open one of the bottom drawers. "Damn. I was sure Grandfather had a stash of cigarettes in here. I don't suppose you have any?"

Sophie shook her head.

"No. That would be expecting too much. So, I hear you're the new managing editor of *Squires* magazine. Quite a coup. After all those years at that little left wing political rag, I guess someone finally noticed you."

Stifling a snide comeback, Sophie managed a polite nod. Left wing political rag, was it? Such a supercilious, condescending little snot. She smiled.

"Are you doing a piece on the reopening of Mother's restaurant for the *Times Register*?"

"I am."

"Staying at Brule's Landing?"

"We are."

"You know, someone asked me the other day if I missed living out there. I thought about it. I decided I missed the clematis on the north facade. That's about it." She leaned over to light the cigarette she'd finally found. "I assume you and Bram will be at the barbecue tomorrow."

Sophie was glad for the change of subject. She rarely wanted to punch anyone out. Chelsea was the occasional exception. Something about her always seemed so unnecessarily critical. As she thought about it, Chelsea was doing a good imitation of her grandfather. "We will. I'm looking forward to it. Are you coming?"

"No."

"I'm sorry to hear that. I'm told there's going to be a pig roast. You're going to miss a wonderful meal."

Chelsea crushed her cigarette in a brass ashtray. "I understand my parents have another houseguest right now."

"Sydney, yes. I suppose you know him."

"I do." She paused. "Sydney was around a lot when I was growing up. I think he was the first man to ever try anything with me. Sexually, I mean."

Sophie's eyes widened. "You're kidding? God, that's awful! How old were you?"

"Twelve."

She swallowed hard. Was it possible Luther and Amanda didn't know? Neither had ever said anything. "I'm so sorry!"

Not unaware of the effect of her last comment, Chelsea answered, "Don't be. It's all past now. Sex isn't that important, anyway."

"Do your parents know?" She had to ask.

Chelsea picked up a pencil and began drawing tight little

circles on a notepad. "It's all ancient history. Let's change the subject. Grandfather hated having an office in his home."

Surely she couldn't be that cavalier about something so painful. On the other hand, if she didn't want to talk about it, she had a right to her privacy. "I'm sorry about your grandfather's death. I'm sure the police will find out who did it."

"Thank you. But then, he lived a long time. He did just as he pleased and he answered to no one. I think a great many people would judge that a successful life."

"Would you?"

Chelsea searched the desktop for an answer. "Yes, I think I would." She looked up, smiling innocently.

"I guess I've been wondering about something," continued Sophie.

"What's that?"

"Well, your grandfather's death followed rather closely on the heels of Lars Olson's murder. I don't suppose there's any connection?"

"What do you mean?"

"Olson was doing consulting for your grandfather's company."

"*My* company."

"Excuse me. Your company." Kind of touchy, thought Sophie. You'd think she would try to hide her acquisitiveness for at least a few days.

"Darling!" Amanda's voice echoed from the doorway. "How wonderful to see you!" She set the box she was holding on the couch and turned to greet her daughter. "Are you all right? Why haven't you returned my phone calls?"

"Hello, Mother."

Amanda glanced at the objects she'd brought down from the second floor. "Mementos, sweetheart. Look here at what I found. It's that copy of Robert Louis Stevenson's poetry I gave you when you were six—the very same book your grandfather gave to me when I was a little girl. How I loved it. I still remember many of the verses by heart. It's funny: I found it on the nightstand in my old bedroom, just like someone had recently been looking at it."

"I was reading it," said Chelsea. "Childhood is a crock. Your friend Claire sent me a signed copy of *her* new book and I mailed it back. It's all a lie. There's no garden. No beauty." She stood and walked to the window, keeping her back to both of them. "I'm putting the house on the market next week."

"What about the furniture?" asked Amanda. "And all your grandfather's personal possessions?"

"Take what you want. The rest will be sold."

"Chelsea, I . . ."

"I didn't expect to see you. I have some work I need to do in the office. Perhaps you and Sophie should leave. You can come back another time."

"But . . ."

"Please."

"All right, if that's what you want." Amanda's voice was full of defeat. She glanced at Sophie for support. "I just thought maybe we could talk for a bit. I wanted to invite you out to the house. Both your dad and I miss you."

"Later, okay?"

"I suppose. But will you promise to call me? Soon?"

"I promise."

Amanda picked up the box and crossed to the door. "Right now, this family needs to stick together. We're all we've got."

"If that's true, Mother, God have pity on us."

11

Shortly before sunset, Sophie found herself walking Jenny Tremlet back to the lighthouse-keeper's cottage where she and Ryan Woodthorpe had lived for the past few months. Together, they strode briskly down the wide front lawn and headed toward the darkening lake.

Before they reached the pine woods, Sophie glanced back at the massive brownstone. The soft evening light made it look as if it had been carved out of solid cocoa. The three-story structure was a simple rectangular design, no gingerbread or ornate moldings. Except for the mullioned windows and the stained glass above the entrance, the house was unadorned. Perhaps Amanda felt the need for some kind of exterior decoration to soften the unyielding severity of solid stone. The perennial garden that circled the house did alter the appearance somewhat, but for some reason it seemed artificial, much like affixing a bunch of pink bows to a slab of concrete.

Sophie waved at Luther who was sitting in one of the redwood chairs on the front deck. He held up his bottled beer in a kind of salute. She was glad they'd had a chance to spend some time together earlier in the afternoon. They'd talked for hours, just sitting by the lake, tossing chunks of stale bread to the gulls.

The fact that one of Luther's guns had been used for the murder of Herman Grendel had really thrown him. But, in his usual ironic style, Luther had made light of the intense police interrogation he'd been subjected to yesterday afternoon. Sophie could see him lean back and look up at the sky. It was good that she could be here now, when both her friends needed her so much.

Jenny pointed to the quickest path, which would take them into the woods, past a thick patch of wild raspberries. As they walked along, Sophie glanced now and again at her companion. Jenny was a quiet young woman with a slow, deliberate manner and a rather pudgy, childlike face. Most of her clothing looked as if it belonged to an older, much larger, sibling. Unfortunately, Jenny didn't look fashionably sloppy. She simply looked lost.

"So, I hear you're helping Jack pull together some of his journals and notes into a book. Is he going to write an autobiography?"

Jenny shook her head, brushing a stringy, dark brown lock of hair away from her face. "Not exactly. Some publishing house in New York said that if he won the election, they might be interested in having something written about it. It's still up in the air. The television ads he's running right now are getting attention in Washington. They're so fresh and innovative. Even funny. Have you seen any of them?"

Among other things, Sophie hated the political season because she couldn't stand all the character assassination that masqueraded as political advertisement. She had to admit that Jack's ads were different. They got specific points across without tossing acid in the face of his opponent. In political terms, it was a unique idea. "Yes, I've seen most of them. They're quite good."

Jenny nodded. "I offered my time in the evenings because I like to feel useful. During the day I run a day-care center out of the cottage. It's for people who live up the shore and commute into Duluth. I need to support myself somehow and I really like children."

"Was it your idea to start the center?"

"No, Amanda suggested it. After her father let me go—"

"I didn't know you worked for Herman."

"I was his housekeeper for about a year. I answered an ad in the Duluth paper. Amanda's daughter, Chelsea, was the one who actually hired me. She fired me, too. We never got along."

That was interesting, thought Sophie. "Any hard feelings?"

Jenny gave an indifferent shrug. "I don't know. Maybe. If it hadn't been for Amanda, I don't know what I'd have done. Jobs are hard to come by up here."

"Do you like living so far from town?"

"Oh, absolutely! Especially now that I've found Ryan." Her voice turned wistful. "He's the finest man I've ever known. He has such a passion for his work. I think that's rare."

As they strolled along, they came to a small clearing. Directly in the center stood a low, dilapidated log structure surrounded by clumped birch. "Ah," said Sophie, "the old sauna. I'm going to have to take one while I'm here."

Jenny shivered. "That cabin is creepy. Any place that doesn't have a window makes me feel like I'm trapped. I suppose you've grown up taking saunas."

Sophie grinned. "Since I was a kid. Both my mother and father are full-blooded Finns. There's nothing like a sauna to relax you, make you feel like a new person."

"Really?" said Jenny. Her enthusiasm wasn't overwhelming.

Presently, they found themselves at the edge of a vast, red-rock beach. Instead of taking the path near the shore, Jenny pointed to a freshly mowed trail through the tall grass. About twenty yards before the lighthouse, they emerged into another clearing. The cottage appeared on their right, nestled snugly into the side of a hill. It was a charming building. Whitewashed walls and a red slate roof. It looked as if someone had recently built a greenhouse onto the south side. A swing set and an old-fashioned wooden teeter-totter sat empty next to a separate metal building Sophie assumed was the garage.

"How did you meet Amanda and Luther? Last time I was here, a young man was living in that cottage. A grad student at UMD."

"Claire Van Dorn introduced us at a meeting of the

North Shore Feminist Association. Amanda never came to the house while I was working for her father. Kind of funny, isn't it? Of course, I'm not very close to my parents either. Anyway, Claire knew Ryan and I were looking for a place to live and that the cottage was empty. Amanda's been so kind to us. Both Ryan and I are terribly grateful."

"And that's how you got to know Jack?"

"Ryan's known him for several years, but since we've been living here, he's taken a more focused interest in Jack's campaign."

"Say," said Sophie. "Maybe you can clear something up for me. It seems I remember Jack was accepted at Stanford shortly after he returned from Vietnam. He got his undergraduate degree there in 1974, that is, if I recall correctly."

Jenny nodded. "Yes, I think that's right."

"I don't suppose you've come across anything about the year he spent in Green Dells, Wisconsin. He was donating time at a place called Damascus Gate."

Jenny thought for a moment. "No," she said slowly. "I don't recall the name. I suppose I could check the records I have and see. Why are you so interested?"

Sophie pulled on her earlobe. "Oh, you know. I just have a mental block about dates sometimes. When I don't remember things exactly, it drives me crazy."

Jenny gave her a shy, sweet smile. "I know what you mean. Ryan is the same way."

Sophie liked Jenny. She wished she could say the same for Ryan. On the other hand, they'd only just met. She knew she had to give him the benefit of the doubt. "I think I'm going to do a little exploring before I head back to the house. Is Ryan home tonight?"

"No," sighed Jenny. "He's been doing a lot of research for some of Jack's speeches. I hardly see him anymore. I guess, for now, that's to be expected." She looked at her watch. "I suppose maybe I'll drive over to the Mudlark later, just to get out. Would you like to come with me?"

"Do you go there often?" asked Sophie. Her curiosity was piqued. She wondered if Jenny was one of the *regulars*.

"Not really. I have a couple of girlfriends in Knife River that I see once in a great while. I just feel like, I don't know, doing something tonight. What do you say? You want to come along?" Jenny pulled on her oversized, lumpy green sweater and looked hopeful.

"Thanks for the invitation, but I'm afraid I'll have to take a rain check. I promised Amanda that we'd have a game of cribbage before bed. I think she needs the company right now. She's still pretty upset about her father."

Jenny nodded, her face full of sadness. "Death is an awful thing. So unreal."·

"Unreal?"

"Yeah, you know. Being human, our spiritual insight is so limited. But sometimes it's a blessing in disguise. Well, I better get inside."

Sophie would have pursued the comment, but saw that the light was fading fast. If she wanted to walk down by the lighthouse and do some exploring, she'd better get going. "Will we see you at the barbecue tomorrow?"

"Yes, you definitely will. Tomorrow's going to be a big day."

"It will?"

"Oh, yes! You can count on it." Her face suddenly flushed.

Sophie wondered if the evening light was playing tricks with her eyes. For a second, Jenny's intensity seemed to border on the frightening. "Well, so, I'll see you tomorrow then."

"You sure will!" She gave Sophie a quick hug and then set off toward the cottage.

Sophie waited until she was safely inside before turning her attention to the lighthouse. Standing this close to it now, she was truly amazed at how tall it appeared. Much taller than she'd remembered. The entrance was through a weathered wooden door. As she tried to push it open, she noticed a newly installed dead bolt. Well, wasn't that just peachy? Amanda had warned her that the inside stairs were badly in need of repair. With Jenny's day-care center so close, it did make sense to prevent the children from getting inside. Oh well, it would be dark soon anyway. She could get the key and come again tomorrow.

Before heading back through the tall grass, Sophie tilted her head and gazed one last time up at the top. Several gulls had perched on the iron railing that circled just under the narrow open windows in the topmost room. If she could have gotten in, she might have found a nest somewhere up there. For some reason, that possibility intrigued her. As she moved around the side, she felt her foot slip on something wet. Down she went, hitting her shoulder against the side of the building and banging her knee on a stone. Damn. The pain in her leg stopped her cold. Why hadn't she been more careful? Propping herself up against the wall, she pulled up her pant leg to assess the damage. It didn't seem too bad. She'd probably have a beauty of a black-and-blue mark in the morning, but that was about it. As she was about to get up, she heard the sound of voices. She looked behind her and saw that she was sitting next to a low, screened window. Since no one else was around, the sounds had to be coming from inside. Dipping her head nearer, she could just make out a dark form moving slowly down the central stairs.

"Watch out for the next to the last step," called a woman's voice. Sophie recognized it at once. It was Amanda's.

"You should get a carpenter in here before winter sets in," said another, softer voice. A moment later Claire reached the bottom.

Both women stood motionless for a moment in the dim, interior light. Neither looked happy.

"So," said Claire, moving to one of the higher windows and glancing nervously outside. "What are we going to do?"

Amanda sat down on the steps, brushing a sticky cobweb off her jeans. "Exactly what we've been planning all along. Nothing has changed."

"I never thought it would be like this."

"I know. I didn't either. But it won't be long now."

Claire groaned. "Don't say that. It makes me feel too much like a ghoul."

"We have no other choice! What we're doing isn't wrong. Surely you see that." Amanda stood and crossed to her, putting a hand on her shoulder and turning her around. "You love me, don't you?"

Claire sagged against the wall. "You know I do. I've never loved anyone the way I love you."

As they kissed, Sophie's eyes opened wide. She leaned closer to the screen to get a better look. She felt guilty watching this intensely private scene, yet she simply couldn't bring herself to look away.

"And I love *you*," said Amanda, touching Claire's hair tenderly. "Listen to me for a minute. We've got a good reason for everything we're doing. You know that. You can't back out on me now."

Claire closed her eyes. "I won't."

"Good, then it's settled."

"Nothing is settled. I just want it to be over."

"It will be. Soon, you'll see. Jack will be in Washington, and . . ." Amanda's voice faltered.

"See! You can't even say it. Where will *Luther* be?"

Trembling, Amanda turned away.

"I know I'm only making it worse. I'm just not thinking straight." Claire took her in her arms. "When will I see you again?"

"You know what the barbecue is going to be like tomorrow. I think we should be seen together as little as possible. We don't want to create any more suspicion than we already have. But later, maybe in the evening, after all the commotion has died down."

"Will you be able to make it to my book signing in Duluth? It's going to be at Beckman Books on Superior Street. Eight o'clock."

"I think I'd better pass. You understand."

Claire seemed terribly disappointed. Her entire body sank. "Sure. I understand. By the way, what did you tell Jack about the files we got from the clinic?"

Amanda stepped a few paces away. "I said I burned them."

"You're not serious? Does he believe you?"

"He has no reason not to."

There was a long pause. "No. Of course you're right."

"Look, right now, nothing is more important than getting him elected. I'm absolutely committed to it. I'm afraid that after what we've done, there's no turning back."

Claire's hand clutched at her throat. "I know."

"I'll try to get away later tomorrow night and meet you at your cabin. It all depends on how everything goes tomorrow. Let's just leave it for now."

Sophie continued to watch as the two women held each other, whispering words of tenderness and encouragement. Finally, Claire unbolted the door. "I love you," she said, an urgency in her voice. A moment later she was gone. Amanda took hold of the handle and leaned heavily against it. Running her hand roughly through her long blonde hair, she jerked open the door, bolted it behind her, and then fled into the growing darkness.

Quickly, Sophie stood. She could see Amanda disappear into the tall grass, her thin body bending into the wind. In the other direction, Claire was climbing a sandy hill to where her car was parked. Feeling absolutely stunned, Sophie sank back down on the grass and drew her knees up, resting her head in her hands. As she sat watching the waves pound the jagged rocks in the distance, she had the queasy sense of the ground moving unsteadily beneath her. Of course, she'd known Amanda and Luther hadn't been happy together for a long time, but this? It wasn't that Amanda had found a woman, it was that she had found *anyone*. Did Luther know? And how could Amanda keep something as important as this from her? Selfishly, Sophie realized that the dissolution of one of her oldest friends' marriage would strike at the very bedrock of her own life. It was unthinkable. Still, neither Luther nor Amanda acted any differently toward the other. Was Amanda waiting for the right time to tell him? How could there ever be a right time for something

like that? And what was all that stuff about Jack and
some clinic's files? Sophie closed her eyes and tried to
calm down as her heart continued to race.

What on earth was going on?

PART THREE

This Little Piggy Ate Roast Pork

But the unkind and the unruly,
And the sort who eat unduly,
They must never hope for glory—
Theirs is quite a different story!
                    from *A Child's Garden of Verses*
                    Robert Louis Stevenson

12

Sydney Sherwin sprawled in a rocking chair on the front deck. Pulling a bowl of mixed nuts closer, he began to pick carefully through the contents. "I only like the cashews," he said, spitting out a peanut that had inadvertently slipped into his mouth. "Would you like some?" He peeked over his sunglasses at Ryan. "They're kind of stale."

"No, thanks." Ryan sipped his freshly squeezed morning orange juice and tried to pretend he wasn't grinding his teeth. "Isn't it kind of early to be drinking Scotch?"

"Nectar of the gods." Sydney smiled, popping another nut into his mouth. "And anyway, it's almost eleven. Sitting outside under a cloudless summer sky makes me feel like I'm a kid again."

The Scotch no doubt helps, thought Ryan acidly.

"What time is everyone supposed to be arriving for the barbecue?" Sydney's pudgy hand fingered another small cashew.

"Around noon."

They both watched in silence as cameramen from WDPC set up equipment on the front lawn. At least two hundred folding chairs had been arranged in front of the deck. This, plus an abundance of standing room, had been organized for the sole benefit of those loyal supporters who would, in a few short hours, be intently listening to Jack Grendel's long-awaited Labor Day speech. Jack was known for being a philosophical, yet charismatic speaker. His supporters were rarely disappointed.

Red, white, and blue balloons and long, crepe-paper streamers had been affixed to the base of the rounded deck, making it look a bit like an extremely patriotic birthday cake. In back of them, the house had been plastered with American flags. Off to the side, a group of men dressed in white shirts with bow ties, striped suspenders, and old-fashioned straw hats practiced the beginning of a Sousa march.

"I suppose Jack and Nora stayed here last night," said Sydney. He yawned, his florid face stretching like rubber. "When I went to bed, you were all still hard at it."

"They did. We needed to do some last-minute polishing on today's new material."

"You're really working hard to get him elected, aren't you, son?"

Ryan's skin crawled at the use of the term *son*. He found Sydney one of the most thoroughly repulsive men he had ever met. Just the suggestion that they might be related turned his stomach. Sydney Sherwin not only looked like a human rodent, he had all the instincts of a sewer rat. Nora Grendel had been quite informative about the real reason for his unexpected visit. It appeared there was something even more potentially damaging to Jack's political career out there than the Lake Superior dumping scandal. If Ryan could only get his hands on the proof! It was like walking a tightrope. Others wanted to control Jack, too, wanted leverage over his future decisions. Ryan was positive he knew who the biggest threat came from, but who would believe it? Certainly not Jack. "Jack is the best candidate for public office Minnesota has seen in the last fifty years."

"Well now, that's kind of a tall statement." Sydney's nose twitched rodentially. He watched a group of young women busily setting up the food tables. "I've known Jack for a lot more years than you. It's kind of hard for me to see him as anything other than the crazy kid I bunked with in Nam. You knew that, didn't you? That Luther, Jack, and I were all buddies over there?"

"Yes," said Ryan wearily. "You mentioned it several times last evening."

"Did I? Yeah, well, but I bet I didn't tell you the whole story." He winked. "It might blow some people's minds."

"What are you saying, Sid?" Ryan didn't even try to hide the disgust in his voice.

A catering truck clattered into the drive on the west side of the building. Two heavyset men got out looking confused. Before they had a chance to climb the steps to the deck, Nora Grendel appeared and shouted impatiently for them to move the van around to the back. She waited until the truck drove away before crossing to a redwood chair and sitting down.

Ryan was a little concerned about how tired she looked this morning. Even though Nora was only a couple of months Jack's senior, her freckled, ruddy complexion often made her seem years older. The delicate tracery of lines around her eyes needed careful attention before the afternoon celebration began. It was critical she look her best today. Everyone had been up entirely too late last night. Thank God Jack looked like a newborn no matter how little sleep he got. In many ways, hc was the perfect political animal.

"I hope those men know how to roast a pig better than they're able to follow simple directions." Nora held up her hand to shade her eyes from the glittering lake. Her luxurious red hair was pulled back tightly into a thick ponytail.

"I can hardly wait," said Sydney, smacking his lips.

Ryan closed his eyes and looked away.

"Did you take care of everything?" asked Nora, leaning over and touching Ryan on his knee.

He nodded.

"Good." Her smile was positively brilliant. "Then let the Labor Day celebration begin."

Around one, Nora took a stroll down by the pit where the caterers were roasting the pig. She wanted to make sure everything was on schedule. Since the coals were very hot but completely covered by a thick tarp, the men had roped off the entire area so that none of the guests could wander in and get·hurt. One of the cooks had been posted since early morning to prevent an accident. The pit itself had been dug late last evening, with the pig going into it around two A.M. It would be at least twelve hours before it was done and ready to eat.

As Nora approached, one of the guests came to her and pointed to something on the far side of the pit. "What is it?" he asked. "Don't you see?"

Nora squinted curiously at the tip of a striped piece of cloth. She immediately recognized what it was. "It's nothing," she said with a quick smile. "Just part of the process." She took the man's arm and turned him around until he was facing the food tables set up under several high-peaked yellow tents. "Why don't you try some of the guacamole and a glass of fresh lemonade? My husband is up there and I'm sure he'd love to meet you."

"Only if you join us." The man grinned.

Nora tried not to rush him. "I'll be there in a few minutes. I need to talk to the cook first. Please, we're asking the guests to stay away from this area."

"All right," he said. "But I'll be waiting."

Nora watched him walk up the grassy hill. Once he was out of earshot, she turned back to the pit. "Pull that thing out of there," she demanded. "I want to see it."

The caterer walked around the back and drew out what appeared to be a partially charred man's silk necktie. "Gee, I didn't see that. I wonder how it got there?"

"Someone's idea of a joke," said Nora under her breath. Except she knew she couldn't dismiss it quite that easily. Something about it had frightened her. As she took it from his outstretched hand, she realized it was one of Jack's. She moved under the rope and approached the edge of the pit. "I want you to uncover the pig. I have to see it."

The cook appeared confused. "But lady, the whole thing is spread with this thick layer of hot coals. Then there's a layer of wet leaves. Under that is—"

"I don't care what it's covered with! Take that shovel over there and uncover part of it. Now!"

The caterer stared at her as if she had lost her mind. Grudgingly, he picked up the shovel.

Nora stood by impassively as he went to work. After a few minutes of careful digging, the head of the pig appeared. Instantly, Nora could feel the tension in her body begin to dissipate.

"That's fine. You can cover it back up now."

With a look of intense disgust, the cook did as he was told.

The crowd fell silent as Jack Grendel took his place behind the podium. All eyes watched as he brushed a lock of curly blond hair away from his forehead and reached underneath the stand for a glass of water. He took a sip before beginning.

"You know, my friends, this means a great deal to me today to see so many of you here pledging your support to this campaign. I much prefer *this* to the fifteen-second sound bites I've been trying to get used to for the last several months. On the other hand, I give you my guarantee, I won't be making a long speech this afternoon. The food smells entirely too good to keep everyone waiting."

The crowd clapped their approval.

"What I do want to talk about is really quite simple. This Republic has finally begun to recognize the luminous stupidity of the very *same* politicians we send back to Washington, year after year, time after pointless time. It's like a game of political yo-yo, and nothing ever changes. Just the rhetoric. Our collective ears can now pick out a political lie quicker than it takes to turn off the TV set. We realize that too much—much too much—is daily being taken away from us, while very little is ever returned.

"In our election process today, no one is allowed to go uncategorized. This one is a liberal. That one is a conservative. We all know the buzzwords. Yet, if we must be pigeonholed to allow for quick and easy analysis by the newspaper columnists and nightly newscasts, let's at least choose those names carefully, and give them a modicum of definition. Therefore, let's talk for a minute about liberals and conservatives.

"I am running for the U.S. Senate as a Democrat. For all practical purposes, that name designates me as a liberal. The question is then, what *is* a liberal? For the last ten years candidates for public office have been desperately running away from that unholy title. I do not. I believe I've finally begun to understand what motivates the liberal and conservative minds. And that motivation, my friends, is at the very heart of our national dilemma."

Almost as one, the crowd grew quiet, giving their full attention to the handsome man behind the lectern.

"I submit to you that the conservative position in this country today is one inherently motivated by fear. Fear of loss. Fear of change. Quite honestly, I understand those fears myself. We all do. It's natural to fear losing power. And as much as we look forward to it, in some sense we all fear the uncertainty of the future. Why? Because it represents change. And change is a terrifying thing. Consequently, in this time of some of the greatest changes humankind has ever experienced—both politically and socially—conservatism is an appealing and highly comforting position. After all, at least we understand the way things used to work. They may not be working all that well for everyone *now*, but again, it's familiar, and change is threatening and we're doing okay; so leave us alone. Don't rock the boat. Sticking with the status quo—indeed, *making it the moral equivalent of righteousness*—means that we'll all stay safe and secure, and as part of the bargain, feel ourselves to be ethical human beings. And that, my friends, in a nutshell, is the fallacy of the conservative position.

"Change is inevitable. Whether we are prepared or not, the future is coming. Past rules and ways of looking at things—even though every sane person agreed they were the very foundation of God's will on earth—may no longer work. Will we have to be dragged, clutching our old ideas to our breasts, into the next century? Or will we embrace change? I believe *that* perspective is what liberalism can offer to this nation.

"The liberal position, although sometimes Pollyannaish and impractical, has always embraced change—*and* human diversity—as good and necessary. One way or another, things *will* change. We can either send people to Washington who will nurture and direct our collective future, or we can send philosophical dinosaurs who will fight against it with the virulent and highly effective weapons of racism, sexism, reactionary religion—those whose fear is so great they would paralyze this nation and send us to our doom. My friends, the stakes are clear. We *have* to believe in our ability to shape the future and live with diversity and, yes, change!"

Thunderous applause followed the statement.

"Let's make a deal," said Jack, holding up his hands for quiet. "Let's decide to take the future into our hands. Even though we're afraid, even though we need to be cautious and practical, let's not let our fears lead us to defeat. 'Look to this day for it is life. Yesterday is but a dream, tomorrow only a vision. But, today well-lived makes every yesterday a dream of happiness, and every tomorrow a vision of hope. Look well, therefore, to this day.' It's my hope, my good friends, that instead of voting our fears in November, this time, this year, for our future, we will vote our dreams! Thank you very much. And God bless you all!"

People leapt to their feet cheering and calling Jack's name.

"Nora, come up here!" Jack waved her up onto the stage. "I want you all to meet my wife."

Looking extremely elegant in a jade-green designer suit, Nora stepped up next to her husband. Their almost-Hollywood attractiveness was not lost on the crowd of supporters cheering from the lawn.

"I hope you'll all enjoy the fabulous food prepared by Olafson Catering here in Duluth. Nora informs me we'll be ready to eat about three o'clock. In the meantime, I'd like to meet and talk personally with each and every one of you. If we work together, if we never lose sight of our goal, we will achieve victory for ourselves, our country, and our future in November. Thank you very much! Have a great Labor Day!"

The crowd continued to cheer as the Sons of Norway Marching Band began to play "Stars and Stripes Forever." Jack waded into the throng, shaking hands with the people closing in around him. Nora shook a few hands and then caught Ryan's eye. He'd been standing quietly at the edge of the deck, observing people's reactions. Together they headed around to the rear door of the house. Jack had his duties to perform. So did they.

13

"Are you coming?" shouted Bram, his voice impatient. He paused at the edge of the front lawn, waving his arms furiously.

From her vantage on a rocky cliff overlooking Lake Superior, Sophie could see people beginning to line up in front of the food tables. She had been enjoying a moment of solitude, breathing in the sweetness of the afternoon lake breezes. Much to everyone's dismay, the sky had begun to turn cloudy during Jack's speech. Large black thunderclouds were now appearing over Duluth. Thankfully, it would be a while before they reached this far up the shore. "Is it time to eat?" she shouted back, picking up the fringed suede jacket Bram had given her for her last birthday. Such a sweet man. They had seen it in a specialty shop on a recent trip to visit some of Sophie's relatives in northern Minnesota. An elderly Ojibwa woman in Cass Lake still made them by hand. Bram knew how much she wanted it and arranged to have it sent to the house the day of the party.

"You better hurry," he called. "There won't be a scrap left after I'm through."

Saying a brief goodbye to the acrobatic gull that had been keeping her company, she crossed the flat rock to the lawn. The house, which loomed high above her on the hill, seemed a forbidding vision in the gloomy afternoon light. Something about it had always felt so cold, so closed off and remote. It wasn't just that it was constructed of stone. It had more to do with the interior darkness. There was no sense of comfort or warmth within its thick, wintry walls. Sophie shook off the melancholy feeling. Today was *not* going to be spent worrying about anything at all. A picnic was supposed to be fun. Amanda had already introduced her to so many people she felt she knew half the crowd.

Bram motioned her into the food line in front of him. They were standing a good twenty yards from the tent. The line was moving slowly because of the vast array of food set out on the long folding tables. Everything smelled so wonderful it was going to be an agonizing wait. In the distance, a group of small children, each holding a balloon, danced on the grassy slope in front of the gazebo. The band was still playing, but had changed from patriotic marches to "Let Me Call You Sweetheart."

"Today, my darling, you look like you've been on a three-day drunk." Sophie touched his prickly face.

"I must say, I like this no shaving in the morning. I should have grown a beard long ago."

Sophie smirked. "Kissing you is like kissing a Brillo pad."

"Well, if it's so damn bad—"

"I didn't say that."

"You like Brillo pads?"

"I could get used to them."

Bram harrumphed. "Lucky for you. By the way, have you gotten through to your son yet? I heard you calling him last night. No use trying to keep secrets."

Sophie's expression turned serious. "Not yet. Norman's wife answered. She said she'd pass on the message, but I don't believe her."

"Maybe you should try calling again?"

"Maybe."

"You seem so preoccupied with it, Soph. I wish you wouldn't worry so much. Things will work out. You'll see."

Sophie stood on her tiptoes and kissed his cheek. To be honest, she hadn't had the heart to tell him what was really uppermost in her thoughts since last night. All morning she simply couldn't get the image of what she'd witnessed at the lighthouse out of her mind. It wasn't that Bram was homophobic. They both had lots of gay friends in Minneapolis. But Amanda was married to a man they each cared about. Claire was a threat to that marriage. Unfortunately, it didn't seem to be just a casual affair. And, adding insult to injury, it was obvious something else was going on. Something sneaky. The more Sophie thought about it, the more she wondered what it could possibly be. Still, she didn't want to say anything to distract Bram from his writing. At least, not yet.

"Good afternoon," called Claire. A large brown spaniel dragged her toward them. "I was hoping we'd run into each other today." Her round face beamed cheerfully as she yanked the dog to a halt.

"Hi," said Sophie, a little disoriented to see the woman she had just been thinking about materialize right in front of her. She caught Bram's eye. "Sweetheart, I'd like you to meet a friend of Amanda's. This is Claire Van Dorn. My husband, Bram Baldric."

Claire held out her hand. "Bram. That's an unusual name. I don't believe I've ever heard it before. Is it short for something?"

"Bramble," said Sophie. "It means a rough, prickly shrub." She patted his face.

"My wife thinks she's a comedian. I try to humor her, otherwise she pouts. No, it's just Bram. Unfortunately, my mother's favorite book was *Dracula* by Bram Stoker. I am his unwitting namesake." He took off his straw hat and bowed.

"I keep telling him he should feel lucky. After all, we could be calling him *Drac*."

Bram glowered.

"Claire is headmistress at the Tate Academy just outside of Two Harbors," continued Sophie, ignoring his look.

"It's a young women's academy," smiled Claire. "I've been there for several years. I taught art history at the University of Minnesota in Minneapolis before I was offered this job. I jumped at the chance to get out of the city. It's so quiet living by the shore. I wouldn't trade it for anything."

Quiet, huh? thought Sophie. Right. "And I believe you're the current president of the North Shore Feminist Association. Isn't that correct?"

"It is. Speaking of the Association, I was wondering if you'd like to attend one of our meetings while you're here? We'd love to have you. Amanda is giving a speech on Wednesday night. She wants to discuss her brother's position on things like child care, the rights of children and the elderly, and other specific issues that affect women."

Before she could form an answer, Sophie caught sight of Luther crossing the lawn toward them. He was holding a bunch of balloons in one hand and waving at them with the other. Plaid seemed to be the order of the day. Luther had exchanged his usual Brooks Brothers attire for that of L. L. Bean. Somehow, even in an old flannel shirt and faded jeans, he still gave the impression of dignified formality. A baseball cap was pulled low over his eyes.

"I don't know," said Sophie, returning her attention to Claire. She wasn't sure she wanted to spend one of her precious vacation evenings sitting in a room listening to a political speech.

"You don't know what?" asked Luther, grinning as he punched Bram in the arm. The dog, obviously recognizing him, began to wag its tail.

"I was saying to Claire," said Sophie, "that I'm not sure I would be able to attend the next Association meeting."

"Ah. Well, we all have to live with life's little disappointments." Luther scratched the dog's ear. "I was always disappointed Claire was never able to attend one of my classes at the university. I think she would have particularly enjoyed my lecture on women as viewed by the great philosophers."

Claire's face grew stony. "As I've told you before, I'm quite aware how men have defined women down through the centuries. It's not my favorite subject."

"Things like," Luther continued, "Nietzsche's infallible solution to all of women's problems." He let one of the balloons go. Everyone watched as it was caught by the wind and carried high into the air.

"What was that?" asked Bram.

"Pregnancy."

Claire's lips tightened.

Sophie could tell the conversation was headed in the wrong direction. Was Luther baiting her? Sophie had never found him a particularly sexist man, yet he did seem to enjoy Claire's all too obvious irritation. Did this mean he knew about her relationship with Amanda?

"And then there's Immanuel Kant. He said any formal learning in a woman would surely weaken her powers to attract a man. If a woman wanted a formal education, she might as well grow a beard. Or words to that effect."

"You don't actually believe that stuff, do you?" asked Sophie. "Come on."

Luther ignored the question. He was on a roll. "And if you like that, you'll love Schopenhauer. He felt woman's fatal flaw was her inability to understand principles, especially justice." He glanced sharply at Claire. "Interesting, don't you think?"

Claire leveled her gaze. "He was full of shit. And if you believe that crap, so are you."

Sophie had to do something before they came to blows. "Luther, Amanda tells me you were thinking of teaching a special class this fall." It was painfully apparent she was trying to change the subject, but so what? Better that than a formal declaration of war.

A sudden gust of wind blew off the lake, causing the ropes on the food tent to strain against their moorings. Sophie glanced at the angry sky.

"That's right," said Luther. "I wasn't really feeling up to it, but if they'd allowed me to teach the Western world's single greatest philosopher, I'd have considered it. As it turned out, no one was interested."

Everyone turned in unison as a rotund, unkempt Sydney Sherwin walked up and slapped a meaty hand over Bram's shoulder. "How you doin', fella? Been lookin' for you folks." He reeked of sweat and alcohol. "What did y'all think of Jack's little speech? I guess the murder of his father is old news. A mild display of bereavement might've been nice, but then, people are fickle. On the other hand, if he gets some bad press over it, I doubt he'll find quite so many adoring crowds." He leaned closer to Claire and whispered, "This little piggy stayed home. Kind of cute, don't you think?"

"What are you talking about?" coughed Claire, waving away his foul-smelling breath.

"You mean no one around here reads the morning paper?" He stifled a burp. "Old man Grendel was the second little piggy to be bumped off in two days. Someone phoned the paper with an anonymous tip."

Angrily, Luther pulled Sydney aside. He looked helplessly at Sophie. "I'm afraid it's true. For Amanda's sake, I had hoped we could get through the day without making it *the* subject of conversation. The gossip will start soon enough."

"But what did this article say?" asked Bram.

Luther eyed Sydney with disgust. "It appears someone called the *Duluth Daily News* and reported that the police found the words *This little piggy stayed home* typed onto Herman's computer screen shortly after he was murdered. The police have been trying to keep it quiet. With the revelation in this morning's edition, it's not going to be a secret any longer."

Sophie was stunned. "But that means . . ."

Sydney moved in closer, wiggling his eyebrows. "This little piggy went to market. This little piggy stayed home. This little piggy ate roast pork . . ."

"Roast pork?" repeated Bram. "No, no. It's roast beef."

"No, honey," said Sophie, "I think he's right. I've always heard it as roast pork."

With the exception of Sydney, the significance of the statement seemed to strike everyone at the same time. Sophie looked from face to face, each expression more aghast than the last. Almost as one, their eyes moved to the food table.

Claire backed up several steps. She yanked her dog to a

standing position. "Using a gentle little children's poem for something so hideous—well, I for one think it's disgusting! If you will all excuse me, I just lost my appetite. It was nice seeing you again, Sophie. Think about that Association meeting." She nodded politely to Bram. "Nice meeting you."

"Hmph," said Sydney, watching her walk away. "No manners." He belched. "God, can you smell those beans! And did you see that mound of potato salad?" He licked his lips.

Luther draped his arm around Sydney's shoulder. "Come on, Sid old boy. I think you've had a bit too much of our ten-year-old Scotch. Not everyone finds your charms irresistible, you know." He started to maneuver him away. "I want you to go sit over there," he said, pointing to a chair under a large oak, "and I'll bring you a plate of food."

"Well, if you insist," said Sydney, lisping slightly. He strided uncertainly toward the tree. "Lots of piggy!" he shouted over his shoulder. "Don't forget!"

Bram shook his head. "I suppose you're going to tell us he's nothing like that when he's not drinking."

"No," said Luther wearily. "He's just the same. I'm sure you've already noticed. I suppose the only reason I can tolerate him is because I've known him so long—warts and all. When we got out of the service, Jack convinced Sid and me to visit Duluth. He said this area was just waiting for enterprising young men to move in and take over. I know that really appealed to Sid. On the other hand, I wanted to go back to school. I'd always hoped to teach. I agreed to a visit, but then I was going to drive back to St. Louis. As you know, a small problem developed. Somehow, I managed to fall in love with Jack's older sister. I never counted on that. She was the most vibrantly beautiful woman I'd ever met." He looked wistfully at the lake. "Needless to say, I changed my plans."

"And see? You made the right choice. You two have had such a good life," said Sophie. "I've often envied you and Amanda." The words came out before she realized what she'd said. Yet, from her point of view, it *was* the truth. Why did things have to become so complicated?

Luther gave her a half smile. "Does it seem that way?"

"Hey, Mr. Jorensen?" A young man yelled from the edge of the deck. "Your wife wants you to come up to the kitchen."

"Right away," shouted Luther. "Well, duty calls." He glanced at Sydney who had already fallen asleep under the tree.

"Looks like you got a reprieve," said Bram. "Don't worry, we'll bring him his food."

"You two got a reprieve, too," grinned Luther. "I hate to bore people with ancient history."

"It's not boring," protested Sophie. "I mean that."

Luther smiled almost shyly. "You're both very kind."

"Can I ask you one thing before you go?" said Sophie.

"Sure. Anything."

"You mentioned you'd like to teach a class if you could teach the philosophy of someone in particular. I guess I'm just curious who that might be."

Luther gazed up at the threatening sky. " '*And blest are those whose blood and judgment are so well commingled that they are not a pipe for Fortune's finger to sound what stop she please.*' "

"Shakespeare," pronounced Bram.

"Exactly." His eyes slipped to the house. "Now, I better go. We can talk more later."

"One more thing," said Sophie, touching his sleeve. "While you're up there, do you think you could find that newspaper article for me? The one about the note found on Herman's computer terminal? I'd like to see it."

Luther cocked his head and stared at her for a moment. "Sure, I suppose. Why not. It's on the desk in my study. Maybe you can figure out what's going on around here. I, for one, would damn well like to know!" He turned to Bram. "Listen old boy, don't eat the entire pig before I get back." He winked.

Bram swallowed hard, casting a longing glance at the heaped plates of food people were carrying away from the tent. "No problem. You know, I know this is out of character, but I may just stick to vegetables today."

"Hey, this is really nice of you." Sydney turned down the volume on the TV with the remote. He was sitting in Luther's study watching a baseball game on a cable channel. He'd finished his meal about an hour ago, just in time to catch the opening pitch. It was now nearly four-thirty. "I've got two hundred dollars riding on this game. I'm betting the Red Sox make it all the way to the World Series."

"Where would you like me to set your drink?" A crack of thunder shook the tiny panes of glass in the windows on either side of the fireplace.

"How about just handing it over." He reached for it, turning his head to glance outside. "Looks like we might be in for a storm. A pity." He snickered. "The picnic may be called on account of rain. You know, I think you mix the best stinger I've ever had. That first one you brought in really hit the spot."

"Why don't you take a sip? See if I mixed this one the same way."

Sydney leaned back in his chair and put his feet up on the footstool. "I will if you sit down and join me."

"Of course, I'll join you."

"No, no, don't sit there. I won't be able to see the TV."

"All right. How about here?"

"Dandy." He took a taste of his drink. "Agh, this one tastes kind of bitter."

"That's funny. I mixed it with the same ingredients as the first. It must be the brandy."

He took another sip, choking slightly. "It's not so bad, I guess. You just have to get used to it."

"I'm sure you're right."

A flash of lightning caused the TV screen to flicker.

"You're awfully quiet. Something goin' on?" asked Sydney.

"I don't know what you mean?"

"Well," he laughed, "if you don't know, how should I?" He took another sip. "I think we may have a no-hitter here.

The third baseman is the problem. That's the hot corner tonight." He watched eagerly as the next man at bat was struck out.

"Is there something wrong with your throat, Sid?"

Sydney set his glass down and sat forward in his chair. "I don't know. Something feels kind of funny." A ripple of pain crossed his face.

"Why don't you try taking another drink. That might help."

"Right. Good idea." He picked up the glass and took several swallows.

"Feel better?"

Slowly, Sydney pulled a handkerchief out of his back pocket and began to wipe his forehead. "Shit, is it hot in here, or what?"

"No. I feel just about perfect."

"Well, I don't." He held his stomach. "I feel awful."

"You know, Sid, you look awful."

"Do I?"

"Yes, you do."

He took another sip. "I hope it's not the stomach flu. I've heard that's going around and I've got an important meeting tomorrow."

"I don't think you need to worry. It's not the flu."

"Well, Christ! It's got to be something. My stomach hurts like hell. And the inside of my mouth feels like a five-alarm fire." He sat forward, doubling up in pain.

"It's probably the cyanide."

"The what?" Sydney's eyes grew wide.

"The cyanide. At least, I think it's cyanide. The bottle just said rat poison. But it's highly toxic to human beings. You're a human being, aren't you, Sid?"

Sydney stared straight ahead.

"I put some in both your stingers. A little more in that last one. Kind of gives new meaning to the name, don't you think?"

Sydney could no longer speak. He clutched his stomach and pitched forward onto the Oriental rug.

14

Amanda slumped against the soft couch cushions, covering her face with her hands. "How could this have happened? I can't believe Sydney's gone!" Her voice shook with emotion.

"I'm going to have to ask each of you in this room some questions," said Detective Wardlaw. Silently, his tired gray eyes moved from face to face.

Sophie and Bram were seated on one end of the living room couch next to Amanda. Claire sat tucked into the other end. Jack and Nora stood stonelike in front of the fireplace, while Ryan and Jenny had taken up positions near the mullioned front windows.

Outside, the storm that had been threatening for several hours had finally broken over Brule's Landing. Sheets of wind-driven rain crashed heavily against the silent house. For once, Sophie was glad the walls were made of thick stone. The crowds outside had dispersed around five-fifteen, shortly after the police had arrived. The thunderstorm had taken care of any stragglers who might have wanted to stick around and gawk.

"Where's your husband, Mrs. Jorensen?" Wardlaw towered over her frail form.

"I imagine he's still upstairs sleeping. He was exhausted by all the commotion and went up to take a nap around four. I'll have someone go up and get him."

Jack draped his arm protectively around his wife's shoulder. "Surely you must realize there were hundreds of people milling around here today. Any one of them could be responsible for Sid's death."

Wardlaw shook his head. "Not possible."

"I don't understand," said Jack.

"This house was locked all afternoon. The only access was through the kitchen. We've already checked the doors and windows for signs of a break-in. None have been tampered with. We've also talked to Alice Oag, the Jorensens' cook. She remembers quite clearly that Mr. Sherwin entered the house about three forty-five P.M. At no time did any stranger enter through the kitchen. Mr. Jorensen left strict orders that none of the guests be allowed in the house. People who needed rest room facilities were asked to use the portable units set up in the parking lot. So, Mr. Grendel, whoever murdered Mr. Sherwin was either someone known to Ms. Oag, who entered through the kitchen—that could be any of you—or someone who came in with a key." He sat down in a chair opposite Amanda. "How many people have keys to your home, Mrs. Jorensen?"

Nervously, Amanda cleared her throat. "Well, of course, Luther and I each have one. And then Jack and Nora both have keys. We gave Ryan and Jenny a set because they're here so much. It was just easier that way. And, of course, my friend Claire has a key. Last winter she stayed with us fairly often. She was helping me redesign the interior of my restaurant."

"Anyone else?"

"No, I think that's it. Except for our daughter, Chelsea. She has one, but she's hardly ever here. We asked her to come to the barbecue this afternoon, but she couldn't make it."

"That's not the information we've been given," said Wardlaw.

Amanda looked up. "What?"

"She was seen entering the house by the side door at approximately three-thirty this afternoon. That would be close to the time Mr. Sherwin died."

Amanda flushed, pulling her collar more closely around her neck. "Surely you aren't suggesting . . ."

"Eight people have keys to this house, Mrs. Jorensen. I

believe we'll find the owner of one of those keys committed a murder."

An oppressive silence filled the dank, storm-darkened living room as Detective Wardlaw stood, rubbing the center of his back. Only the crackling fire seemed to relieve some of the growing tension.

Bram took hold of Sophie's hand, squeezing it tightly.

"What about the note we found?" asked Jenny. The sound of her voice seemed to startle her. She looked hesitantly around the room, making sure she hadn't said the wrong thing.

"What note?" asked Jack.

"Another note was found next to Mr. Sherwin's body," sighed Wardlaw. "After this morning's article in the Duluth newspaper, I suppose there's no point in trying to hide what's going on here. The note found today in Mr. Sherwin's hand clearly links his death with that of your father, Herman Grendel, and Lars Olson. From a quick examination, it appeared to be typed on the same typewriter as the first note." He turned his back to the fire. "Now we've prepared a room upstairs where we can talk privately. For your protection, our conversations will be taped. I'd like to start with you, Ms. Tremlet, since you found the body. If you'll come with me?"

Jenny quickly fell in behind him as he left the room.

Watching them go, Amanda reached for the handkerchief Bram held out to her. The tears she'd been holding back now came in a flood.

Sophie felt completely helpless as she watched her friend cry. She slipped her hand around Bram's arm, feeling comforted by his presence.

"It'll be okay, Sis," said Jack, trying to sound hopeful. "Really. The police will find out who did it."

"Claire," sniffed Amanda, "would you be a dear and wake Luther? Tell him he's wanted downstairs right away. Oh, and while you're up, would you mind getting my pills? You know the ones I mean. They're in my purse. It's hanging on the coatrack next to the front door."

"Of course," said Claire. "I'll just be a minute."

Ryan dropped down on a chair opposite Sophie, stretching his arms and legs to relieve some of his nervousness. "How do they think Sydney was—?"

"Poison," said Nora, cutting him off. She drew out a cigarette from a brass box on the mantel.

"Don't smoke that damn thing in here," snarled Jack, stepping away from her.

"Excuse *me*, your lordship."

"And cut the crap. I don't have time for it today."

Sophie noticed a smile creep around the edges of Ryan's mouth. Was he enjoying this?

"Sophie," said Amanda, dabbing at the edges of her eyes, "be a dear and get me a glass of water, will you? I'll need it for my pills."

"Sure," said Sophie, more than glad to get out of the room. She was beginning to feel like an unwelcome intruder inadvertently witnessing a private family tragedy. The last thing Amanda and Jack needed right now was an audience. "I'll be right back."

Nodding to a heavyset policeman who had been observing her from the doorway, Sophie crossed to the dining room, past the long Duncan Phyfe table covered in lace, and walked at last into the darkened kitchen. A flash of lightning illumined the empty food trays stacked haphazardly on the wide counter. Mechanically, she turned on the faucet and reached inside the cupboard for a clean glass. As she watched the water trickle into the sink, she tried to clear her mind and think.

Wardlaw was undoubtedly right. Someone in that room had indeed murdered three people. But facing that fact was frightening, not just because of the horrible deaths involved, but because these people were her friends! Never in her life had Sophie come upon a situation like this. Nothing had prepared her for the cold revulsion she was feeling. Yet somehow, the most surprising part of it was the intense curiosity she'd experienced ever since she'd heard Jenny's scream and had run into the study to see what was wrong. Under the circumstances, curiosity seemed an appalling reaction to something so horrid. Yet, there it was.

It was that child's verse that was so diabolical. Only a sick mind could twist something so sweet into something so evil. But think, now. What were the verses? *This little piggy went to market. This little piggy stayed home. This little piggy ate roast pork.* And what was the next verse? *This little piggy had none. None* of what? None of the roast pork? None of the festivities surrounding the eating of the roast pork? Or none of something completely unrelated? It was the puzzle that fascinated, even though the reality was almost too horrible to contemplate. If she could only crack the code, she might be able to prevent a death. Sophie knew she had one important advantage over the police. They didn't know the people involved as well as she did. Maybe, just maybe, she might be able to help. Except, what if Bram wanted to leave? That was a strong possibility now that the peace he needed so badly to complete his book had been totally shattered. Yet how could she leave at a time like this? Her friends needed her. It was unthinkable!

Sophie filled the glass and walked quietly back through the dining room. Hearing footsteps on the stairs, she made a quick decision and hid behind one of the large oak doors just as Claire came into the foyer. Watching through a crack, Sophie saw her approach the coat stand, where Amanda's purse was hanging, and reach inside for the pills. Carefully, Claire drew out a large brown plastic bottle. It didn't look like any prescription container Sophie had ever seen before. Holding it closer to a lamp, Claire appeared to be reading the print on the back. Sophie couldn't see her expression, but the hesitation told her something was wrong. Hurrying now, Claire felt in the pocket of her sweater for a tissue. After wiping the bottle clean of finger-prints, she stuffed it into the pocket of a gray suede jacket hanging next to the purse. Still glancing around, she stuck her hand inside the purse again and, this time, drew out the correct container. Sophie took it as her cue to move from behind the door.

"Oh," said Claire, whirling around. "You startled me. I didn't hear you coming."

"Amanda asked me to get her a glass of water." She held it up. "For the pills."

"Of course. I should have thought of that." Absently, she touched the gold chain at her neck. "I expect we have a long evening ahead of us."

Sophie nodded.

"I was going to do a book signing later this evening at Beckman Books in downtown Duluth. I called and told them I couldn't make it. After I explained the situation, they understood." She sighed. "Well, I guess there's nothing else to do." With a look of frustrated resignation, she turned and walked into the living room.

Sophie took a deep breath and followed.

15

"Lower your voice," said Sophie, pulling Bram into a nook under the back stairs. "We've got to talk."

"If you'd tried a little harder, I'm sure you could've found a more uncomfortable spot." He stooped to avoid hitting his head. "To someone who is barely five-three, this may look inviting."

"Shush and help me think. These are our friends, for pity's sake. We've got to help them."

"I'm going to say this once, darling—"

"Don't call me darling. You only call me darling when you're going to say something nasty."

"—and I expect you to listen. I think we should check into renting that cabin farther up the shore. Things have already gotten out of hand around here, and I, for one, have the sense to leave! I know you feel a certain loyalty to Luther and Amanda. Even Jack and Nora. But—"

"A certain loyalty! One of them may be accused of murder! What if this detective screws up and accuses the wrong person?"

"If the police make an arrest, they'll have plenty of evidence. Don't worry. Besides, they're professionals. They know how to handle things like this."

Sophie wasn't convinced. "You know, I got a pretty good look at that third note Wardlaw found in Sydney's hand. It was typed on an old manual typewriter. All the *t*'s were slightly below the rest of the letters. I doubt it would be too hard to trace. And another thing. There was something else printed on that paper. I took a second to memorize it. What do you make of this? *But the unkind and the unruly, and the sort who eat unduly, they must never hope for glory— theirs is quite a different story!*"

"Charming." He scratched his chin. "You know, it does kind of ring a familiar chord. I'm sure I've heard it before."

"Well, you're the English lit major. Unless it's a direct quote from Ezekiel or Jeremiah, I might not recognize it."

Bram grinned. "Let me think about it."

"And another thing. Remember that newspaper article I saw on Jack? The one that said he was going to donate a year of his time to a place called Damascus Gate. Unless I'm losing my memory, that was the same year he supposedly entered Stanford."

"What's your point?"

"The point! The point is he couldn't be in two places at once."

"I'm sure there's a simple explanation."

"Really? Then why did Amanda get all weird about it when I mentioned it to her this morning? We were having a cup of coffee in the dining room and she asked where I'd seen the clipping. When I told her, she said it was a mistake. Tried to make light of it—you know, newspapers are so inaccurate. Poked me in the ribs. Laughed about my doing an occasional job for the enemy. She changed the subject almost immediately."

"All right, I'll grant you, it does sound like she was trying to hide something. But what's it got to do with these murders? It seems like a rather big leap in the dark to me."

"Maybe. But there are an awful lot of secrets around here. Something's not right."

"What do you mean? I haven't noticed any secrets. You're exaggerating."

"I am not."

"Name one other secret."

Sophie squared her shoulders. "Amanda and Claire are having an affair."

Bram's head banged against the sloped ceiling. "Christ!"

"Yes, and they've got some information on Jack—something Amanda told him she'd burned."

Gingerly, he rubbed the top of his head. "I don't know how you do it, Soph. You shouldn't have taken a job as managing editor of that arts magazine. You missed your calling. You should be a gossip columnist."

She flashed him a sickly smile. "This is not gossip. Look, all of this is important. You can sneer if you want—"

"No, you're right. I didn't mean to sneer. I'm just frustrated like everyone else. I mean, what the hell's going on?"

"I don't know, but there's more." She thought of Claire finding that mysterious bottle in Amanda's purse.

"More? Like what?"

"I'll fill you in on everything later, okay? Right now I want to get back in that living room and see how Amanda's chat with Wardlaw went. I think Luther's supposed to talk to him next."

"Sophie," said Bram, firmly grasping her by the shoulders, "promise me something. Tell me you're going to show the police that note you found under our windshield wiper."

"All right," she said. "Anything you say."

"Good."

"On one condition."

Bram raised an eyebrow.

"That you make an attempt to work here for a few more days. I need some time. Please, honey. I can't just pick up

and leave right now. I promise I won't put myself in any
danger. Scout's honor." She held up her right hand.

"Sophie—"

"Oh, come on. If we leave, it's going to be cold cheese
sandwiches and tepid beer. You know those cabins don't really have any decent cooking facilities. And Alice has cassoulet on the menu tomorrow."

He closed his eyes. "You know that for a fact?"

"I do."

"Well, I suppose I could consider extending our sojourn.
But only if matters calm down around here. I know this
sounds selfish, but I've got to finish those last four chapters. And you, my dear, have to keep your promise to talk
to the police."

"Of course. First thing in the morning."

Luther opened the door quietly and entered the bedroom.
Wardlaw was sitting in a leather armchair by the window,
his face barely visible in the diffuse light from a small table
lamp.

"Thank you for coming, Mr. Jorensen. I assume by now
you've been told what's happened here today."

Luther nodded, sitting down and pulling a pipe out of his
sweater pocket. "Do you mind?"

Wardlaw pushed an ashtray toward him. "I understand
you were taking a nap when the death occurred. Your wife
mentioned you'd been asleep for quite a while."

"I suppose our Puritan forefathers thought it a lazy habit,
but it's one I enjoy."

Wardlaw watched Luther fill his pipe and then press a
lighted match to it. "Do you often take such long naps?"

He sucked on it for a moment before answering. "To be
truthful, I haven't been feeling well lately. I get tired easily.
I don't have much stamina, so I take naps. They seem to
help."

"Did you fall asleep right away?"

"As soon as my head hit the pillow."

"And you heard nothing unusual?"

"Unusual? No. My wife came in to get a sweater out of

the bureau drawer. I'd say I'd been in the room for about ten minutes. I imagine she thought I was asleep since I had my eyes closed."

"How did you know it was your wife?"

"I peeked."

Wardlaw cleared his throat. "Were you aware that your daughter, Chelsea, was here this afternoon?"

Luther bit down hard on the pipe stem. "No. I wasn't aware of that."

"She came to the lodge to meet Mr. Woodthorpe."

He arched an eyebrow. "You know that for certain?"

"We do. According to Mr. Woodthorpe himself, she arrived around three-thirty. He got her a plate of food and they spent an hour together in the east sun room. Are they good friends?"

"Perhaps," said Luther, his voice thoughtful. "And perhaps not."

"Jenny Tremlet led me to believe she and Mr. Woodthorpe were planning to be married."

"I think that may be a bit premature."

"I see. I'm curious, Mr. Jorensen. How would you feel about Ryan marrying into your family?"

Luther smiled. "It won't happen."

"Why is that?"

"Because my daughter isn't stupid. May I say, Detective Wardlaw, that your interest in the potential conjugal interrelationships between my friends and family is most touching. But perhaps we should get on to something more pertinent."

"All right." Wardlaw opened his briefcase and lifted out a brown, plastic bottle enclosed in a clear, plastic bag. He set it on the table between them.

Luther stared at it indifferently.

"Do you recognize this, Mr. Jorensen?"

He picked it up. "I think it's the poison I bought last spring. We had a small mouse problem downstairs in the furnace room. I find mice an embarrassment, don't you?"

"When was the last time you saw this bottle?"

"I don't know. We store that kind of thing in an old cupboard. It's not locked. It seems I do remember bringing it up for Alice, our cook, about a month ago. I think she said she saw a mouse in her bedroom. You can ask her about it if you like. She was terribly distraught." He placed it back on the table.

"But you haven't seen it personally for the last month?"

"No, I haven't."

"Then how did it get into the pocket of your gray suede coat?"

Luther jerked the pipe out of his mouth. "It what?"

"One of my men found it a few minutes ago. If I'm not mistaken, it's the same substance that killed Mr. Sherwin."

Luther looked hard at Wardlaw. "You found it in *my* coat pocket?"

"Yes."

He began to laugh. "If I'd tried to murder Sydney, I certainly wouldn't hide the poison in anything of my own. Surely you can't believe I had anything to do with this?"

"We'll have to get the fingerprint report from the lab before we come to any conclusions."

Luther shook his head. " *'For murder, though it have no tongue, will speak with most miraculous organ.'* "

"What was that?"

"Why, that was Shakespeare, Detective Wardlaw." A slow smile appeared on his face. "This doesn't make any sense, you know. But then, I suppose I'd be the perfect scapegoat."

"Why do you say that?" Wardlaw looked genuinely confused.

Luther shrugged. "Oh, I am sorry. I was just thinking out loud. It's an obnoxious habit, I agree. I meant nothing by it." He crossed his arms. "Are we finished?"

"I'm not done with any of you," said Wardlaw, the first hint of strain in his voice. "But for now, that will be all." He got up, stuffing the tape recorder, notes, and bottle of poison into his briefcase.

After he was gone, Luther rose and turned off the table lamp. He crossed to the window and pushed it open, breathing in the gentle, rain-scented night wind.

16

Wardlaw leaned across the desk, taking the sheet of paper from Sophie's hand. The bright morning sunlight streamed in through an open window behind him. Sophie had driven into town right after breakfast, giving Amanda the excuse that she wanted to spend the day shopping. Amanda had begged off, saying she was simply too upset to come along. After a whispered phone conversation, Amanda had retreated to her bedroom carrying a bottle of aspirin. Luther hadn't come down to breakfast at all. As Alice was clearing the buffet table, she mentioned that he'd taken a walk along the water. And Jack and Nora were still asleep upstairs in the bedroom next to Bram and Sophie.

"How did you receive this piece of paper?" asked Wardlaw, laying it down on the desktop and pressing a button on his intercom.

"Someone put it under the windshield wiper of my car the night the Gasthaus reopened."

A young man entered the office. Wardlaw handed it to him and told him to take it downstairs for analysis.

"Did you find the woman with the poodle?" he asked, peering over his bifocals. "The one mentioned in the note?"

Sophie knew she was being carefully scrutinized. Thankfully, Wardlaw didn't seem angry that she hadn't shown him the note last night. "Yes, well, actually I drove over to the Mudlark the next afternoon. The woman in question's name is Dolores Benz."

The detective nodded.

"She apparently saw Lars Olson get into a car with

someone the night he was murdered. She didn't know who it was."

"We've talked with her at some length," said Wardlaw, picking up a pencil and jotting a few words down on a notepad. "Why do you suppose someone sent you this message?"

Sophie shrugged. "Beats me."

Wardlaw studied her for a long moment. He was obviously busy. "Is there anything else?" he asked with undisguised impatience.

Sophie was somewhat embarrassed. There *was* something else. Something that had happened earlier in the morning, but something she wasn't sure she wanted to share with the police. If Bram found out she'd held it back, he'd hit the ceiling. Perhaps it was best to tell everything. After all, the police weren't the enemy. "Well, to be honest, this morning I found another note slipped under my bedroom door. My husband was up before dawn. He's trying to finish some important writing this trip. I would guess the note was pushed under after he left, otherwise he would have seen it."

"Did you bring this note with you?"

Sophie drew it out of her purse and handed it over.

Opening it, Wardlaw adjusted his glasses and read, *"Find the Child's Garden, find the murderer."* He looked up. "What do you make of it?"

Sophie shook her head. "I have no idea. I did wonder why the words *Child's Garden* were capitalized. It's kind of odd, don't you think? The thought occurred to me that maybe the two notes could be from someone who wants to help catch the murderer, but someone who, for whatever reason, doesn't want to be identified. At least, that's the first thing I considered."

"And now?"

"Well, I don't know. I suppose it's possible it could even be from the murderer himself. Or herself. But I don't understand why. I saw the note that was found yesterday in Sydney's hand. The messages sent to me were typed on a different typewriter. An electric I would guess." She looked earnestly at Wardlaw, hoping he could give her an answer. "I don't know, maybe the murderer *wants* to be caught. He's trying to give clues."

Wardlaw smiled for the first time. "You have an active imagination, Ms. Greenway, but in this case, I don't think so."

"Why not?" Sophie was terribly upset. Unfortunately, Wardlaw knew things he wasn't about to tell her. That unavoidable fact made her furious. Couldn't he break his rules, just this once, and tell her what was going on?

"Because of the nature of these murders," continued Wardlaw, "we've asked the FBI to help us develop a psychological profile of the perpetrator. These are not serial murders in the strict sense. There's nothing random about them. The murderer, whoever he or she is, has everything very well thought out. For the moment, I don't believe you and your husband are in any danger. Otherwise, we'd advise you to leave Brule's Landing. We're positive one of the eight people with keys to that house is our man, so to speak. I know some of those people are your friends. That makes these notes all the more interesting."

Sophie pulled on the short wisps of hair around her ears. Damn haircut. She couldn't wait till it grew out. "What are you saying?"

"Your presence at that house right now could be a big help to us. That is, if you'd be willing to cooperate."

"Cooperate?"

"Exactly. Tell us what's going on in there. Call me if you see anything suspicious. Anything at all."

"You mean be your spy." The suggestion disgusted her.

Wardlaw dropped the pencil he was holding. "If you like."

Sophie didn't. She started to get up.

"I can see I've approached this the wrong way. Please, just give me one more minute of your time." He folded his hands on his desktop and tried another, this time a bit more grandfatherly, smile.

Sophie could see the fatigue in the deep lines around his

eyes. Those lines hadn't been there the first time they'd met. She felt momentarily sorry for him.

"Three people have been murdered, Ms. Greenway. No matter what you might think of them personally, they each had a right to their lives. Unless we stop the individual who's responsible, there's going to be another murder. Perhaps even two. The point is, you can help. I'm not asking you to sneak around corners, ransack personal belongings. I'm merely asking you to keep your eyes and ears open, and if you see something you think we should know, give me a call. That's it. Nothing more."

Sophie thought about what she'd seen yesterday. Claire removing the poison from Amanda's purse and slipping it into Luther's jacket. Later in the evening, when she'd had a chance to talk to Luther privately, he hadn't seemed very upset about it. At the time, she'd found his reaction strange. But the question right now was, what would the police make of Claire's actions? "Detective Wardlaw, there is one thing . . ."

Wardlaw took off his glasses and set them carefully on the desktop. "Yes?"

"Well, yesterday, just after you left the living room with Jenny Tremlet, I happened to see something."

His frown deepened.

"Actually, I saw Claire Van Dorn take a large, brown plastic bottle out of Amanda's purse, wipe it clean of fingerprints, and put it into the pocket of Luther's jacket. I understand now that you think it was the poison that killed Sydney."

Wardlaw looked past her, obviously ruminating over what she'd just said.

"To be honest," continued Sophie, "I don't think Claire knew what it was when she first found it. Amanda had sent her out of the room to go upstairs and wake Luther. She'd asked Claire to get a bottle of prescription pills out of her purse on her way down. I don't know why Claire did what she did. Perhaps to protect Amanda. But it's not right to let you think Luther had anything to do with hiding that bottle."

Wardlaw scratched his chin. "It seems we need to talk to Ms. Van Dorn again. I appreciate the tip."

Sophie nodded. She didn't feel entirely at ease about what she'd just confided, but it was probably best to tell the truth.

"Anything else you'd like to tell us?" asked Wardlaw.

Sophie could tell he figured she was holding something else back. She decided to ask the sixty-four thousand dollar question. "Who do you think the murderer is?"

"I don't know."

"But you have a theory."

He nodded.

"And you're not going to tell me."

"I may be wrong, but I doubt you'd like my answer. I will say this much. I know you're very concerned about all this. The fact is, the murderer could easily be a man *or* a woman."

"But what about Lars Olson? How could a woman have done that?"

Wardlaw leaned back in his chair. "I see you've given this some thought. All right, let me explain something to you. We're pretty sure Olson walked from a car to the spot under the bridge where he was tied up and gagged. He'd been drinking, and the autopsy showed a slow-acting sedative in his system. It wouldn't take any physical strength to simply wait until he collapsed and then take a rope and tie it around his neck. The bridge is low at the base. Easy to get to. No one saw anyone dragging a body. There was a bluegrass festival in Canal Park that night. Lots of people were milling around. Even though the murderer picked a remote spot under the bridge, someone would have seen something blatantly suspicious." Wardlaw leaned forward and rubbed his sore eyes. "If Mr. Olson was lucky, he never regained consciousness."

"And the other two murders—"

"A gunshot—and poison."

"Are you saying you think the murderer *was* a woman then?"

"I'm not saying anything one way or the other, Ms. Greenway." He flipped his notebook closed.

Sophie knew the conversation was over. "Well, I suppose I better get going. I've got a long list of things I need to accomplish today."

Wardlaw stood. "We'll need to run some tests on those notes you've given us. Perhaps they'll offer some further information. But one word of caution. As I said before, my feeling is that you're not in any danger. At least not right now. But it's just a feeling. If you and your husband choose to leave, in the long run that might be the wisest thing to do. In any case, things could change. Please don't get involved in this any more deeply than you already are. And call me if you have anything to report or if you need my help." He handed her his card. "My home phone is at the bottom. If you need me, don't hesitate to use it."

He walked her to the door, extending his hand and attempting one final, somewhat sad, smile. As Sophie got on the elevator and waited for the door to close, she caught a glimpse of him as he turned back into his office.

The expression on his face made her shiver.

17

"I'm afraid we don't seem to have a copy of that particular article," said a tall, gangly young man. He bent across the counter, his thin fingers playing with a paper clip. The sign above his head read DULUTH DAILY NEWS—ARCHIVES DEPARTMENT. "Have you tried the public library? They keep old copies of the newspaper on microfilm. We haven't changed over yet. Sometimes things get misplaced."

Misplaced my ass, thought Sophie. She glared at him.

"I've already tried the Duluth library, the library in Clouquet, and I've even called the main library in Minneapolis. Nobody seems to be able to locate it." Angrily, she reflected on the wild goose chase she'd been on all day. The article on Jack Grendel, which she'd first seen in Herman Grendel's office, had been completely excised from public record. The question was: why?

The young man scratched his cheek. "Yeah, it is kind of strange that nobody has it. Well, I suppose I could have someone else look through our files."

Sophie held up her hand. "Don't bother. It would be a waste of time." She picked up her gloves and hurried out of the office. There was no use pursuing a dead end. It was admirably clear she had wasted the better part of the day chasing a phantom.

Sophie regretted the mistake she'd made at the picnic yesterday. In front of Amanda, she'd asked Jack about the clipping—told him of the scrapbook she'd found in his father's house. Amanda seemed angry that she would bring it up again. Jack, on the other hand, casually explained that he'd intended to spend some time as a volunteer at the clinic, but was accepted at Stanford, one thing leading to another, and he never went. Simple. No big deal. Indeed, it had sounded completely innocent over sponge cake and lemonade. If it hadn't been for Amanda's reaction earlier in the day, Sophie would probably have dropped the whole thing. Yet, even if Jack was a good actor, Amanda's nervousness had told her much more than either intended. Something was amiss. Somebody was hiding something. It was a funny feeling to think she was being *handled*, kept at arm's length by two of her oldest friends.

Passing a phone booth in the lobby, an idea occurred to her. She pulled out her phone credit card and stepped into the booth. A second later she was talking to an operator in Green Dells, Wisconsin.

"Can you repeat that name?" asked a clipped, female voice.

"Damascus Gate." Sophie matched the woman's overly precise manner.

"Are you sure it's in Green Dells?"

"I am."

"All right, just a minute."

The line cracked a couple of times as the operator searched for the number.

"It's not part of the Saltzman Clinic, is it?"

Sophie was becoming impatient. How hard could it be to find any given number in a small town? "I don't know. I've never heard of the Saltzman Clinic."

"Oh, here it is. It was under St. Luke's Lutheran Church—Damascus Gate Center. Here's your number."

Sophie wrote it down and hung up. Once again, she punched the buttons.

"DGC," said a distracted male voice. He sounded busy.

"Hello. I'm calling long distance. I'm hoping you can help me."

"Yeah?" Another phone was ringing in the background.

"I understand you use volunteers at your clinic."

"We're not a clinic. We're a halfway house. And yes, we do use volunteers sometimes. Drug rehab is expensive. Volunteers help defray some of the cost."

Drug rehab, mused Sophie. "I was told you began as a center to help injured vets returning from Vietnam."

"That was a long time ago. And even then, drug rehab was a big part of what we did."

"Do you recall a volunteer by the name of Jack Grendel? He would have donated some time at your facility back in 1969."

The man started to laugh. "Are you kidding? Do you know anything about halfway houses? We should remember a volunteer from twenty-five years ago?"

Sophie was not going to be put off. "Please, this is very important. We're trying to ... establish that this young man, ah ... actually made it back from Vietnam. Don't you have any records you could check?"

"Yeah, we got records. But twenty-five years ago, my God, I wouldn't know where to look."

"It's important," said Sophie.

The voice hesitated. "All right, I suppose I could run

down to the basement and see what I can shake loose. What was that last name?"

Sophie pronounced it carefully and then spelled it. She waited as the man dropped the phone on the desk. After what seemed like an eternity, he returned.

"Our files from back then are pretty messed up—office duties weren't a high priority. Anyway, I couldn't find anything with that name on it. If he was here, I would think something would've shown up, but I can't say for sure. I did ask Pastor Iverson—he was one of the men who started the center. He couldn't place the name either."

"I see. Well, thanks for your time. If you do run across anything, let me give you my number. Ask to speak with Sophie Greenway—no one else, okay? And don't say where you're calling from."

"I get it," said the guy. "Don't worry. We know how to be discreet."

Sophie waited while he wrote everything down. After he hung up, she grabbed her purse and gym bag and headed for the nearest women's room. She felt a bit like Clark Kent searching out a phone booth in which to change into his Superman costume. If she didn't hurry and get into her disguise—heavy padding, a woman's curly black wig, Twins T-shirt, sweatpants, tennis shoes, and a plaid blazer—she'd be late for her dinner reservation at the Gasthaus Rethenau. It was perfect casual attire for northern Minnesota. She'd fade into the woodwork. Before she left Minneapolis, she'd promised the food editor at the newspaper an accurate and typically colorful review of the current culinary offerings at Duluth's finest German restaurant. The food at the opening didn't truly reflect the menu or service. To do it justice, she had to have a meal there and base her comments on that experience. It was a tough job, but then somebody . . . et cetera.

After donning her new identity, she stepped into the chilly, misty afternoon. The stiff wind off the lake caused her to pull her leather coat more closely around her body. This morning may have felt like summer, but this was Duluth. One minute it was July, the next January. Sophie remembered how much her mother used to grumble at having to pack for their trips to the North Shore. You have to pack for every season, she would say. With three children and a husband that was no small accomplishment. Her father, not being responsible for these minor, insignificant ministrations, always felt the changeable weather was one of Duluth's most charming features.

Leaning into the wind, Sophie dashed across the street to her car. After a short but scenic drive along London Road, she found herself seated comfortably at a linen-covered table in a dark, cozy corner of the main dining room. It was still early for the dinner meal, so the room wasn't crowded. Sophie studied the menu as she sipped her German beer. The schweinepfeffer in horseradish cream with spätzle and braised red cabbage caught her eye.

"Good evening," said a familiar voice.

Sophie looked up. "Claire. This is . . . how did you recognize me?"

"Your ring." Claire nodded to her hand. "It's a tigereye. I noticed it the first time we met."

"You're very observant."

"Don't worry. You don't look anything like your normal self."

"Thanks. Will you join me?"

"Just for a minute. I can't stay. It's movie night at Brule House, and Amanda's invited me for dinner."

"Movie night?"

Claire unwound a silk scarf from around her neck and unbuttoned her raincoat. "Several months ago Luther finally broke down and bought a VCR. Amanda thought it was a silly waste of money, but she's really gotten into it lately. We all have standing invitations to come for a movie on Tuesday nights. Sometimes dinner. Ryan and Jenny are usually there. And Jack and Nora, when they're in town. Didn't Amanda say anything to you about it?"

Sophie shook her head. Just one more thing Amanda had failed to mention.

"Well, with everything that's been going on, I'm sure it just slipped her mind. You won't be very interested in dinner after you've eaten here, but come down to the rec room when you get home. That's where everything is set up." Claire held a newly matted and framed print under one arm. "I came to give this to Gilly. She's the new night manager. Her brother is the handyman here, and I want him to hang this in Amanda's office. Do you like it?" She held it up.

Sophie did. It was an etching of two Raggedy Ann dolls sitting at a small table, having their morning tea. "Very nice."

"Amanda liked it so much I thought I'd buy it for her. So, are you doing a review for that Minneapolis paper?"

"I am."

She pulled out a chair and sat down. "Tell me, how did you learn so much about food?"

Sophie took a sip of her beer. "Well, my parents own the Maxfield Plaza. It's a lovely, Old World hotel in downtown St. Paul. It's now considered a landmark, part of the historic register. There's a wonderful restaurant on the top floor, so I'm afraid I grew up rather spoiled. On the other hand, when I was young, my enthusiasm for food was fairly indiscriminate. The delight I've found over the years in learning *how* to discrim:i.ate is at the heart of my more mature appreciation. It's something I'd like to pass along. I have no formal training, just a good nose and a keen palate—and a witty writing style that has earned me more attention than I perhaps deserve. I've also traveled to Europe and the Far East on occasion as a culinary adventurer. I simply love to eat!" She patted her stomach.

"And this new job? Managing editor of *Squires*. I used to have a subscription to that years ago."

"It was started in 1959 by a man named Hillary Squire. He was a great devotee of the arts and didn't find any of the current magazines to his liking. His son took it over several years ago, but Hilly didn't like the way things were headed. Actually, when it came time for a change of guard, he called me. He'd seen my work at the *Midwest Forum* and was very impressed. I worked my way up from staff writer to associate editor in less than two years. I've been managing editor there for the last eight. But *Squires* is more what I've always wanted. I couldn't be happier."

"How wonderful for you." Claire waved at a waitress. "Coffee," she mouthed.

The young woman came over immediately with a cup and a fresh pot. "Hi, Ms. Van Dorn!"

"Good evening, Beth," smiled Claire. "How's that paper coming?"

"I haven't finished it yet." She placed the cup next to the napkin and poured the coffee. "I'm off at eight and then I'm going over to the library to do some more research."

"Have you met Beth?" asked Claire, nodding to Sophie. "She's in one of my classes at the academy."

"Nice to meet you," said Beth, extending her hand. "You are?"

"Martha Finchly." Sophie shook hands warmly.

"I'll be back in a few minutes for your orders." The young woman rushed away into the kitchen.

"I didn't know you taught anymore," said Sophie, pouring the last dregs of her bottled beer into her glass. "I guess I just thought you . . . administered."

"I did for the first few years, but I missed teaching entirely too much. Since I'm the head honcho, so to speak, I can pretty much do as I please." Claire held the coffee cup to her lips, her expression turning serious. "That was awful yesterday, wasn't it? I can't stop thinking about it. That horrid Sydney Sherwin was a disgusting little man, but still, such a tragedy."

"Terrible," agreed Sophie. "I've been mulling it over in my mind all day. These *pig murders*, as they're being called, are happening for a very specific reason."

"Pig murders?"

"Haven't you seen the morning paper? It's the headline. PIG MURDERS CONTINUE."

Claire shivered. "Leave it to the press. Picking up on that children's poem. It's disgusting."

"I think Detective Wardlaw was right. Someone with a key to Brule House is no doubt behind everything. The only thing is, there can be a lot of motives for murder."

Claire nodded, carefully unfolding her napkin and laying it in her lap.

"For instance, what if someone had an important secret they wanted kept quiet? What if it was something so important they were willing to kill to prevent it from getting out?"

"Sounds like a stab in the dark to me." Claire looked out the window.

"Maybe."

"The police are doing their job, Sophie. They'll figure it out sooner or later."

"Were you called down to the police station today?"

"Me? No. Well, to be accurate, I haven't been home since early this morning. But I'm sure Wardlaw realizes I have no motive. I hardly knew Sydney and I only knew Herman Grendel socially. There's not much to talk about."

"Uhm," said Sophie. "I suppose you know Luther was asked to come in after lunch."

Claire shook her head. "That's too bad. I'm afraid the police think he had some rather strong feelings about each of the victims. From what I hear, he may be their primary suspect."

Sophie groaned. "I was afraid of that."

"I know he's a close friend of yours, but even *you* must admit he's a strange man. Hard to figure. Who knows what's going on in that mind of his?"

"For that matter, who knows what's going on in anyone's mind? Oh, come on, Claire. You don't really think Luther had anything to do with those murders."

Claire leaned forward, elbows on the table, her head resting on her hands. She seemed to be thinking. "All I can say is, I wish I knew. It's a nightmare. You know, when I talked to Amanda this afternoon, she said the police had even called her daughter down to the station today. And then about an hour later, I ran into Chelsea coming out of a department store. She seemed pretty shook up. She even forgot to be sardonic for a moment."

Sophie couldn't help but laugh. She wanted to detest Claire for what she might be doing to Amanda and Luther's marriage, but somehow she couldn't. She knew better. Amanda was hardly the kind of personality who was easily swayed one way or the other. If anybody was doing the swaying, it was probably Amanda herself. But just why had Claire hidden the poison in Luther's jacket? "I understand they found the poison that killed Sydney in Luther's jacket pocket."

Claire looked up.

"It's crazy to think the murderer would incriminate himself by planting the murder weapon in something of his own. That would take an unusually Machiavellian turn of mind."

Claire's hand brushed at her cheek in a tentative, unsure gesture. She shifted uncomfortably in her chair. "Yes, I did think of that."

"I wonder how the poison got into Luther's jacket."

Claire realized she was staring and turned away.

"Let's not play games anymore. I saw you."

"What?" Claire's head snapped up.

"You can cut the pretense. I know you put it there."

Her body stiffened and she started to get up.

"Sit down," said Sophie. "I don't think we're done just yet."

"I'm not going to stay here and be toyed with."

"I'm not toying. I want to know why you put it there. Why haven't you told the police?"

"The police?" Claire was aghast. "Are you serious? Surely if you know I planted it in that coat, you know why! I panicked. I couldn't let anyone think the poison was in Amanda's purse. I didn't even know it was Luther's jacket. Not until later."

"You trust the police to solve the case, but not enough to tell them the truth?"

"But . . . she's my friend! I had to protect her."

"At Luther's expense?"

"Oh, you don't understand. You just want to judge. It's simply too complicated to go into. And anyway, they haven't arrested him. That bottle they found is only circumstantial. Nobody saw anybody kill anybody. Nothing ties anyone specifically to the scene of the crime. And what was it you just said? No murderer would hide the murder weapon in something of his own. By that reasoning, Luther is off the hook."

"So was Amanda."

Claire's lips tightened.

"By the way, I stopped at the police station this morning. I've already spoken with Detective Wardlaw. He knows you put it there."

Claire's face froze.

"If there is a Machiavelli at work here, you're definitely not it. I suggest *you* better do something, and fast. Explain to the police what really happened."

"I . . ." Claire appeared to be deciding whether she could bolt from the room without creating a scene. After a moment's reflection, she leaned back in her chair. "All right. It was a stupid thing to do. I'll stop at the station first thing tomorrow morning."

"Good."

As a last-ditch effort at maintaining her dignity, Claire picked up her coffee cup and then realized her hand was shaking so dreadfully she might drop it. Carefully, she set it back down. "You must hate me. You must think what I did was awful."

"At this point, I'll give you the benefit of the doubt. Perhaps it was just poor judgment. I'm a friend of Amanda's, too. I understand wanting to protect her." And wasn't that exactly what this whole conversation had been dancing around? Why had the poison been in Amanda's purse in the first place? Was someone trying to implicate her in the murder?

Claire rose and tried to smile. "Thank you. I appreciate your understanding. Believe me, I would never intentionally hurt Luther. Never." Holding her body very tightly, she turned and walked quickly out of the dining room.

It was a funny thing. In a strange way, Sophie did believe her.

18

Jack parked his car in the driveway and walked up the gravel path to the front door of his home in east Duluth. The light rain that had been falling since early afternoon had finally stopped. In the growing dusk, the rocks and plants appeared flat and glossy, much like a strange, surrealistic painting. The wind would dry them soon enough. As he climbed the wooden steps to the deck, he heard a foghorn sound in the distance. It was a sound from his past. The sound of home. He turned to see an ore boat drifting slowly toward the harbor.

Home. It seemed a funny word to use so casually. Minneapolis had never felt like that to him. Nothing except Duluth had ever satisfied his need for solitude and physical beauty. He hated the thought of leaving it behind.

As he entered the softly lit interior, he tossed his briefcase on the sofa and loosened his tie. Sitting open on the bar was a half-empty bottle of wine. "Nora?" he called, surprised at the anger in his voice. "Get in here." He poured himself a Scotch.

Nora glided into the doorway, a stemmed glass in one hand, a cigarette in the other. "Yes, dear?" The sweetness in her voice was a sarcastic exaggeration.

"I just had a call from my sister."

"Ah, and what words of delight did the lovely Amanda have to pass along?"

"Knock it off. This is serious. It seems Luther's been down at the police station most of the day. While he was being questioned, one of the officers let something very interesting slip."

"Oh? And what would that be?"

Jack tossed back his drink and set the glass down hard on the bar top. "It seems they've found several people who swear they saw you and Lars Olson in a tavern up the shore several hours before he was murdered."

Nora held the cigarette to her lips.

"Well?"

"Well what?"

"Is it true?"

She sat down and drew her legs up underneath her. "Yes. It's true."

Jack sat down opposite her. "I want an explanation."

"Don't glower, dear. It's unbecoming."

"What did you have to talk to him about?"

"You want the truth or the lie I'm going to tell the police?"

"Cut the crap."

Nora flicked some ash into an ashtray. "I was trying to protect you."

"Protect me?" The anger in his voice suddenly changed to confusion.

Nora nodded. "Did you know your father was directly responsible for dumping several hundred barrels of industrial waste in Lake Superior? It was back in 1979. You were executive vice president that year."

Jack didn't take his eyes off hers. "Olson contacted you?"

"He did. He called me last week. Said he had some important information we might be interested in."

"Why didn't you tell me?"

"He asked me not to say anything until I'd talked with him."

"He wanted money?"

"Among other things. You didn't answer my question. Did you know?"

Jack brushed a well-tended hand through his blond hair. "No, not at the time. But I was told about it. Recently."

"By whom?"

"My niece."

"Chelsea? Well, of course. Why not? Since she's been working directly under your father for the past few years, she could easily have found out."

"We've always been close. You know that. She wanted to warn me. If it gets to the press, there could be some negative political fallout."

Nora snorted. "Not to mention negative financial fallout for Grendel Shipping. Chelsea owns the company now. The cleanup will cost millions."

"Possibly more."

She watched him. "There's something you're not telling me. I can feel it. You've struck some kind of deal, haven't you? Chelsea's financial support for your campaign in return for a political favor. What is it? You keep the federal dogs off her heels until she can see what's really in those barrels? Get the whole thing cleaned up without any government supervision? Ryan's not going to like that. He doesn't make deals that could hurt the environment. You better see that he doesn't find out."

"He won't. And don't get the wrong idea. I don't need to make deals with Chelsea. I'd have her support no matter what."

"Lucky for you your father left the company to her. If he was still alive, you wouldn't be getting a penny for your campaign."

"Don't make it sound like that. Do you think I wanted my father dead?"

Nora finished her wine. "Someone did."

"Drop it."

"You're a fool, Jack."

"You might be surprised."

She stretched her arms above her head and leaned back, closing her eyes. "I doubt that. You're a rich kid. You've always been insulated by money. You've never learned how to fight dirty. Sometimes, I don't think you've got what it takes to win."

"And you do?"

She narrowed her eyes and watched him with a catlike intensity. "One day you'll be glad I was on your side.

We're very different, you and I. You sit around with your books and ideas—as if they made any real difference."

"Never underestimate the power of thought, Nora."

She pulled a headband off her long red hair and shook it loose. "Horseshit. We need to cover your political ass, or you may find it displayed rather unattractively on *Prime Time News.*"

Jack burst out laughing. "I knew I married you for something besides that gorgeous body."

"Careful. Amanda and Claire probably have you wired for sound. I think you just said something gratuitously sexist."

Jack reached for her hand. "Don't worry. Things will work out the way we both want. Come the new year, we'll be in Washington. That's a promise. Now," he said, standing and picking up his briefcase, "you have to get ready. We're expected for dinner at Brule's Landing. Amanda's planned dinner and a movie."

Nora groaned. "We just got home."

"Be nice. And repack that overnight bag of mine while you're at it. I'm meeting with my staff there early tomorrow morning. We'll be spending the night again."

"Lucky us."

"Besides," he added, "a little rest and relaxation might be good for both of us. Amanda thought I was looking a bit pale." He stood over her, running his hand lightly around her neck. "I haven't had an evening off in quite a while. Maybe tonight we can catch up on more than our sleep."

Nora grinned. "All right. I'll consider it. But on one condition. I get to pick the mood music tonight. 'Hail to the Chief' is getting kind of old."

19

"We missed you at dinner." Alice Oag, the Jorensens' cook, smiled. She sat heavily on a stool in front of a long wooden worktable cutting up fresh peaches. Her silver-gray hair was haphazardly pinned away from her face, revealing a high forehead and shrewd, somewhat rheumy eyes. "Your husband had three helpings of my famous cassoulet. He even had room for dessert." She spoke with a certain awe.

"That sounds like Bram." Sophie smiled. "He adores your cooking." She poured herself a cup of steaming Norwegian egg coffee. "What are all the peaches for?"

"Homemade peach pie. Mr. Jorensen's favorite. Mr. Grendel is having a big meeting here at the house tomorrow morning. Some kind of strategy session for the next debate." She gave Sophie a knowing look. "Everyone will be staying for lunch."

Sophie sat down at the table and watched Alice slice deeply into the center of a particularly lovely peach, removing the pit. She had known the Jorensens' cook for just over ten years. Alice had come to their employ shortly after they'd moved to Brule's Landing. Her sturdy, no-nonsense approach appealed to Sophie. And Alice definitely knew her way around a cassoulet.

"I don't mind telling you," continued Alice, pulling another bowl of peaches closer to her, "I'm pretty upset about what's going on around this house. If you ask me, poor Mr. and Mrs. Jorensen are being harassed by the police. And with Mr. Jorensen so tired all the time. Can't they see the man is ill? They should leave him alone." She poked her paring knife threateningly at Sophie. "Never in all the years

I've worked for the Jorensens have I once considered leaving their employ. Not until now. I mean, I don't feel safe." She shuddered, slipping the skin from another peach.

"I'm curious," said Sophie. "How well did you know Sydney Sherwin?"

Alice scowled. "Well enough. He was an evil man. You may not believe in evil, but I do. I don't know why he came back here, but you can bet it was to cause trouble."

One of the few things Sophie had not lost faith in over the years was her belief in human evil. She could easily grant that Alice was right. "What about Chelsea? Were they . . . friends when she was a child?"

Alice sighed. "Poor Chelsea. She's always been such a lost soul. I don't blame her parents though. They love their daughter very much. The thing is, both Luther and Amanda were so busy when she was growing up, they didn't make much time for her. I know Chelsea felt isolated when they moved to Brule's Landing. There weren't many children to play with this far out of town. Anybody who showed her any attention, at least when she was young, she would follow around like a little puppy. I don't mind telling you it was a sad sight. If I remember correctly, Sydney did take her on a skiing trip once. I always thought it was kind of funny, him offering to take her and all. He wasn't one to spend much time with children. I think it was the first winter we lived here. Chelsea must have been eleven or twelve. You know, it was her uncle Jack who really made time for her. She would just light up when he'd come through that front door. They're still quite close. I've often wondered if Mr. Jorensen isn't a little jealous of Mr. Grendel's relationship with his daughter. I think he'd like to go back and change some of the things he did—or didn't do—when Chelsea was young. He's said as much. Mrs. Jorensen, too. But there's no use now. What's done is done."

Sophie held the coffee cup to her lips, mulling over what Alice had just said. "Let me ask `you another question. What do you think of Claire Van Dorn?"

Alice made a sour face. "Well, it's none of my business, you understand. I hate to speak ill of people. She's okay,

I guess. She used to be here all the time. Last winter Mrs. Jorensen even insisted she be given her own room upstairs. They were working on the restaurant renovation and sometimes they'd work late into the night. Lots of times they'd come into the kitchen here to make a snack after I'd gone to bed. I could hear them giggling like two schoolgirls. And then other times they'd be very secretive, whispering to each other. I know it got on Mr. Jorensen's nerves. Can you blame him? He tried to be pleasant, but I think her constant presence upset him more than he let on. Since Mr. Jorensen got sick, she hasn't been around as much. But she's here tonight, God love her." Alice nodded to the basement door. "They're all down in the rec room watching a movie. Something about a python. It's supposed to be a comedy, not that I can see anything particularly funny about a snake." She stabbed another peach.

Sophie could hear laughter coming from the stairway.

"Chelsea called a few minutes ago. I took the message. She'll be coming out for that breakfast meeting tomorrow. When Mrs. Jorensen came upstairs a few minutes ago, I mentioned that her daughter was going to be here in the morning. She got so excited I didn't have the heart to tell her it wasn't a social call." She shook her head. "It's sad, isn't it—that people can't get along better? Oh, that reminds me. You had a phone call, too."

Immediately Sophie thought of the man she'd spoken with at Damascus Gate. "Was there a message?"

Alice set down the knife and wiped her sticky hands on a damp towel. "Let me think. No, no message. It was from someone named Rudy. He just asked for you and when I said you weren't here, he thanked me and hung up."

Sophie was stunned. "That was my son!"

"Is that right? Sure, I remember now. He lives out West somewhere."

"Montana."

"Well, he has a nice voice. Very polite."

Sophie's mind was racing. Why had he called? Was it possible that Norman's second wife had actually given him her message? Did she dare call him back? What if Norman answered? If he found out Rudy had called her, there might be a very nasty scene. Rudy didn't need that. She didn't either. But he'd called her! Bram was right. Maybe there was some hope after all.

"Oh, he did say he was over at a friend's house. Maybe that's why he didn't leave a number."

Sophie's heart sank. He wasn't home. Even if she got up the nerve to call, he wouldn't be there. Her soul ached to hear her son's voice.

"Are you all right?" asked Alice. "You look kind of flushed."

Sophie stood and walked to the sink, splashing a handful of cold water into her face. "It's nothing."

"Your son sounded fine," said Alice comfortingly. "Really. You shouldn't worry."

She attempted a smile. "I'm not. As a matter of fact, this is really great news." If he'd called once, he might try again. She had to hold that thought. As she returned to the worktable, she could feel the adrenaline pumping through her body. The evening would be a total loss if she simply spent it stewing. She had to find something to occupy her time. "Say, Alice, I was wondering. I know how much Amanda has always loved to garden. Did she and Chelsea ever do it together?"

Alice cocked her head. "No, not that I remember."

"There's no *child's garden* around here then?"

Alice seemed confused. "I don't think so. There's a small rock garden up near the gazebo. Could that be what you're thinking of?"

Sophie sipped her coffee. "No. But thanks anyway." She decided to shift subjects. There was still the matter of the typewriter on which the murder notes had been typed. She knew the police had searched the house quite thoroughly last night, after Sydney's body had been found in Luther's study. But they hadn't found it. Maybe she'd get lucky. "Listen, Alice, I need to write a letter to a friend. Is there a typewriter around here that I could use? I don't want to bother anyone."

Alice got up and crossed to the stove, turning up the fire

under a kettle of water. "Let me think. Well, there's the
computer Mr. Grendel bought for Ryan to use in his speech
writing. Very fancy. It's in the east sun room."

Sophie shook her head. "Sorry. It's not an IBM. I
wouldn't know how to use it."

"No, me either." Alice nodded her approval. "Well then,
I think your husband is using one. I suppose he brought that
with him. Would he let you borrow it?"

"I have strict orders not to bother him until he comes out
of his lair."

Alice smiled at the allusion. "Yes, he is kind of a bear,
isn't he? You know, I've never told you this before, but I
think you two make such a cute couple."

"Cute?"

"Oh, you know what I mean. When you first brought
Bram up here, I wasn't sure what I thought. I have pretty
high standards, if I do say so myself. My own husband,
God rest his soul, was one in a million. But Bram was forever coming back into the kitchen, poking through the pots
on the stove, peeking in the ovens. He always wanted to
know what was for dinner, how I did this or that. I like that
in a man. He has down-to-earth interests. And all the while,
we were becoming friends. He kind of sneaks up on you,
you know that? Before you know it, you like him."

"I know," smiled Sophie.

"Tonight he wanted to know where I got the sausage for
the cassoulet. He wouldn't leave me alone until I told him
all about this smokehouse in Two Harbors where they
smoke Lake Superior whitefish and trout—and occasionally
do some garlic sausage. You know, a cassoulet is only as
good as the marriage of the wine and sausage. As far as
I'm concerned, if there's a secret, that's it. He wrote everything down and I think he's going to drive over and get
some—or make you do it." She winked. "I told him he
should buy some of the whitefish, too. A trip to Duluth is
never complete without it. I even gave him one of my secret recipes, one of Mrs. Jorensen's favorites. You see, I
bind the fish in a rich béchamel sauce with fresh dill and

basil and then bake it in a puff pastry. I usually serve it in the summer with slices of fresh lime."

"Stop." Sophie laughed. "I've just had dinner and you're making me hungry all over again."

"You know, with all our talk about food, I never got to ask him about that book he's writing."

"Are you sure you want to know?"

"Sure!"

"Well, for starters, it's a novel. *Forests of the King.* I guess you could say it's science fiction."

Alice scrunched up her nose. "Give me a good mystery any day."

"Me, too. But the book will be fun."

"What's it about?"

"Well, it's set in America in the year 2216. The country has been completely reforested and the populace is worshiping Elvis Presley as a god. You know how everyone calls him The King today? Well, Bram wanted to explore—"

Alice held up her hand. "That's okay. You don't need to go into detail."

"He's fascinated by time travel. Unusual cultures."

"Has he ever visited the Iron Range?"

"Alice, be nice."

"Pardon me, but I grew up in Calumet. Sometimes I can't help myself. Anyway, getting back to your original question about a typewriter. It seems to me there used to be an old manual around here somewhere. I haven't seen it in years. You might try the attic."

"Thanks," said Sophie.

"Don't let the cobwebs scare you. There's some fascinating stuff up there. You never know what you're going to find."

"That sounds like just what I want."

20

The stairway to the attic was narrow and uncarpeted, with faded rose wallpaper peeling from the top of the wall. The light switch was at the base of the stairs. Sophie flipped it on as she began her ascent. The attic itself appeared to be one long room lighted by a single, bare ceiling bulb of minimal wattage. She gave the space a brief examination before deciding on a plan of attack. It was simply filled to overflowing with furniture, old clothes, books, cracked mirrors, and boxes of assorted memorabilia. She made a mental note *not* to tell Bram about it. With his penchant for collecting, it would be next spring before they got the U-Haul loaded. She shuddered when she thought of their basement at home in Minneapolis.

Edging her way in between two large oak chests, she began searching through the contents of a long shelf. Finding an old typewriter in this warehouse of antiquity would be like finding the proverbial needle in a haystack. Books, magazines, even an old stereopticon lay buried under a thin frosting of dust.

A velvet patchwork quilt was stuffed haphazardly onto one end of a bare wood shelf. As she brushed past it, it fell to the floor. A centipede slithered away. Shuddering, she stepped carefully around the quilt. As she did so, she noticed a gray metal case that had been hidden before. That was interesting. It didn't even look dusty. The initials J.M.G. were stamped in gold letters on the outside next to the word REMINGTON. Jack M. Grendel. So this was *Jack's* typewriter case. She picked it up, realizing immediately that it was empty. Damn. Rotten luck. But where was the typewriter it had once contained? It was obviously an old manual. Could it be the same one on which someone had typed those sinister *piggy* notes?

Returning it to the shelf, she continued to poke through the assortment of junk. Under one of the dormer windows she spied an old Tiffany lamp. She inched in front of several badly water-damaged cement statues and leaned down to take a better look. It was truly a work of art. Some of the glass was cracked and a couple pieces were missing, but the design was still lovely. As she studied it, she thought she heard the sound of footsteps on the stairs. Curious who might be coming up, she turned her head.

"Welcome to the junkyard," she called.

The creaking stopped.

That was odd. If someone was out there, why didn't they answer? She called again. "Hello? Who's there?"

Again no reply.

Perhaps it was just her imagination. Old houses were full of odd noises, things that went bump in the night. She waited a moment longer, but when everything seemed quiet, she went back to examining the base of the lamp.

Outside the room, the stairway creaked again.

This time there was no mistaking it. Before she knew what was happening, the light was switched off, plunging the musty chamber into total blackness. Her heart started to pound. Damn, why had she let herself be so vulnerable? The silence in the room was enormous. Any sound, any perceived movement sent jolts of adrenaline into her system. She had to get out.

In the darkness, the junk-filled space would be almost impossible to navigate quickly, but she couldn't simply whimper in a corner, offering herself up like some helpless, sacrificial lamb. All her adult life she'd hated that part of herself that, in her youth, had acquiesced to a fascistic, fanatical religion, a crazy church with a mad, charmingly evil leader, and a husband whose basic motivation was not love but self-aggrandizement and absolute control. A victim felt powerless. A victim saw no choices. But Sophie Greenway was never going to see herself that way again. She wasn't going down without one hell of a fight.

Crouching on all fours, she began to crawl toward the door. Her hand grasped the first solid object that could be used as a weapon. The words Wardlaw had used earlier in the day echoed in her ears like a taunt. *Not in any danger,* he'd said. Not in any danger? So much for his infallible police instincts. She banged her head on the edge of something sharp. Christ! She was bleeding. She could feel the sticky liquid ooze from her scalp and dribble down onto her forehead. Wiping it away, she stopped for a second to catch her breath. It didn't take the instincts of a guard dog to notice that, for some reason, no one was making any move toward her. She waited a moment longer. Could it be that someone had flipped off the light switch down below merely to scare her? She listened. The room was absolutely still. The only sound she could hear was heavy breathing. Her own.

Well! She brushed off the dust on her hands, feeling more than a little embarrassed by her rather obvious overreaction. Somebody must like playing games. Carefully, she scrambled to her feet. Her eyes had finally begun to adjust to the darkness. She could now see a faint light coming from the partially open doorway. Taking a deep breath, she walked swiftly toward it, managing to bang her hip only slightly on the edge of an antique dresser.

Just as she had suspected, the stairway was empty. The floor below was quiet. She tugged her sweatshirt indignantly over her jeans and started down.

Entering the second floor hallway, she headed immediately for her bedroom. She could hear Bram's typewriter plunking away in the tiny cook's quarters at the end of the corridor. The familiar sound warmed her. He was only a few feet away. It had taken a few minutes, but the prankster's intentions were beginning to come into a kind of perspective. She was no longer scared. No. Now she was pissed. *Extremely* pissed.

As she passed the partially open bedroom door next to hers, a figure stepped farther into the darkness, waiting until Sophie had entered her own room. Then, looking both ways down the hall, the figure proceeded quickly to the stairs, the long red hair disappearing into the easy anonymity of the basement rec room.

Jenny ran her finger along the smooth wood of a stately grand piano that sat near a series of windows in one corner of the living room. She knew Luther played it on occasion. Amanda had said she'd tried to learn many years ago, but seemed to have no talent for it. They'd purchased it on Chelsea's ninth birthday, and given her lessons until she was fifteen, when she'd announced, apparently rather dramatically, that she no longer had any interest in music and refused to go into Two Harbors for her lessons. Jenny wished she'd had something this fine to practice on as a child. The ancient upright her mother had saved for years to buy couldn't even hold a tune. To Jenny, that flat, slightly dissonant sound was the sour, unmistakable chord of poverty.

She passed in front of the antique couch and sat down in Amanda's favorite comfy chair by the fireplace. Next to it on the floor was a sewing basket. Amanda wasn't much for knitting or crocheting, but she occasionally did some embroidery. Jenny knew she would find a needle and thread somewhere in the basket. She'd noticed a button about to come off of Ryan's favorite chambray shirt. Before the next movie started, she wanted to sew it on. It would only take a minute.

She pulled off the wicker top and began her search. Lifting a light blue spool of thread out of a narrow tray, she quickly spotted the pin cushion. As she reached for it, she noticed a tattered, leather-bound book tucked into the side. Silently, she read the title: *A Child's Garden of Verses* by Robert Louis Stevenson. Interesting. She'd been looking for some more poetry for her day-care children. Sometimes, before they went down for a nap, she liked to read to them. Amanda had loaned her her own copy of Claire's new book. The kids loved the poems. It seemed to help calm them down. Jenny had read the inscription in the front so many times she knew it by heart. *To a kindred spirit*, it had said. *Perhaps here and now we have the beginnings of a new child's garden, filled with joy and hope. My love to you always, Claire.* Slipping this new book into the pocket of her baggy wool sweater, she selected a needle and stood. She had one more errand to perform before heading back downstairs. Luther had asked if she would find a sweater for him. The basement rec room could be cold, even on an early fall night.

Saying a silent goodbye to the grand piano, Jenny walked straight to the back hallway and into Luther's study. He'd said he'd left a sweater on the footstool near the TV. There it was. Jenny liked this room. She liked the heavy furniture. Sometimes it seemed like the only comfortable spot in the entire house.

She sat down at Luther's desk and reached into her pocket for the book again. Such a beautiful little volume. She opened it up to the center and read: *Faster than fairies, faster than witches, Bridges and houses, hedges and ditches; And charging along like troops in a battle, All through the meadows the horses and cattle.* Perfect. Her children would love this.

"Jenny!" said a deep voice from the doorway. Ryan stood framed against the dark passage. His short, muscular body looked tense, his fists clenched. "Everyone's waiting for you! Come on."

Jenny dropped the book on the desktop. "I'm so sorry, sweetheart. Really, I just stopped to look for a needle and thread and—"

"Fine. I don't want to hear it. Forget that poetry book, just come on." The look on his face said everything was not *fine.*

She stood, brushing a stringy hair away from her face in an apologetic gesture. "Sure. Right away, hon." Before she could get to the door, he'd turned on his heel and left. She could hear him in the kitchen talking to Alice. Ryan was a good man, but he sometimes had no idea how he affected other people. He shouldn't talk to Alice that way. *Ordering* her to make more popcorn. Couldn't he just ask nicely? He was oblivious to her intense dislike of him. To Ryan, she was probably just some old woman. He didn't need her, therefore, she wasn't important. No, that was unfair. He was just so stressed right now. Jenny knew she'd added to that stress and that's why he'd been so short with her tonight. But he would get over it. Later in the evening, he'd be as affectionate as ever. She knew she could count on that.

As she crossed to the doorway, Sophie suddenly appeared in front of her.

"Jenny!" said Sophie, a look of surprise on her face. "Hi! I thought you'd be downstairs watching the film."

It was then that Jenny remembered why she'd come into the study in the first place. "Luther asked me to fetch him a sweater." She rushed over and picked it up. "Are you coming down? We're just about to start an old Tyrone Power movie. Something about a bullfighter. Amanda said it was really good."

Sophie smiled. "I guess I'm kind of a party pooper tonight. I'm awfully tired. I thought I might see if Luther had something interesting to read before bed." She glanced at the walls of books.

Jenny nodded. "I'm sure you'll find something. Well, I better get going. I'll probably see you tomorrow then." She hurried out.

"I hope so," said Sophie to her disappearing back. She sank down in the leather chair behind Luther's desk and picked up a well-worn, leather-bound volume of what looked like poetry. Her eyes locked on the title. *A Child's Garden of Verses.* My God, it was a book! This had to be the meaning of that note! She opened the front cover and read the words,

> *To my darling daughter on her sixth birthday. This book belonged to me when I was a little girl. I wanted nothing more than to live in the garden for the rest of my life. It's a special, magical place, Chelsea. I hope you love it, too.*
> *Your loving mother.*

Sophie looked up. *Find the Child's Garden, find the murderer.* That's what the note had said. But? She'd found the book in Luther's study. Did that mean? No, impossible. Then again, the book had been given to Chelsea. But that was hardly likely. The original owner was Amanda. Did that make her the murderer? God, how could she sit here and think something like that?

Sophie was beginning to feel like she was at the center of a vortex, and no matter how hard she resisted, she was going to get sucked down along with everyone else. She gazed at the book in her hand, her heart sinking. Another clue that led nowhere. Well, maybe it led somewhere, but how was she supposed to interpret it? This was too much for one day. Turning off the lamp on Luther's desk, she dropped her head in her hands and pressed her fists hard against her temples. Fighting back the emotion she was almost too tired now to suppress, she tried her damnedest not to cry. Tonight it was going to be a losing battle.

PART FOUR

This Little Piggy
Had None

These shall wake the yawning maid;
  She the door shall open—
Finding dew on garden glade
  And the morning broken.
                 from *A Child's Garden of Verses*
                    Robert Louis Stevenson

21

Bram ambled aimlessly into the bedroom eating the last bite of a slice of cranberry bread. This morning his attire consisted of a pair of ratty old jeans, a red flannel shirt, and a silk top hat.

"Nice hat." Sophie stood in front of the mirror brushing her uncooperative hair.

"Oh, do you like it?" He took it off and held it at arm's length. "I kind of like it, too. Found it downstairs in the rec room. I think I'll have to get a cane and tails to go with it. Then we can go dancing." He grabbed her and began leaping around the room.

"Bram? Stop!" She couldn't help but laugh as he pulled her down on the bed.

"All right. But what shall we do now? I can think of a few suggestions." He wiggled his eyebrows.

"What do you mean?" asked Sophie, keeping him at arm's length. "No writing this morning? Am I actually going to see you today?"

"If I sit in that room one more minute and stare at that blank piece of paper, I'm going to go insane. There's no telling what I might do!" He began to pull the hair away from the sides of his head and drool.

"Stop it," said Sophie, hitting him on the arm. "You know I hate it when you drool."

"You do? You should have said something years ago. Before it became a habit."

"Listen to me for a minute, bean brain. I've got a great idea."

"I'm all ears." He flopped on his back and pulled the hat over his face.

"Let's take a sauna."

He didn't move.

"Bram? Did you hear me?"

From under the hat came a deep, rumbling yes.

"Well?"

"Well what?"

"Isn't that a great idea? Remember that sauna out in the woods? We took one together there several years ago. You know, I could use a break today, too. Something restful. Remember those two wooden benches? The shower right outside?"

"How could I forget? The flora and fauna got quite an eyeful."

"They're used to it." She waited. "So, are we on?"

Bram rolled over onto his stomach, propping his head on his hands. "How do I say this politely, honeybunch?"

"Don't call me obnoxious names. We took a wonderful sauna at cousin Sulo's cabin before we got married."

"I do remember that. Yes, indeed, I do."

"You loved it!"

"I loved seeing you naked in the middle of the day."

Sophie smiled. "How about in the middle of the morning?"

"This isn't fair."

"Why?"

"Because now I can see you naked anytime I want—without benefit of that thirteenth-century torture chamber designed by *your* ancestors for the sole purpose of terrifying the rest of the world. God thunders to the poor soul: *Be good or I'll drop you back on Finland!*"

"Stop."

"Well, it's true."

"Oh, don't be such a coward," prodded Sophie. "You'll love it."

"I will not."

"Then I'll have to find someone else to do it with."

"Naked?"

"What do you think? After all, I am a full-blooded Finn."

"I think I better save you from yourself." He took the top hat and dropped it over her face.

"Great! I'll go down and ask Alice to have someone open it up for us and get a fire going. It's chilly this morning. Perfect weather for a sauna." She tapped the hat into place on top of her head. "You go get us two big bath towels and I'll meet you in half an hour out on the front deck. Just wear a robe."

"I know what to wear," he snapped. "I just hope this isn't a mistake. My horoscope wasn't very promising this morning. You probably aren't interested, but it doesn't look like a very auspicious day."

"We'll work on it," said Sophie, moving in a bit closer.

"Are you sure you remember how to find this place?" asked Bram, nearly tripping over a large rock.

"Calm down. We're almost there. I can smell the wood fire."

"Oh, goody. I can hardly wait." He kicked a branch out of his way. "All these trees look alike to a city fella. I'd much rather be fishing. Sometime before we leave, I'm going to call old Farley Barnes and get him to take me out in his boat."

"Tell him to leave the six-pack on the dock, or I may never see you again."

"Yeah, Farley's kind of a good old boy."

"The color of his neck has less to do with it than the shape of his liver. There," said Sophie as they came to a small clearing. She pointed at a dilapidated log structure, complete with smoke belching from the low chimney in the rear. Running ahead, she pulled open the door. Inside, the room already appeared to be heating up nicely.

"It's dark in there," groused Bram.

"Do I detect a slight whine? Come on, honey. There's a light. See that power line over there? Here." She flipped the switch. "What did I tell you? All the comforts of home."

He peeked further into the doorway. "It smells like a wet mitten."

"Does it? It's probably lined with cedar. Most people find that rather pleasant." She found the bucket of water that had been left next to the wood stove and tossed a dipperful over the heated rocks. Immediately, steam billowed into the air. "Just wait till that heat really starts pumping."

Bram climbed the steps and surveyed the space distrustfully. "We're going to die in here," he mumbled. Removing his robe, he paused in the center of the room, lethargically staring at a bad crack in the ceiling.

Sophie dropped her own robe over a bench and unfolded the beach towels. "Actually, I have quite a lot to tell you. You didn't come to bed until after I was asleep last night."

Bram watched her stretch out on one of the bare wooden benches. "Later," he said, sitting down next to her. He ran his hand gently up her leg. "I hope you brought along tweezers because I think we may need them before the morning is over. I do so love these exotic vacations, Sophie. I really do."

An hour later he lay on the bench looking like a dead flounder. "Christ, can we consider ourselves roasted through now?" He raised a limp arm.

"What happened to all your energy?"

"You have to ask?"

Sophie laughed. "Just a few more minutes. Besides, we haven't finished our discussion." She got up and pulled another log off the pile in the corner. "This is great for our skin."

Bram raised his head slightly and rolled his eyes.

"What's this?" asked Sophie. Spying something underneath a log, she lifted a pile of twigs and tree bark off a small typewriter. "My God, will you look at this!"

Bram propped himself up on one elbow. "Looks like a typewriter."

"Brilliant. Being locked in a room for the last four days eating Popsicles and making paper airplanes hasn't dimmed your powers of observation one bit. I don't suppose you have a piece of paper on you?"

"Do I look like I have a piece of paper?"

Sophie studied him for a moment. "No." She brushed a spiderweb off the top of the machine. "This could be the typewriter the police have been looking for. The one the death notes were typed on."

Bram sat up and whistled. "They combed the place all day yesterday looking for that."

"Too bad one of them didn't get the urge to take a sauna. Listen, we've got to get this out of here right away."

"I think we better be careful, Soph. After what you said happened last night, I'm not so sure we should get involved any more than we already are. Let's just leave it here and go call the police. Let them take care of it. After all, even you have to admit this has turned into a pretty dangerous business. No one is immune. Just because you think so many of these people are your friends—"

"They *are* my friends, don't you see?"

Bram shook his head. "I'm not so sure. I think you're being blinded by your loyalties. The police seem to think Luther's involvement is central. Look at the facts."

"I am! But I know some things the police don't. For instance, there are several secrets surrounding Jack's senatorial campaign that might be significant. What if he had a bad drug problem back in the late Sixties? People might go to extreme lengths to keep that under wraps."

"People? You mean like Jack?"

Sophie stiffened. "Not necessarily. Anyone who feels he has something important riding on the election might be forced to act in his own best interest."

"Maybe he sold secrets to the Vietcong."

"What?"

"Maybe that's the secret. You know, Sixties stuff. How to tie-dye your underwear. The correct way to pass around a roach clip. Or maybe how to start a commune and convince your goofy girlfriends to do all the work while you sit on the porch and smoke weed. Important information like that."

"Bram, be serious."

"I've talked to a lot of folks who've known Jack for years, Sophie. No one has ever hinted at a drug problem. Don't kid yourself. He's got enemies. If someone had information like that, it would have hit the papers long before this. My gut instinct tells me you're barking up the wrong tree with that Damascus Gate thing."

"Then what was he doing in Green Dells?"

"Well, pardon my mentioning this, but one of the most famous mental health facilities in the country is located just outside of town. The Emmet Saltzman Clinic."

Slowly, Sophie turned around. "What are you suggesting?"

Bram scratched his prickly chin. "Nah. Everyone says how cool Jack is under pressure. He isn't the type."

"There is no type. Mental illness can affect anyone. What if Damascus Gate was a cover?" She thought for a moment, trying to reach back and pluck a specific comment from her memory. "As I think about it, when I mentioned Green Dells to Jack, he did use the term clinic. So did Claire the night I overheard her talking with Amanda in the lighthouse. Why didn't I catch that before? Damascus Gate isn't a clinic. It's a halfway house."

"I don't know, Soph. You have no proof. Then again, I suppose it's possible Jack could be hiding some sort of latent psychological instability." He shook his head. "No, I think you're really reaching. Best to leave it alone." He pulled himself to a sitting position.

"I can't! I know it's a chilling thought, but unless somebody gets to the bottom of this very soon, someone else is going to die. We simply can't turn our backs on that."

"I suppose you have a theory for who the next little piggy will be. All the people I've talked to have been falling all over themselves trying to figure it out."

"Yeah, it's driving me nuts. Wardlaw thinks everything has been planned in advance. *This little piggy had none.* None of what? Money? Fame? A new car? I just feel so useless."

Bram smiled, wiping a drop of sweat from the tip of his

nose. "You may have found the most significant piece of evidence so far." He nodded to the typewriter. "Don't be so hard on yourself."

Sophie gave a small cough. "Isn't it getting kind of smoky in here?"

Bram looked around. The room did seem to be filled with a thin haze. "Maybe the vent is blocked or something."

Sophie eyed the wood stove.

"I suggest we leave," he said cheerfully. "Being steamed is one thing. Being smoked is an entirely different matter. Here's your robe." He tossed it to her. "I'll meet you outside by the shower. The squirrels are already waiting out there with their binoculars. I saw them on the way in." Getting into his own, he tiptoed to the door. "Sophie?"

"What?"

"Do sauna doors ever swell shut?"

"What?" She moved in front of him and tried the handle. It turned easily enough, but the door wouldn't budge. "Damn." She tried again. "I'll bet someone's slipped something through those metal brackets outside. I doubt we can force it open. I'll try to put the fire out."

Bram pushed his body hard against it. "No! Don't do that. It'll just make the smoke worse."

"We've got to do something!" Sophie could feel the panic rising in her chest.

Amanda stepped out of the tall grass at the edge of the beach and stopped. In the distance she could hear the sound of children laughing. Glancing momentarily at the white-washed cottage, she noticed several small boys playing on the swing set in the front yard. Today was Wednesday. She was pretty sure Jenny took care of five or six children today. It was a cool, cloudless morning. The gulls were dipping and diving off the rocky point near the lighthouse. "There you are," she called, spotting Luther sitting alone on a rock. "I thought I'd find you out here."

Hearing her voice, he raised his head. "You found me." The wind flattened his dark hair hard against his forehead.

"You look like a pirate." She smiled, shading her eyes from the sun as she approached. "My pirate."

"You can join me if you'd like. I'd enjoy the company." He moved over slightly. "Are you out for a walk?"

"No. I came to find you."

"Sit with me then."

She did as he asked, taking his hand in hers. "How are you feeling today? I didn't see you at breakfast."

Luther shrugged. "The same. No worse really."

As they sat for a few minutes in companionable silence, Amanda found herself wishing he would put his arm around her, just like the old days. Something inside her ached for the way things used to be. Yet, surely both of them knew their marriage had reached the point of no return. The old days were long dead. Strange that her body still responded to his touch. Life, unlike art, was never black and white, with neat beginnings and clearly defined endings. She could feel him stir. "What is it?"

He shook his head. "Nothing."

"Luther, I was thinking . . ."

He turned to look at her.

Under the intense gaze of his blue eyes, Amanda felt oddly uncomfortable. "Well, you see, it struck me this morning how strange it is that one's life can end up so different from what one planned."

He gripped her hand tightly.

"Luther, what I'm trying to say . . ."

"Please," he said, quickly standing up. "You don't have to say anything."

"But I do. Don't cut me off. We never talk anymore."

His face was a dark silhouette against the bright sun. "I think we'd best get back to the house. I'd like to clean up before lunch."

Amanda knew it was no use. Quietly, she rose. "Of course. We'll talk later—when you feel more rested."

Luther led the way through the tall grass. They paused briefly at the edge of the woods to pick and eat a few late raspberries still clinging to the tangled vines. As they reached the lawn in front of the house, he stopped. "I smell something." He sniffed the air.

"It's probably the wood fire in the sauna. Sophie asked Alice to have someone get it ready for her this morning."

Luther turned around. "And I hear something. Don't you?"

"I don't hear anything. Come on. Let's get back before you're completely exhausted."

"Listen." He cupped a hand over his ear. "Someone's pounding on something—and shouting. Don't you hear it? Something's wrong, Amanda. Come on!"

Reluctantly, she followed him back into the woods. They took a familiar shortcut, jumping over rocks and fallen branches. Luther reached the clearing first, rushing to the cabin door and pulling away the piece of wood that prevented it from opening. Bram burst out, collapsing on the dirt path. "Sophie!" he gasped, pointing over his shoulder. Luther took a huge gulp of air and disappeared into the smoke. An instant later he reappeared carrying Sophie in his arms. He laid her on the ground next to Bram and brushed the tangled hair away from her face. "She's breathing," he cried. He looked up, shouting at Amanda. "Run, damn it! Call 911! Tell them it's an emergency! Tell them to send someone from Two Harbors!"

Amanda seemed paralyzed. She stood staring at the open door.

"For God's sake, Amanda, hurry! There's no time. She's inhaled a lot of smoke. Run!"

Amanda appeared to be startled by his words, as if they had brought her back from someplace far away. She looked at Sophie and then at Bram. "Of course," she whispered. "Right away."

"She's going to be all right," said one of the paramedics a few minutes later. He held an oxygen mask over Sophie's nose and mouth. Bram sat on the grass next to her, gently rubbing her arm. Every so often he would reach up and scrape a tear away from his cheek.

"We need to get you two to a hospital," said the woman

standing next to Luther. "You have to be checked over. I think the doctor will want to admit you both for observation."

Sophie brushed the mask away from her face. "No, I'm fine. I'll be fine. I don't want to go to a hospital."

"Well, we're both going," said Bram. "So shut up."

Sophie closed her eyes.

"Barring any complications," said the standing paramedic, "you should be able to come home tomorrow."

Home, thought Sophie. That seemed so far away. Her chest ached as she tried to sit up.

"No you don't," said Luther, crouching down. "These folks will take care of everything. You just lie still. Amanda and I will come into town later this afternoon to see you." He laid his hand on Bram's shoulder.

"Thanks," said Sophie, blinking up at him. She was slowly beginning to realize just how weak she was.

The paramedic kneeling next to her lifted the oxygen mask back over her face. "Both of you are going to have sore lungs for a few days."

"No marathons," said Bram, squeezing her hand.

"None for you either," said the paramedic. He glanced at Amanda. "It was a good thing you found them. They could have died in there."

Amanda nodded.

"We're going to have to report this to the police. Someone stuffed a pile of rags into the vent behind the cabin."

Bram coughed several times, trying to rid his lungs of the foul smoke. "Oh, one more thing. There's a typewriter inside there sitting on a woodpile. The police need to come get it right away. It may be important evidence in a murder investigation." He shivered as he watched Sophie lying so still, her eyes closed, her face frighteningly pale. A wave of anger passed over him. Somebody was going to pay for this, damn it. Somebody was going to pay dearly.

22

Jenny buttered a piece of toast as she looked out the kitchen window at several little boys who were playing in the sandbox next to Ryan's new greenhouse. Two more children would be arriving at the cottage in less than an hour. She loved to watch children play. So intense. So serious about their pleasure. And so absolutely unaware of the kind of world they were growing up into.

"Nora is coming over in a few minutes," shouted Ryan from the other room.

Wonderful, thought Jenny. She bit off a corner of the toast. What a treat so early in the day.

Ryan swung into the kitchen, adjusting his tie as he crossed to the refrigerator. He stopped abruptly when he noticed her sullen look. "I want you to be nice to her, Jen. At least try to get along." His deep voice registered perfect calm.

Jenny knew the tone well. She dropped the toast on her plate with a loud thunk. "What's wrong with us, Ryan? It seems like all we do lately is argue."

Ryan ignored the question and reached inside the refrigerator for a carton of milk. He was always terribly thirsty after his morning run in the woods. "Tonight is the Northern Environmentalists annual meeting in Duluth. Remember? I told you about it last week." He drank directly from the carton. "Well," he said between gulps, "are you planning to go or not?"

Jenny picked at her toast. She hated it when he treated her like that, ignoring her comments. He was so self-important. So morally superior. "I don't like her, Ryan. And

I don't think I should have to hide my feelings in my own home. After all, even you said how manipulative she is. How she's done plenty of things behind Jack's back—things he would never approve of. If you ask me, nobody needs a wife like her."

"Nobody's asking your opinion," answered Ryan, shutting the refrigerator door. He grabbed his briefcase and headed into the living room. "Damn junk," he muttered, kicking a toy truck out of his way. "Why don't you pick these toys up once in a while?"

Jenny followed. "That's just the problem. You used to ask me my opinion. You trusted me. But Nora's gotten you involved in things you're afraid to tell me about, hasn't she? Bad things."

"That's crap, Jenny. I don't know where you get these ideas. You know, ever since—"

"Ever since what?" she snapped. "Ever since this?" She put her hand on her stomach. "You can't even say it, can you? I'm going to have a baby. Our baby."

Ryan sank into a chair.

"It's your child too, you know."

"I know." He rubbed the back of his neck. "You wouldn't dream of being unfaithful to me. I'm a lucky man."

"But you'd be unfaithful to me, wouldn't you?" Her words stung like acid.

"What do you mean?"

"Oh, go fuck yourself," she said angrily, striding back into the kitchen. She rarely asserted herself. It felt good.

Ryan shouted from the living room. "Jenny, come back in here. We're not done talking."

"I am," she called. She dropped the toast into the wastebasket.

He appeared in the doorway, his face flushed. "I want to know what you meant by that last comment."

"I should think you of all people would know what 'go fuck yourself' means."

"Jenny, you know I don't like you using that kind of language. You just do it to hurt me. Now, I demand to know what you meant."

"Okay, don't go fuck yourself. How about, go piss up a tree. I believe that means essentially the same thing."

He grabbed her roughly by the shoulders. "Why are you doing this? You're trying to start a fight, aren't you? I don't get it. If it isn't the pregnancy, what is it?"

"Damn you, Ryan. Don't you blame this baby for your sleeping around. If you didn't want a child then you should have let me use my diaphragm. You're the one who said, 'No, no, honey, if you get pregnant, that's great! Don't spoil the moment.' "

Ryan's hands tightened around her shoulders.

"That's right. Hurt me. Slap me around."

Quickly he released his grip. "I'd never do that. You know better than to say something like that!"

"No? Is it against the Ryan Woodthorpe code of ethics? But sleeping with Chelsea Jorensen is acceptable, right?"

He looked momentarily surprised. "You're crazy. I don't know where you got that idea."

"Nora Grendel," said Jenny. "Last night. In case you hadn't noticed, she loves to drop little hints. Did she suggest it? Good for your career? Do you love Chelsea, Ryan? Or is this just one more deal you're trying to cut in the great cause of your own political future. You disgust me sometimes. You're so transparent."

He turned around, his expression full of frustrated rage. "There aren't many politicians in this country today committed to saving our earth. Who says I wouldn't make a good leader? I love the North Shore, Jenny. No, I take that back. I don't just love it, it's *part* of me. Part of my soul. Don't you feel it, too? All around us this vibrant, trembling life. It needs someone to protect it. The protection of a lover. My protection! Most people aren't interested in environmental issues. They only vote because they prefer futility over complete passivity. But just wait until the rivers turn foul. Wait till the land is so choked with poison, we can't even eat the food. Then they'll listen. They'll look around for good men like Jack and me to lead them out of the muck. But we have to get elected first. Think about that, Jen. If I had enough money and power, I could make a real difference. This is a bigger issue than just you or me. I'm totally committed to Jack and Nora—and yes, to my own career."

Jenny kicked a toy bear across the floor. "Never have I heard a more eloquent, creative argument for being a pure bastard. Those are words, Ryan. Nothing more. What about our baby? Doesn't its *'vibrant, trembling life'* concern you?"

"Just drop it," he snapped. "You obviously don't understand." He turned and left the room.

"I hate you!" She picked up a plastic helicopter and threw it at him.

The doorbell sounded. Ryan crossed to the door and opened it. "Nora," he said, glancing over his shoulder. "I'm all ready for the meeting. Just let me get my briefcase."

Mutely, Jenny stood in the kitchen doorway.

"Good morning, Jennifer." Nora peeked curiously into the messy living room. "Lovely morning isn't it?"

"See you later," said Ryan curtly. He left without a backward glance.

An empty silence permeated every corner of the little cottage after he had gone. With her fists thrust deep into her long, baggy sweater, Jenny shuffled back into the kitchen and put on the teakettle. Her mind was a blur of emotions. She hated fighting. It was totally against her nature. Inside, she felt like putty. Was she doomed to feeling forever humiliated? Incomplete? No artist would dare call something as unformed as she was a finished work. She sat down at the table and watched the boys still playing contentedly in the sand. Why couldn't life be that simple? Safe? How frightened she'd always been of finding her way in the world. Ever since she'd left home at fifteen, she'd been scared, deprived of some necessary nourishment she could only call love.

When she'd first met Herman Grendel and was offered the housekeeping position, she was barely making it. After she was fired, she'd blamed Chelsea. Even though Ryan tried to convince her otherwise, she knew it was her doing. But Amanda had been there with the offer of the cottage and a suggestion for another way to support herself. Since moving to Brule's Landing, her life had finally begun to make sense. Something inside her was beginning to thaw. She was starting to feel almost—what was the word Luther had used the other night? Legitimate? Amanda's love had done that for her and she would never forget it. When she and Ryan moved in together, the world was already beginning to feel like a good place. He just made it better. She'd loved him almost immediately. His interest in her ideas and his sensitivity to the natural world fascinated her. She'd never met anyone quite like him before. But something happened. What had changed? Was it the baby? She'd only found out last week. She thought Ryan would be so happy, but his reaction confused her.

Jenny shivered and hugged herself, staring at a heap of stuffed animals in one corner of the room. Elephants. Bears. Bunnies. A zebra. A dragon. What had Amanda said once? Men fall in love with themselves through the adoration of their women. Was that the problem? Had she simply stopped adoring him?

She stood and trudged to the stove, pouring hot water into a mug. Getting down a tea bag from a tin in the cupboard, she dropped it into the water and returned to her seat by the window. So what if Ryan left? What difference would it make? Bitterly, she laughed, feeling her body begin to quake. Men did that to you. Hadn't she always known? Romantic feelings had to be borne, much like the aftermath of a long illness. Perhaps that, ultimately, was what relationships were. Lucky Chelsea. If she could only think of it that way, maybe she wouldn't hate her so much. Chelsea had simply caught the same virus. But it didn't help. Not really. Jenny knew she'd always wanted to be both free and safe. Maybe, in the end, that was what was truly impossible.

23

"We've been waiting for that cretinous pencil-necked gasbag for the last two hours," complained Bram as he leaned against the deep windowsill in the hospital room. He was completely dressed except for his shoes.

"If you're referring to Dr. Quist, I'd speak a little more softly," answered Sophie. "He could be standing right outside."

"Hmph. Wishful thinking. I hate all this inane procedure. It makes me feel like I'm five years old."

"We only finished lunch ten minutes ago. The nurse said he'd be in to sign our release papers sometime this afternoon. I think we should be prepared for that to mean anytime before dinner." She fluffed the short reddish gold hairs around her ears.

As Bram continued to sputter, Sophie heard the sound of a soft knock on the door. "Come in," she called.

Bram turned just as Jenny stuck her head into the room. "Are you two up for a visit?" She inched hesitantly inside.

Today her choice of clothing was decidedly less baggy. She wore a dark brown dress with a high neck and long sleeves. Sophie found it unusually severe for such a young woman. Almost chillingly so. "Sure," she said, swinging her legs off the bed. "Come in. You didn't drive all the way in from Brule's Landing just to see us, did you?"

Jenny seemed embarrassed by the question, her hand fidgeting with a small button at her neck. "Well, no, not exactly. Of course, I knew you were here. Amanda told me. Actually, I had to come in for an appointment this afternoon. But I did come early." She smiled, brushing her hair behind her ears. "I was so sorry to hear what happened to you yesterday. Such a horrible thing for someone to do." She glanced curiously at the oxygen equipment still sitting in the corner of the room.

"Would you like to stay for a few minutes?" asked Bram. He waved his hand to an uncomfortable-looking orange plastic chair at the foot of his bed. "We'd enjoy the company."

Jenny glanced at her watch. "I really should be getting downstairs. I don't want to be late."

"An important appointment?" asked Sophie.

"Yeah. Kind of. I suppose it's no secret any longer. I told Amanda this morning. I'm pregnant. Ryan and I are going to have a baby."

How awful! thought Sophie. "How wonderful for you." She quickly masked her look of horror.

"Yeah, I'm pretty excited. I've always wanted a child—I love children. I just wish . . ." She looked down at her feet.

"Wish what?" asked Bram.

Jenny shook her head. "Oh, nothing really. Just, well, that Ryan was a little more . . . involved. Not that he isn't happy," she added quickly. "He's just so busy right now. You understand."

"Completely," said Bram.

Sophie couldn't imagine Ryan as a father. He was too much of a child himself.

"By the way, I should have said something to you the other night. I didn't find any record of Jack's volunteering time in Wisconsin in 1969. I'm sorry. Maybe you should ask him yourself."

"Thanks," said Sophie. "I'll do that."

"Well, I better get going. I have an appointment with an obstetrician at one. When will they be releasing you two?"

"Within the hour," pronounced Bram. "If not, Soph and I are going to storm the nurses' station. We may even be forced to take hostages."

Jenny cocked her head, smiling without the slightest

trace of humor. "Well," she continued, her eyes slipping to the door, "see you both later. Maybe tonight at dinner?"

"It's a date." Bram smiled. As soon as she was gone, he slapped his knees and stood.

"You're not going to start pacing again, are you? You're wearing a groove in the linoleum."

"It'll give them something to remember me by."

"I doubt anyone will ever forget your visit to North Shore General. You've made your usual impression."

Bram raised an elegant eyebrow.

"And anyway, staying here last night gave me some time to think. I seem to have come to a dead end with that Damascus Gate business. If Jack did volunteer there, there's no way to prove or disprove it. And what's the difference anyway? If only Amanda hadn't acted so strangely when I mentioned it, I'd have dropped it long ago."

"Perhaps you should drop it now."

Sophie ignored him. "But what if he was never there? What if the real secret had to do with that other place you mentioned? What was the name?"

"The Emmet Saltzman Clinic."

"That's it. What if Jack spent a year there?"

"I doubt they use many volunteers, Sophie."

"Exactly. I know I haven't wanted to admit the possibility of a problem, but what if he was a patient?"

"All right, I'll say this much. Whoever is behind these murders has got to be more than a little nuts. If Jack really was mentally ill, maybe he was never completely cured."

"That's unfair."

"Is it?"

She swung her feet off the bed. "The problem is, we can't prove anything. No real clinic is going to give out confidential information. So, as I see it, any suspicions we might have are just another dead end."

"Well, not necessarily."

"What do you mean?"

"Do you have the phone number?"

"No, but I can get it." She picked up the receiver and dialed Wisconsin telephone information. After jotting the number on a notepad, she hung up and tore off the top page. "Here you go. What are you going to do with it?"

Bram began shaking his arms wildly, making sounds like a duck.

"Knock it off, you idiot! They're going to be in here any minute with a straitjacket."

"I have had years of professional voice training, my dear. If these people don't understand my methods, let them *learn*. I need to warm up my vocal cords."

Sophie shook her head.

"Just watch now." He winked as he dialed the number. After a few rings a receptionist answered, "Saltzman Clinic."

"Medical records," snapped Bram using his deepest, most authoritative radio voice.

"Just a minute."

He smirked at Sophie.

"Records," said a bored male voice.

"This is Dr. Darrel Thorndyke of the Thorndyke Psychiatric Clinic in Duluth, Minnesota. I'm sure you've heard of us." He paused, waiting for a response.

"Yes, of course, Dr. Thorndyke. How may I assist you?"

"My secretary just informed me that records we requested over a month ago still have not arrived. I don't mind telling you, this is *not* acceptable. I can't stress that too strongly. This matter concerns one of our most important and *sensitive* clients. I felt I should call personally to facilitate the matter."

"I'm sorry," said the young man. "We do have a procedure here that—"

"I know all about your procedures. And, rest assured, we've complied with everything you've asked of us. But, do I see that file on my desk this morning? No, I don't. I do not! Now, what is your name?"

"My name?" said the man quickly. "It's Theodore."

"That's not the name I was given," said Bram impatiently. "You weren't the one my secretary talked to. Do you have someone else working in that department?"

"Well, I suppose she could have talked to Rose. She's

here Monday, Wednesday, and Friday afternoons. I'm kind of new."

"I thought so. I don't remember you. My association with the Saltzman Clinic goes back many years. Fifteen years ago I was on the board of directors. I will tell you truthfully, Theodore, I have never had a problem like this before."

"I'm very sorry, Dr. Thorndyke. Maybe you could give me the name and I could look it up for you. I might be able to find out where the problem is."

"That would be fine, Theodore. Just fine. And believe me, I won't forget this. I'll be in town next month to give a lecture on quintessential renderings of homeopathic instability. It's my specialty. And I'll be sure to mention to Dr. Blatten-Vorgstein how helpful you've been. Now, the file we're looking for is the one on Jack Grendel." He spelled the last name carefully.

"Yes. I'll be right back."

Bram took a small bow as Sophie sat in rapt attention on the bed. A minute later papers began rattling on the other end and Theodore returned.

"That file has already been sent to Minnesota, Dr. Thorndyke. We no longer have any of the records here."

"That's ridiculous!" said Bram. "Very unprofessional. Can you explain that to me?"

"Well, it *is* sort of unorthodox, I guess. We usually just send copies and keep the permanent record here on file. All I found was his name, the address where the file was sent, and the empty folder."

"Give me the address," said Bram impatiently.

"Well, I'm not sure . . ."

"Theodore, this snafu is costing me time and money. If I have to contact your supervisor . . ."

"It was sent to Mrs. Amanda Jorensen, Box 1298, Duluth, Minnesota. That's it."

"I see," said Bram. "Amanda Jorensen. Well. You've been a great help. Next time I talk with Emmet Saltzman, I'll tell him what a good job you're doing."

"But . . . Dr. Thorndyke?" The voice grew apprehensive. "He's been dead for over thirty years."

"Oh, I am sorry," said Bram quickly. "I'll have to make a point of sending his family some flowers. Thanks, Theodore." He hung up.

Sophie jumped up and grabbed him, hugging him tightly. "You did it!"

"Of course," he said serenely. "O ye of little faith." He stuck his tongue in his cheek. "False humility is only thinly disguised smugness. The file was sent directly to Amanda."

Sophie whirled around. "I knew it. I knew he was there. Both he and Amanda lied to me. But why?"

"I should think that would be obvious."

The door swung open and in walked an extremely thin Dr. Quist, a clipboard under one arm. "And how are we feeling today?" he asked, sitting down on the orange plastic chair. He crossed his sticklike legs and eyed them both noncommittally.

Bram stood over the chair, glowering. "*We* are just dandy. We would be even dandier if you'd sign that inane procedural shit and let us out of here."

The doctor studied him for a moment and then turned to Sophie. "How do your lungs feel?"

"Sore."

"That's to be expected. I need to examine you both one more time. If everything checks out, you'll be out of here in fifteen minutes. Or we can sit and snarl at each other." He looked up at Bram. "What shall it be?"

"Thank you, doctor," said Sophie. "That would be fine. Where would you like me to sit?"

The doctor stood. "On the edge of the bed." He glanced dismissively over his shoulder. "I'll be with you in a minute. Take off your shirt."

24

It was after two before Bram and Sophie were finally released from the hospital. After a short stop at one of their favorite cafés for a piece of homemade blackberry pie à la mode, Bram dropped Sophie off at Canal Park while he headed into town to visit an old friend who worked at one of the local radio stations. Sophie couldn't stand the thought of being trapped one more minute inside some huge, stuffy building. She needed fresh air after breathing the stale hospital variety all night.

Canal Park was one of her favorite spots—or, at least, had been until Lars Olson was found murdered beneath the Aerial Lift Bridge. The mental image of his body hanging from one of those huge girders would forever taint her feelings about the place. And the worst of it was, she was almost certain there was going to be another murder—and soon.

As she pulled out the remnant of her hospital lunch to feed to the gulls, she spotted Jack and his niece, Chelsea, walking arm in arm down the long concrete walkway that formed one side of the narrow canal. They appeared to be deep in conversation. Sophie sat down on a bench and tossed crumbs into the grass, all the while watching them approach the base of the bridge.

Together they stopped and peered over the side. Powerful waves crashed against the concrete barrier with enough force to throw spray high into the air. After a few moments, Jack put his arm around Chelsea and gave her a hug. In response, she whispered something into his ear and they both began to roar with laughter. Feeling inside his raincoat pocket for his keys, Jack kissed her on the cheek and headed off toward the parking lot. Chelsea turned and watched him go.

Sophie took it as her cue to toss the remainder of her snack at one large, particularly noisy gull. Picking up her purse, she crossed the grass to the stairs leading down to the walkway. She got within a few yards of Chelsea before being recognized.

"Sophie! You're the last person I expected to see here today." Chelsea was wearing an elegant sand-colored silk blouse and darker, fawn-colored slacks. She was the picture of tailored perfection.

"Bram and I were just released from the hospital. I assume you know what happened."

"I was at the house yesterday when Father came in with the news." Her tone was crisp, expressing no sympathy.

"Of course. I did know you were coming out yesterday morning. For Jack's meeting."

Chelsea nodded. After a nicely judged pause, she continued with the same studied indifference. "You look well."

"I'm a little sore when I breathe, but otherwise just fine." Out of the corner of her eye, Sophie noticed an ore boat glide slowly into the harbor behind them. Normally she would be more than excited about watching such a huge vessel thread its way through the narrow channel and out into the vastness of Lake Superior. Today, the sight barely registered. "I saw Jack leave a few minutes ago. Do you get together with him often?" She knew the question was nosy, but didn't care.

Chelsea's eyes searched the horizon. "Uncle Jack and I are very close. We always have been. If I'd had my way, he would have been my father, not Luther. Unfortunately, we don't get to pick and choose our parents."

Or our children, thought Sophie.

"My mother and father are in extreme demand by the rest of the world, you know. At least they were when I was growing up. I used to figure that meant they were very important." She laughed. "I didn't realize all it really meant was that they were totally self-consumed."

"Aren't you being a little hard on them, Chelsea? After all—"

"You're their good friend, right? You're lucky. They make better friends than they do parents. At least they don't forget *you* exist. But no matter. It's all past. And the past no longer interests me." She said the words coldly, her flawless complexion looking almost like a painted, Oriental mask. "There's very little worth remembering anyway. Just Uncle Jack. You know, when I was eleven years old, my uncle and I were roughhousing on the front lawn. I suppose I was giggling and trying to get away from him or something. I don't really remember. But as I was running toward the cliff, I tripped and rolled over the side. I landed on a ledge about three feet down. I must have scraped my knee pretty badly because I started to cry. I remember Jack's face appearing above me. He looked a hundred feet tall. He reached down and drew me into his arms and ran all the way back to the house.

"I can still remember the feeling of his body, so strong and warm. But the odd thing was, he was shaking. I'd never seen an adult do that before. He carried me into the house and sat me down on the kitchen counter. I can still see the look on his face. He was crying. Actually crying! And it was for me. No one had ever cried for me before. I was so intrigued, I totally forgot my injury. He cleaned off my knee and put something on it, but it was his tenderness and absolute concern that I remember. He told me that day that I was the most important person in his life. He couldn't bear to see anything bad happen to me and that I could always count on his protection. He held me for a long time. I think we finally ended up tickling each other and laughing, just like always, but I'll never forget that one moment. Nothing he's done since has ever led me to believe he's changed his mind.

"At the time, I didn't realize how dangerous that fall could've been. The thing is, even though the ledge stopped my fall, Jack saved my life that day. And I'll never forget it. I'd do anything for him, Sophie. Anything."

Sophie was struck by the story. She had no idea how

miserable Chelsea's childhood had been—or how bonded she and Jack had become. "But you were close to your grandfather, too, weren't you?"

Chelsea twisted a lock of shiny blonde hair around her finger. "I suppose. In a way. But it seems like people have always wanted something from me. My parents wanted a quiet, undemanding little doll, who looked cute when brought out at parties and who would grow up healthy and happy with no real input from them. My grandfather was the opposite. He was willing to give me all the time and attention I wanted. That fooled me at first. I wasn't used to it. But, in the end, all he really wanted was to mold someone into his own image. I was available. When I moved in with him, the year I turned seventeen, I knew I was unformed, raw. He taught me a lot. But the only person to understand who I really was, and love me for *that*, was Uncle Jack. He wanted me to be whatever made me happy. No strings. No demands. He listened to my ideas without superimposing his own. Do you know how important that is?"

"You're lucky," said Sophie. "Some people never find that." She thought grimly of her own son.

"I know."

"You must be very proud of him—running for senator like he is."

"I am. Very."

"He wants it pretty badly."

"And he'll get it."

"You're so sure? It seems to me that he may have an Achilles' heel."

"What do you mean?"

"Well, if I'm not mistaken, he spent a year at a mental health facility shortly after his return from Vietnam."

Chelsea stood very still. "You've got to be kidding. That's ludicrous!" She burst out laughing.

Sophie was momentarily taken aback by the response. "How can you be so sure? You weren't even born yet."

"Because I know my uncle. I've never met a man who is more mentally healthy. Where did you pick up such a ridiculous rumor?"

Sophie shrugged, feeling a little embarrassed. "It's the truth."

"You can rest assured it has no basis in fact. I can't believe all the rumors that get started in these campaigns. Did you know he's supposed to have had three illegitimate children by some woman in Arizona? And he wears a toupee? I think someone even swore he sleeps with his chauffeur. I mean, he doesn't even *have* a chauffeur. Get a grip, Sophie. People throw around a lot of mud. Most of it never sticks."

Her reaction did seem to be genuine. Perhaps she didn't know the truth. And anyway, it might have nothing to do with the recent murders.

"I can see where you're coming from," said Chelsea. "You think Uncle Jack has something to do with these recent deaths in Duluth. Well, rest your mind. He's totally innocent. He's incapable of something like that. Jack is the most gentle man I've ever known."

Sophie found it an extremely naive statement. "All right. Let's say that's true. On the other hand, not everyone around him may be quite so gentle."

"What do you mean by that? Who are you referring to?"

"Well, Ryan Woodthorpe for one."

A faint smile touched her lips. "You don't like him?"

"No. I don't." Sophie turned at the sound of a horn blast. The ore boat was alerting the bridge that it wanted to pass underneath. The bridgeman responded with two blasts of his own and a few seconds later, the bridge began to empty of cars. "Ryan's going to be a father, you know."

"What?" Very deliberately, Chelsea turned until she was facing Sophie.

"He and Jenny Tremlet are having a baby."

"How do you know that?"

"Firsthand. Jenny came to see Bram and me at the hospital shortly after lunch today. She had an appointment with an obstetrician. She seems pretty happy about it. I understand you know her."

"We've met."

Amidst the clanging of warning bells, the bridge began to rise. Sophie's eyes were pulled to the spot where Lars

Olson's body must have been tied to the bridge. As the huge ship moved into the channel, she felt the deep horn blasts resonate inside her body. She waved at the boatmen standing high on the ship's top deck. Several waved back. The boat appeared to be from Greece. She'd always wondered what it would be like, sailing through the November gales on Lake Superior, out through the St. Lawrence, and on to the Atlantic. The seamen's lives were undoubtedly hard, yet ship life must surely have its pleasures. The boat moved swiftly through the canal and out into the lake.

"I'm just like a kid," she said, watching it advance toward the horizon. "I'm always so ridiculously impressed." She turned and to her surprise, found herself alone.

25

Alice Oag sat perched on a high stool in the lodge's kitchen, busily frosting a chocolate layer cake. It had been a quiet day. The ancient radio that rested on a tall stand next to the table was tuned to her favorite classical station. She'd always loved opera. Tonight, *Tosca* was being broadcast live all the way from New York City. Her favorite aria, "Recondita armonia," would be sung by the greatest living tenor, Luciano Pavarotti. Just thinking about it gave her goose bumps. She followed the melody in her mind, the last few notes swelling with a brilliant intensity. The metal spatula she held cut through the moist kitchen air as she directed the imaginary orchestra, remembering every flourish, never losing track of the violins. She stopped midverse when she noticed Sophie standing in the doorway, watching her.

"No, no, don't quit," said Sophie, leaning against the

door frame. "You're having such a good time. I didn't mean to interrupt you."

Alice straightened her apron. "You must think I'm a terribly silly old woman."

"I do not! Really, I just thought I'd see what you were up to. The house seems so quiet. Bram and I just got back from town and he's gone up to work on his book. We stayed to have dinner with some friends."

Alice began filling a cloth pastry bag with frosting. "How are you feeling?"

"Much better, thanks. The doctor says we should both be back to normal in a few days." She walked over and warmed her hands next to the stove. "It's getting chilly out there. And the fog is rolling in. We almost missed the turn into the drive."

Alice peeked out the window. "The six o'clock news advised people not to travel after dark. It's only going to get worse." She scraped the last bit of frosting out of the bowl. "That was awful, what happened to you yesterday. I don't mind telling you, Mr. Jorensen's been in a terrible mood ever since it happened."

"I know. He and Amanda stopped by the hospital yesterday evening. They were both pretty upset. To be honest, Bram and I were going to stay in town tonight. We only came back to the house to pick up our things. Except, by the time we got here, the visibility on the highway was so poor we decided it was better to stay one more night rather than risk driving in this soup." Sophie hesitated before adding, "But we will be leaving tomorrow."

Alice looked up from the cake. She appeared genuinely upset. "For good? Are you driving back to Minneapolis?"

"No, not yet. Bram still needs some quiet time to finish his book. He's going to work in the hotel room for the next few days. I wanted to stick around a while longer, see if I can be of some help. I just feel like there should be something I could do." She sighed and looked out at the fog.

Grimly, Alice shook her head. "I don't blame you for taking a room in town. It's not safe in this house anymore. If I had any brains, I'd probably leave, too." She twisted the top of the pastry bag shut and stood, pulling the cake stand toward her.

Sophie crossed to the table and sat down. Since she felt somewhat at loose ends tonight, she might as well watch Alice decorate the cake. "Where is everyone?"

"Well, Mrs. Jorensen had her dinner sent up on a tray. She has a bad headache. If you ask me, it's going to be a long time before she's over her father's death. This has all been pretty hard on her. And Mr. Jorensen said he didn't feel much like eating. He's been reading in his study all evening. I'm going to bring him a pot of tea and some sandwiches a little later. He needs to eat something."

"Are Jack and Nora here?"

"Sure are. Last I heard they'd gone to the east sun room to do some work."

Sophie glanced into the silent dining room. She wasn't particularly upset at the prospect of spending another night at Brule House. It felt like the same old place. Just like always, the house was quiet and dark. Someone had built a fire in the living room fireplace. The wonderful scent of burning pine beckoned to her even as she sat at the kitchen table.

Alice scowled at the cake. "A chocolate layer cake can cure just about anything. I thought I'd do my part to try and change the mood around here." Her expert hands deftly began to decorate the sides. As she finished, she made a large swirl in the center and dropped a cherry on top. "All done," she announced. "Would you like a piece?"

Sophie patted her stomach. "Of course I would. But I think I'd better pass. There's altogether too much good food around here." She pushed away from the table. "I think I'm going to go and sit by the fire in the front room for a few minutes before heading up to bed."

Alice nodded her approval. "If you need anything, just give me a holler." She carried the cake over to the counter and crossed to the sink to begin washing up the mixing bowls and pans. "See you in the morning," she called over her shoulder.

* * *

Jack looked up from a stack of papers he'd been reading and leaned back in his chair, making an arch of his fingers. He peered over them at Nora, who had just entered the sun-room holding a large goblet full of wine. "I wondered where you'd gone. I see now that I should have guessed." His eyes dropped to the glass. "Didn't you get enough of that at dinner?"

"Guess not." She took a sip. "Well?"

"Well what?"

Nora narrowed her eyes in disgust. "Have you thought anymore about what I said?"

"No."

"Jack, you've got to address this!"

He shifted some papers into a folder. "Why did you wait until now to tell me?"

"Because I wasn't sure the file still existed until this af-ternoon."

He was silent.

"Well? Don't you have anything to say? Your sister told you she'd burned it. There's only one good reason she wanted to hold on to it."

"What do you mean?"

"Do I have to draw you a picture? Your sister is your one blind spot, darling. You don't see how controlling she is."

"Nora, I'm not going to listen to this."

"With that file in her possession, she has a great deal of power over your future decisions."

"She would never blackmail me. I'm sure of it."

Nora shook her head. "The day after you told her you were going to run for the Senate, she handed you a list of issues she wanted you to champion—and all her little fem-inist dos and don'ts."

"Some of those dos and don'ts, as you put it, I happen to agree with. You might take a moment out of your busy schedule to read some of the position papers she's given me. Most of them are very well thought out and well doc-umented. I've used them in several of my campaign speeches."

"Well, don't kid yourself that the scope of her interest lies in merely feeding you statistics. Just look at the money she's given over the years to her pet causes. Through you she has a chance at *real* clout. Under all that sisterly charm beats the heart of a power broker."

Jack began to laugh. "You should listen to yourself. Don't you think this is a case of the pot calling the kettle black?"

Nora made a sickly smile. "Someone needs to speak to you about your periodic use of cliché. It's a liability."

"I'm just a homespun kind of guy. And anyway," he said, his expression growing serious, "I'm nobody's puppet."

"No? Maybe not willingly, but what if—six months after we get to Washington—she threatens to send that file to, say, The *New York Times*? That is, unless you vote her way on something very specific."

"It won't happen."

Nora let out a screech and flopped backward on the couch. "You're impossible. Do you know that? Amanda lied to you, Jack. And there are other things about her you don't know. As I think of it, two can play at the game of blackmail."

"What do you mean?"

"Oh, just drop it. You never give me any credit. One day you'll see how much I've helped."

"Nora, I hate it when you speak cryptically. Either say what you mean or shut up." He picked up his favorite dagger-shaped letter opener, poking the tip into his palm.

"You shouldn't speak to me like that, *dear.* Remember, you're supposed to be Mr. Wonderful."

He yawned. "Don't worry, Nora. I have everything under control."

"That's not good enough. You need a plan to deal with your sister—with *everything* that's been happening."

"This may come as a shock, but I've had everything planned from the very beginning."

Nora was surprised by the hard edge in his voice. "Well,

that's a start. But who's speaking cryptically now? What specifically are you going to do about that file?"

"Wait."

"Wait?"

"Look, there are other people who know about the time I spent at the Saltzman Clinic. You don't need the actual file to make an accusation."

"Most of them are dead."

"What are you saying?"

She looked away.

"I paid Sydney off."

"But he wanted more. That's why he drove all the way up here in that flashy piece of tin."

Jack drummed his nails on the arm of his chair. "Luther's not dead. He knows. And thanks to you, Ryan knows. You made a mistake there, Nora. Never trust a zealot—even if you *are* attracted to him."

"Don't be absurd!"

"No? I suppose he might even tell Chelsea. If he does, he'll regret it. Did you know they are seeing each other? She's muscling in on your territory. I told her I thought she should be careful." He laughed. "God, if you think you've seen Amanda at her controlling best before, just wait till she finds out Ryan is hustling her only daughter. That goes for Luther, too. He's never had much time for Master Woodthorpe."

Nora pretended a smile. "Very funny. The atmosphere in here is getting a little ... close. I think I need some fresh air."

"Suit yourself." He opened his briefcase and removed a stack of papers. "I'll be in here going over these briefs. On your way out will you ask Alice to bring me a thermos of coffee?"

"Of course. *Dear.*" She crossed to the door and disappeared into the darkness.

26

Sophie stood next to the fireplace, hand on her hip, staring intently into the crackling flames. She'd just tossed another log onto the fire and was deciding whether it was positioned correctly on top of the others. As she reached for a poker, the phone began to ring. "I'll get it," she called to Alice, who she could hear still washing up dishes in the kitchen. Walking briskly into the front foyer, she picked up the extension that sat on a thin piecrust table next to the stairs. "Hello," she said into the receiver. She noticed a stack of mail leaning against a small crystal bowl filled with mints.

"This is John Wardlaw. I'd like to speak with Sophie Greenway."

"Detective Wardlaw. Hi. This is Sophie." Absently, she picked up a mint.

"You're a hard person to track down, you know that?" He sounded relieved. "I'm sorry it's taken me so long to contact you. I didn't find out about the sauna incident until late this afternoon. The Two Harbors police handled it and I still haven't seen any of the paperwork. I should have been informed about it immediately."

Sophie could hear the frustration in his voice.

"Anyway, I was wondering what your plans were?"

She hesitated. "My plans?"

He cleared his throat. "Do you intend to continue staying at Brule's Landing? In all honesty, I have to tell you that I feel partially responsible for what happened to you and your husband yesterday. I should have taken the potential threat to your safety much more seriously."

"I'm not sure there was anyway you could have convinced me to leave."

"I realize that. But I should have tried." He paused. "I really have to insist that you find somewhere else to stay."

Sophie thought about the incident in the attic. Was the person who switched off the light the same one who tried to trap her and Bram in the sauna? And what did it have to do with the murders? "Are you any nearer to finding this murderer?" she asked. She could hear phones ringing in the background. It was nearly nine P.M. and yet there he was, still at work.

Wardlaw was momentarily silent. "Yes," he answered slowly. "The typewriter you found in the sauna was used to type those notes. I think we may be close to an arrest."

"But you can't tell me who, right?"

"No. I'm sorry. It's not something I can discuss. By the way, you haven't received any more notes, have you?"

"No, I haven't. Not since the one about the Child's Garden. Turns out it was a book of children's poetry by Robert Louis Stevenson. I found a copy that belonged to Amanda when she was a child. She'd given it to her own daughter for her sixth birthday. The thing is, I don't know where that leaves us."

"Interesting," said Wardlaw. "I don't suppose you've run across anything else that might be of help to our investigation?"

"Nothing. And to answer your earlier question, Bram and I are leaving in the morning. We only came back here to pick up our belongings, but because of the fog, we decided to stay the night."

"See to it that you two stick together. Stay in the same room for the rest of the evening, if at all possible. And if you can lock your bedroom door before you turn in, do so. I'm not trying to scare you, I just want you to appreciate the seriousness of your situation."

Sophie felt herself begin to shiver. She knew that for many years, she'd resisted any urge to feel afraid. Fear was something from her past. Admitting fear into her life now might mean that she wasn't in control. That thought was almost worse than any tangible threat she could imagine. Yet, she knew intellectualizing things didn't make them go away. In her gut, she realized that she had mentally forced herself to take an impossible emotional position. She *was* afraid. She couldn't continue to ignore it.

"And one more thing, Ms. Greenway. Do you still have my card? The one with my home phone number on it?"

"I do. It's in my wallet."

"Well, don't hesitate to call if the need arises."

"Thanks," said Sophie.

"All right. Take care. Perhaps we'll talk tomorrow." The line clicked.

Sophie replaced the phone and stood for a moment, looking up the stairs. She could hear Bram's typewriter plunking away. Had they made a mistake coming back here? Surely nothing was going to happen tonight. For days she had refused to consider that any one of her friends could want to hurt her, but her resolve was beginning to crumble. Nervously, she picked up the mail and began flipping through the letters. The top postcard was from Bram's daughter. Margie was in her first year of college and taking care of the house in Minneapolis while they were away. Halfway through the stack she came across a small, white envelope with her name typed on the front. No address. No postmark. She turned it over and drew out a piece of typing paper. Stepping nearer to the floor lamp, she read:

> You must leave.
> Your life is in danger.
> Consider yourself warned.

Sophie could feel a prickly sensation creep down her back. She had to get upstairs right away and show it to Bram.

"Are you all right?" asked Alice.

Sophie looked up. Alice was standing in front of her, her shrewd blue eyes fixed on Sophie with a look of intense concern.

"Did you get some bad news?" Alice nodded to the note in her hand.

"It's . . . an invitation. I'm fine. Really."

"That's good. You had me worried there for a moment. Anyway, I just brought Mr. Jorensen a pot of tea and some sandwiches. I mentioned that you and your husband had come back, and he wanted me to find you and ask if you'd mind coming back to his study for a few minutes." She paused, tugging self-consciously on her chocolate-stained apron. "Do you think you feel up to that?"

Sophie stuffed the note into the pocket of her sweater. "Sure. Of course. I'll go right now."

"Fine," said Alice. "I think he could use the company tonight. He's kind of down."

Sophie nodded her thanks and crossed to the rear hallway. She was sure she could make the conversation brief. And anyway, Bram wasn't going anywhere. As she approached Luther's study, she was struck by the haunting melody coming from his open door. Moving closer, she peeked into the room. Luther sat quietly in front of the fire, reading. He seemed even thinner today than the day she'd arrived. He wasn't eating well, that was more than apparent. How could he, with everything that had been happening? As she watched him, he looked up.

"Sophie! I called the hospital earlier today and they said you and Bram had already been released. Come in. Please." He snapped the book shut and stood, turning down the volume on the stereo receiver. "I had hoped you'd be back this evening. How are you feeling?"

"We're both fine," said Sophie, sitting down in a comfortably overstuffed chair opposite him. "Just a little sore when we breathe."

Luther noticed her looking at his record library. "Are you a fan of Mahler? This is his first symphony. Alice has been after me all evening to listen to *Tosca* on the radio, but for some reason, I've lost my taste for Puccini. I find him a bit, how shall I say, saccharine?"

Sophie nodded.

"Will you join me for some tea and sandwiches?" He

glanced at the tray sitting on the table next to him. "Alice just brought this in. I'm afraid I wasn't very hungry at dinner."

In the firelight, Sophie couldn't help but notice how terribly drawn his face looked. It worried her that he wouldn't open up and talk more about his illness. He was too much of a stoic sometimes. Too much like her.

As if reading her mind he said, "Do I frighten you?"

"No!" She knew her response was too vehement and much too quick.

Luther lifted the tray down onto a low table between them. "Have you already had your supper?"

"Bram and I ate with friends in Duluth before driving back here." She sighed. "We were hoping to relax a bit, have some fun, a few laughs. But all anyone wants to talk about are these awful murders. At least at dinner tonight, I would have preferred a different topic."

Luther poured tea for both of them. "People seem to be doing little else. It's a wonder we get our teeth brushed in the morning."

"One of our friends said the police were about to make an arrest. I just talked to Detective Wardlaw a few minutes ago. He confirmed it."

Luther nodded. "I see. Did you know I'm their prime suspect?"

Sophie's head snapped up. "What? Are you serious? I can't stand this anymore. You've got to tell me the truth, Luther! You didn't have anything to do with any of this, did you?"

Luther tried to smile but his face wouldn't cooperate. "No. But don't worry. If I'm arrested, perhaps it's for the best."

Sophie was aghast. "How can you say that!" She couldn't believe her ears.

He shrugged. "Let's not kid each other. You and I realize the murderer is someone we both know, probably intimately. Bottom line is: he's got to be one of my family or friends. If that's true, better me than him."

"But that's ridiculous! You *want* to be a martyr?"

"Do you really care that much?"

Sophie could see tears forming in his eyes.

"Believe me, I'm not the stuff of martyrs. It's just . . .
I'm the logical scapegoat. Claire knew that when she hid
the poison in my jacket. In case you're wondering, she told
me several days ago what she did. In many ways, I don't
even blame her because I'm a willing scapegoat." He
paused, clearly struggling with something. "I suppose my
own pride has kept me from telling you this. I asked
Amanda to keep it quiet. I didn't figure it was anybody's
business but mine. The truth is Sophie, I'm dying."

Sophie felt a sharp pain in her lungs.

"I believe at this moment you look worse than I do." He
waited for her to recover before continuing. "I think of
most things now with a kind of lethargic indifference. *Most
things,*" he said, his jaw tightening. "Not everything."

"I'm so sorry. I had no idea. Amanda just said you were
on some kind of awful medication."

"I am. She wasn't lying."

"It's monstrous to think that you would willingly spend
your last days in prison. How can the police even suspect
you? I mean, for one thing, you have no motive."

Luther laughed. "But my dear, I have an infinite assortment of motives. I made the mistake of telling the police
the truth. One must never do that, if one wants to appear
innocent."

Sophie wrapped her arms around herself. "But, for instance, you hardly knew Lars Olson."

"On the contrary. I knew him only too well. He was
chancellor of UMD for many years before he left to go to
work for Amanda's father at Grendel Shipping. I saw him
almost every day." He looked into the fire. "He had eyes of
immense emptiness."

"You didn't like him?"

He smiled. "I hated him. Perhaps as much as or more
than any man I've ever known. He was one of those pathetic individuals who mistake the university for the universe."

"And you told the police that?"

"I also happened to mention that I detested Herman Grendel and Sydney Sherwin. Nobody liked old man Grendel—except maybe his banker—so that didn't set me apart from the crowd. As for Sid, we long ago realized how much we loathed one another. I felt that our continuing relationship was nothing more than an odious habit."

"But none of that is necessarily a motive for murder."

"You think not?" He bit into his sandwich. "I beg to differ. I'll tell you something, Sophie. I may be wrong, but I think I know who the murderer is. And for what he's doing, I don't blame him. I wondered at first if I was going to be one of the victims myself, but I don't think so anymore. I don't really want to go into all of this, because I could be wrong. But if I'm right, I pray the real murderer is never discovered. Let them haul me away. I'll go gladly." He chewed his sandwich, thinking hard about something. "You know, our lives are made up of small events that wear us down. It's not the great crisis, but the small details that mold us into what we eventually become."

Sophie stared at him, blinking back her tears. "You seem so philosophical about everything. I don't understand that."

"Well, I *am* a professor of philosophy." He could see she wasn't amused. "No, that wasn't funny. Perhaps it's my illness—or the drugs." Again he couldn't help but laugh. "The eternal question still remains. Does one mellow or does one rot? I think, in my case, the rot's won."

Sophie wanted to cover her ears. Her old friend, dying! Yet something he'd said had rung false. What was it? *He's got to be one of my family or friends. If that's true, better me than him.* Luther had his strengths and weaknesses just like anyone else, but one thing Sophie knew for sure: he wasn't a noble man. There were only two people on earth for whom he might willingly give up his last days of freedom. One was Amanda. The other was his daughter, Chelsea. Did that mean he thought one of them was responsible?

"I'm sorry, Sophie. This is all pretty heavy stuff. Try a sandwich."

A door slammed somewhere down the hall and Nora

steamed past Luther's study shouting, "*You just do that!*
See if I give a good goddamn!"

"Ah, domestic bliss," said Luther, sipping his tea. "If the
press were only around to record our typical evening festivities."

"What are you reading?" asked Sophie, responding to
what she felt was his desire to lighten the conversation. She
glanced at the two books next to his chair.

"Well, this first volume here"—he held it up—"is that
thing I published many years ago on ethics in everyday life.
It's entitled, interestingly enough, *Ethics in Everyday Life.*
I used to lack imagination, but I've changed. Jenny bor-
rowed it a few weeks ago and just returned it before dinner
tonight. I hope she has gleaned the essence and will pass it
on to her squirrel of a boyfriend. Ryan could use a little re-
fresher course, if you ask me."

"What's the other volume?"

"Ah," said Luther. "My solace. Shakespeare. It's a pity
he can't offer me a heaven. At least not the heaven I was
taught as a boy." He opened the book and leafed through
the first few pages. "Here's something. It's from
Richard II." Slipping on his glasses he read:

> O, but they say the tongues of dying men
> Enforce attention like deep harmony.
> Where words are scarce, they are seldom spent
>   in vain;
> For they breathe truth that breathe their words
>   in pain.

Looking up, he continued from memory:

> More are men's ends mark'd than their lives
>   before.
> The setting sun, and music at the close,
> As the last taste of sweets, is sweetest last,
> Writ in remembrance more than things long
>   past.

Slowly, he closed the book.

Sophie set her cup down on the table. "I suppose I should be going."

Luther nodded. "But one last thing. Please believe me, I'm sorry you walked in on all this. It was my intention to keep my problems to myself."

"You idiot." She fought to control her voice.

"You go on, now. I'll see you in the morning."

Sophie wanted to say something eloquent, something to ease his pain, but knew it was impossible. Instead, she just said she'd be down for breakfast about nine.

Luther smiled. "It's a date. Before you go, would you turn the volume back up on the stereo? This next part is my favorite." He leaned back and closed his eyes.

Sophie did as he asked. The last movement was just about to begin. Stepping quietly to the door, she turned and for a moment, watched him resting. Of all things, a slight smile appeared on his lips. She stood listening to the music as it rose into the chilly room, lighting the darkness.

27

Ryan carried a huge pink begonia into the greenhouse and set it down on the potting bench. Turning it around and around, he eventually found the best angle.

"Is that the new variety you were telling me about?" asked a voice from behind him.

Whirling around, Ryan looked startled. "Sure is. Isn't it a beauty?"

The figure was seated on a bench next to one of the growing tables.

"I didn't hear you come in."

"No. I saw that you were busy in the other room. I didn't want to disturb you."

Ryan appeared puzzled, but shrugged it off. Busily, he began to snip off some of the dying leaves. "You seem kind of preoccupied this evening."

"Do I?"

"Yeah. Something wrong?" He pulled a wastebasket out from under the table.

"No. Actually, I just made a decision. I always feel so much better when something is finally decided."

"Really? Sounds serious."

"It is."

"Are you going to tell me or is it a secret?"

"No. It won't be a secret after tonight."

"So? I'm waiting." He stopped and turned around.

"Kind of a foggy night."

"Yeah, it is. What does that have to do with anything?"

"That's a pretty scarf over there. The one wrapped around that pot. Don't I recognize it?"

Ryan's mouth tightened. "What are you getting at? If this is about . . ."

"About what, Ryan?"

Ryan flexed his arms and shrugged.

"Now, this is an interesting plant right next to me here. Look at what I found stuck in the dirt."

Ryan stepped back. "Hey, that's a gun."

"Twenty-twenty vision. Good for you."

"What are you going to do?"

"Do? Why Ryan, where's your imagination? I'd hate to think it's escaped you at a time like this. What do you usually do with a gun?"

"I don't know. I mean, look, I can explain." His eyes darted from side to side, looking for a way of escape.

"Explain? I don't think that's necessary. You already know how I feel."

"It's not what you think!"

"It's not? Oh, but I think it is. And we both know it, don't we? As a matter of fact, I've already warned you."

"But this is ridiculous. Give me a chance to explain."

A gunshot shattered one of the glass panels behind him. "God! Shit!" Ryan backed into the table, knocking the begonia over the side. The next two shots hit their target.

Slowly, Ryan slid to the floor.

"We can't forget our calling card. I'd like to think people could recognize a pig when they see one, but for those who can't . . ." A piece of typing paper was placed in Ryan's hand. "There."

Before the light was switched off, a potted geranium was set decoratively on top of his chest.

PART FIVE

This Little Piggy . . .

When the bright lamp is carried in,
The sunless hours again begin;
O'er all without, in field and lane,
The haunted night returns again.
                    from *A Child's Garden of Verses*
                         Robert Louis Stevenson

28

Sophie poked her head into the deserted dining room, lustfully examining the contents of several chafing dishes elegantly displayed on the sideboard. She tugged at the waist of her jeans. For some reason they seemed smaller than the last time she'd worn them.

No one seemed to be stirring. Bram had left with some friends earlier in the morning to go fishing. He said he needed a break before he tackled the last two chapters. Sophie was elected to take the car and scout out a hotel in Duluth. She wanted some time to explain the move to Luther and Amanda before she left. Bram had insisted that they would understand. Sophie wasn't so sure.

Backing out of the dining room doorway, Sophie bumped smack into Alice who was backing around a corner of her own. "Good morning," she said cheerfully, laughing at their mutual surprise.

Alice burst into tears.

"Are you all right?" asked Sophie, reaching out a hand to steady her.

"I can't talk about it right now." She yanked her arm away and ran into the kitchen.

What on earth? Sophie followed the sound of voices and found Claire and Amanda seated on the couch in the living room. Amanda was clearly angry.

"There's more at stake here than your career, Claire!"

"But what if she says something to the board of trustees? I could lose my job, my reputation—everything I've worked for."

"You're exaggerating." Amanda turned when she saw Sophie enter.

"What's going on?" asked Sophie. "Where is everyone? And what's wrong with Alice? I merely said good morning and she burst into tears."

Claire withdrew her arm from around Amanda's waist. "I'm afraid it's Ryan. Alice found his body about seven-thirty this morning when she went over to the cottage to give him a message. No one was answering the phone. She found him lying on the greenhouse floor. He'd . . . been shot." She shuddered. "One of those pig notes was found in his hand. *This little piggy had none.*"

Slowly, Sophie closed her hands around the back of a chair.

"There was no sign of a fight or a forced entry."

"Please," said Amanda. "Come sit down. We all need each other's support at a time like this."

Sophie sat down on the piano bench. "Have the police been here?"

"Come and gone," continued Claire. "They only stayed at the house for a few minutes. They spent most of their time over at the cottage."

Amanda put her face in her hands and began to sob.

"It's Luther," said Claire, her voice gentle. She rubbed her hand soothingly across Amanda's back. "The police have arrested him. Another gun was taken from the case in his study. They haven't found it yet, but they seem sure Luther is responsible."

Sophie wished she knew what to do. It was a horribly impotent feeling to just sit and watch Amanda cry. Amanda did look a sight this morning, as if she'd been abruptly awakened and simply tossed on an old robe. Her hair wasn't combed and, without the help of her usual makeup, the tracery of age was clearly visible in the texture of the skin around her mouth. Deep lines around her eyes made her look every day of her forty-five years. "What about Jenny? Where was she last night?"

"That's just it," said Claire. "Jenny wasn't around when the police arrived this morning. Their bed hadn't even been slept in. While they were examining the greenhouse, she drove up. Apparently she claims she and Ryan had a bad fight last night. She said she left about seven and drove around until almost midnight. She found a motel up the shore and spent the night. She didn't want to drive back because of the fog."

"Did she say what the fight was about?"

"If she did, I didn't hear."

Sophie folded her arms protectively over her chest. "Not much of an alibi, if you ask me."

"It would seem they think they have their man." Claire glanced cautiously at Amanda.

Snuffling back tears, Amanda pulled a tissue out of the pocket of her robe. "Worst of all is what Nora told them."

"And what was that?"

Amanda wiped her nose. "She said she went out for a walk last evening around ten. She and Jack had had another one of their . . . disagreements. She wanted some fresh air. I don't know why, but she took the path through the pine woods. As she passed the cottage, she just happened to look inside. She said she saw Ryan and my daughter Chelsea having a rather intense discussion. You can imagine how she made it sound. The police insist they need to talk to Chelsea about it. I called just as soon as they left to warn her. She's got to deny it!"

"But if it's true?"

"Of course it's not true. What business would she have with him? Nora's just trying to make trouble. Trying to throw suspicion away from herself. I mean, what about her? She had plenty of opportunity!"

"But no motive," interjected Claire.

"Well, maybe not, but it won't work. My daughter is completely innocent. And I've already called a lawyer about getting Luther released. He'll be home in a few hours."

Claire cleared her throat. "I think it may take more time than that, Amanda. You have to be realistic."

Amanda glowered.

"This kind of stress could be too much for Luther," said

Sophie. "He should tell what he knows. Maybe they'd let him go."

"What do you mean by that?" Amanda's face momentarily registered intense distress.

"Well, ah . . . all I meant to say was that he knows he's innocent. He needs to make them understand that!" Something told her it wasn't prudent to mention that Luther thought he knew who the killer was.

Amanda continued to stare. "That's good of you to worry, but Luther will be fine. He knows the police want to interrogate Chelsea and he's very upset about it. He demanded that Wardlaw leave her alone. After all, they have him, why do they need to bother her?"

"Excuse me, Mrs. Jorensen." Alice drooped against the edge of the archway. "Mr. Jorensen is on the phone for you."

Quickly, Amanda followed her out into the hall.

Turning slowly to Claire, Sophie waited until Amanda was out of earshot before saying, "She's in bad shape. I've never seen her so on edge."

"I know." Claire reached for the pack of cigarettes Nora had left lying on the coffee table. She seemed embarrassed as she tapped one out. "In times of stress I always break my own rules. Old habits die hard." She picked up a lighter.

"I know about the Saltzman Clinic, Claire. And the file Amanda was supposed to burn. I also know about your relationship with her."

Claire's hand shook as she lifted the cigarette to her mouth. "Jesus, do you have this entire place bugged?"

"Are you going to answer me?"

"I wasn't aware there was a question."

"Why didn't Amanda burn that file?"

Claire inhaled deeply, blowing smoke directly at her. It was a stalling gesture, yet Sophie knew there was more than a hint of defiance in it as well. "Well, I suppose she thought it might give her some leverage over Jack. Maybe even Nora."

"I can't believe she'd do that."

"No? Then you don't know her as well as you think."

"That's an awful thing to say!"

"You wanted the truth, didn't you?" Her entire body seemed to deflate. "Okay, maybe I'm wrong. To be honest, I don't know any more. It just seems like, when you enter this house, there's a rule that you have to leave your conscience at the door."

"That's bullshit."

"You think so?" Her glance was sharp. "Well, maybe it's just me. I've let my emotions cloud my judgment and I'm trying to find someone to blame. It's happened before, but this time I'm in way over my head."

"What do you mean?"

Claire smoked the cigarette absently, letting some ash fall onto the Oriental rug. "Are you sure you want to hear this?"

"I'm not leaving the room until I do."

"All right. But remember, you asked for it. To be honest, it might feel good to actually tell someone the truth." She sat up straight, squaring her shoulders as if readying herself for a battle. "About a month ago Amanda came to me. Jack had asked if she would help finance some TV ads he wanted to run. Since she was mortgaged to the hilt with the renovation of her restaurant, she came to me with what she thought was the perfect solution. As you know, I'm the current president of the North Shore Feminist Association. Amanda is the treasurer. It's a large organization, well over three hundred members. A dozen or so are quite wealthy. Last year alone we took in over one hundred thousand dollars in philanthropic donations. During the past few years the Association has started a rape crisis center and a shelter for battered women, and sponsored several studies on prostitution and sex education in the schools. We're a very active and committed group of women. In the last six months, our focus has become largely political. Thanks to Amanda, we're now supporting Jack for Congress.

"You have to understand that the next sixty days will be the most expensive months of the entire campaign. Unfortunately, but predictably, the big money in the state is backing Jack's Republican opponent. When Jack asked for the money, I know Amanda felt she *had* to do something. That's why she came to me and asked if we could borrow Association funds to help him with the TV promotion. She said after he'd won—and all the polls do show him way ahead—he'd be in a strong position to pay back campaign debt very quickly. She made it sound like a sure bet— almost like I'd be a traitor to my ideals, as well as to *her*—if I didn't go along with it. I know Amanda is an old friend of yours. One of the reasons I'm telling you this is because I think you can understand how persuasive she can be when she wants something. And, as you know, with me she had even more power."

Sophie knew she was telling the truth. "But if something happens to derail Jack's campaign, you could both go to jail. I assume you didn't take a majority vote to authorize use of Association funds."

Claire made a tiny strangling sound inside her throat. "No." The word came out low and raspy. She gave herself a moment to regain control. "And now . . . there's another complication. Nora found out about my relationship with Amanda. She's threatening to tell the trustees of the academy that I'm a lesbian. I've been running from that all my life, Sophie. But with Amanda it was finally going to be different. We talked about being open with our love. Standing our ground and letting the chips fall where they may. Even having a ceremony after Luther . . . You have to understand, Amanda wouldn't think of leaving him when he's so ill. If circumstances had been different, I believe she would have left him long ago. I've never once pressured her. I needed some time myself to think through what I was going to tell the academy. But you can imagine how fast they'll have me packed and out of there, if they find out this way. Nora wants that file. She threatened to put the worst spin on the information she possibly could unless I persuade Amanda to hand it over. You know the kind of accusations she's going to make. If I'm gay I'm obviously a child molester. None of the girls would be safe from my marauding eye. Garbage like that. I've talked to Amanda, but she absolutely refuses to give in. There's this sick kind of power struggle going on between her and Nora. Unfortunately, I'm caught in the middle. Christ, I don't even get it. She can copy the report if she wants. Anything, only *I* don't want to be her sacrificial lamb. It seems to me that some people are really good at recruiting others into their own personal army. If you're not constantly acquiescing to their way of seeing things, then you're a traitor." She began to wring her hands. "I didn't mean that. I'm sorry. It's just that I'm so upset. I love Amanda more than I thought I could ever love anyone. I've done all I could to help her. But I won't see my life ruined because of it. Nothing is worth that!"

Quietly, Amanda reentered the room. Her eyes moved back and forth between them, taking the measure of what had just been said. "You two seem to be having an interesting discussion. Did I miss something?"

Sophie could feel sparks coming out of her eyes.

"It's nothing." Claire put out her cigarette. "What did Luther have to say?"

"He wants me to come into town with his medication. With all the commotion this morning, he forgot to take it." She walked around behind the couch and stood over Claire, placing both hands on her shoulders. "I'm too upset to drive. I need you to take me."

"But my morning classes?"

"This is an emergency. Can't you cancel them just this once?"

Before Claire could answer, Sophie asked, "What about Jack and Nora?"

"They left shortly after the police arrested Luther," said Amanda. "And Alice left a few minutes ago in the van. She wanted to spend the afternoon at her sister's."

"Well," said Sophie, "why don't I give you a lift. I thought I might go into town today anyway." She didn't think that now was the time to tell Amanda that she and Bram were leaving.

"No, really, that's all right." Claire stood and faced Amanda. "Why don't you get dressed and I'll go call the school? I'll meet you by the car in a few minutes." She dropped the package of cigarettes into her pocket and quietly left the room.

Amanda remained standing behind the couch. "There's breakfast set out in the dining room if you and Bram get hungry."

"Bram went fishing with some friends earlier this morning. I'm supposed to meet him later at Castle Rock Tavern for dinner."

"Is that right? Well, you won't mind staying by yourself for a little while, will you? I shouldn't be gone more than an hour or two. We'll make a pot of tea and have a long talk when I get back."

Sophie hesitated. She didn't really want to stay alone in the house, but she couldn't simply leave without explaining matters to Amanda. Don't be such a big baby, she told herself. "Fine," said Sophie, trying to sound chipper. For some reason, the prospect of having tea with Amanda positively set her teeth on edge.

"Something bothering you?" asked Amanda.

"Why, no." Sophie smiled. "Not a thing."

29

Sophie stopped chewing her breakfast sausage and laid down the morning paper. Upstairs, she was sure she heard the sound of a door closing. "Hello?" she called, embarrassed at the timidity in her voice.

No answer.

She waited a moment longer, contemplating what she should do about it. The house was almost too silent for her liking. The quiet only added to her growing sense of apprehension. So what if she was alone? Wardlaw would have fits if he knew, but what could she do about it? She'd promised to wait for Amanda to return and she wasn't going to break that promise. She owed her that much. Besides, she could take care of herself. Pushing her plate away, she walked briskly into the kitchen and snapped on the radio. That was better. A little human companionship, even if it was only sound waves.

The breakfast she'd just finished was beginning to feel like moldering pudding inside her stomach. She should have stuck to orange juice and a muffin. As George Bernard Shaw used to say, you don't get tired of muffins, but you don't find inspiration in them either. Perhaps a stroll out by the shore would help her digestion. It was a windy day, the sky an intense cobalt blue, the temperature in the mid-fifties. Perfect early fall weather by anyone's standards. She poured herself a mug of coffee and wandered back into the dining room.

Hadn't she always loved being alone? When she'd first moved to Montana with Norman, before Rudy was born, she couldn't wait until he left in the morning (bad sign) so she could walk through the huge old farmhouse, listening to every nuance of the quiet, reveling in her newfound freedom. At college there had never been enough space or solitude. The dorms were crowded and everyone ate together at long tables in the dining hall. The rest of the time you were either in class or working. The only real privacy to be found was inside one of the tiny prayer closets. Roommates often commented on her righteousness. Why, sometimes she'd stay in that prayer closet for hours. Even now she laughed when she thought of it.

Stopping in front of a large window, she leaned her head against the cool glass. Big, puffy clouds sat low on the horizon. The sky was so brilliantly blue, it almost hurt her eyes. What was it everyone called the North Shore? The Norwegian Riviera? If Duluth, with all its charm, and the lake, with all its primitive beauty, were transplanted somewhere inside Europe, people would be falling over themselves to get there. As it was, Duluth's American image was slightly worse than Booger Hollow. She'd never been able to figure that out.

Sipping her coffee, she moved down the long hall to the sunroom doorway. She gave the room a quick perusal. Stacks of files sat neatly on one end of the desk. An ashtray filled with stale cigarette butts rested on a table next to the Queen Anne love seat. Compliments of Nora, no doubt.

She ran her hand lightly along the polished mahogany around the edges of the heavy, antique desk.

"It's a beautiful piece, isn't it?"

Sophie jumped at the sound of the voice. Coffee spilled from her mug onto the Oriental rug.

"I'm sorry. Did I frighten you?"

She turned. "No. I mean, yes! I didn't hear you come in."

"I parked in the back and used my key in the side door. Where is everyone?"

She backed up a step, resting her hand on the desktop for support. "Alice is at her sister's house. Amanda and Claire drove into Duluth."

"And Bram?"

She swallowed hard. "Yes, well, Bram . . . he went out for a short walk. I expect him back any minute."

"You seem kind of upset. I suppose it's Ryan's death. That was terrible, wasn't it?"

Sophie nodded.

"And poor Luther. Wouldn't it be incredible if he really was the murderer? I can't imagine what would make him do something so hideous, but the police seem convinced he's guilty. My own personal opinion is, they may be right. Don't say anything to Amanda. I don't want her to worry any more than she already does." Jack entered the room and shut the door behind him.

"What are you doing back here so soon? I thought you and Nora had left for the day."

"Nora wanted to do some shopping, so I dropped her off. I happened to run into my sister and Claire coming out of a drugstore downtown. They said you were here all alone. Bram had gone fishing."

Sophie managed a lame smile. "Well, yes, actually . . ."

"It's all right. I startled you. But surely you're not afraid of *me*? We're old friends."

"Of course. I don't know what you thought, but I wasn't reacting to you—just to being here all alone. I guess I'm kind of jumpy today." She hoped that was the truth.

"That's understandable. Have a seat."

"What?"

He moved behind the desk and sat down. "I came back specifically to talk to you. Please." He smiled his usual, easy smile. "I suppose you can stand if you want. I just thought you might be more comfortable sitting."

"No, I . . . sure. I'll sit." She glanced at the closed door. Why had he done that? No one was even in the house.

"Amanda tells me you found out about the year I spent at the Saltzman Clinic. Since you know that much, I thought you might be interested in hearing the whole story."

Sophie gripped the coffee mug tightly. "Jack, you have to understand."

"No, really, it's all right. I don't know how you did it, but I'm impressed. I thought I'd covered my tracks better than that. I can trust you, can't I? I don't want you to repeat any of this."

"Of course!"

"Good." A shaft of sunlight struck the top of his head, turning his curly blond hair into a kind of halo. "Shortly after I got back from Vietnam, I had a breakdown. A lot of guys did—for some, it took a bit longer. But in one way or another, I suppose we all reacted to what we'd seen and done. Luther, Sid, and I were staying at my father's house at the time. I was trying to convince them to settle in Duluth. I didn't know what I'd do if they left. We needed each other; no one else understood what it was like over there. Everyone thought that since we still looked the same, we were the same people inside." He laughed, and then sighed. "For me, it was a terrible transition.

"One evening, I got very drunk. I started some stupid fight with Sid and eventually he and Luther left. Amanda wasn't living with us at the time. She'd already moved out.

And Dad had gone out to walk the dog. I don't even remember it happening. Dad said I met him at the front gate naked and waving my service revolver. He tried to get it away from me and drag me inside before the neighbors noticed what was happening. London Road isn't exactly a secluded spot. Somehow—I still don't see how this is even possible—I shot the dog. He'd been given to me on my fifteenth birthday and I loved him like my life. The next day I was on an airplane to Wisconsin. Dad had a friend at the clinic in Green Dells. Luckily, he had the presence of mind to put a cover story in the paper. Some people we knew were on the same flight so he couldn't lie about the destination—just the ultimate destination.

"I'd been accepted at Stanford for the beginning of winter term. I still hoped I might be able to make it, but my recovery took longer than anyone expected. The doctors helped, but they didn't cure me. I did that myself. I also made some good friends while I was there. One woman in particular, an old Italian lady—Anna Casati—used to talk to me every night after dinner. She told me things about the history of this country I'd never heard before. If anyone is responsible for my interest in politics, she is. When I finally got to Stanford, I couldn't get enough American history. It became my major and eventually the basis for my Ph.D." He turned and looked thoughtfully out the window.

"The problem is that mental illness, as viewed by the American public, automatically disqualifies one for political office. It's even worse now than when Senator Eagleton was dumped by George McGovern. You have to understand that our national character is essentially middle class. It's highly suspicious. That means, anything we don't immediately understand—anything that doesn't fit the common mold—is suspect. It doesn't matter that there *is* no absolute norm for human behavior or that our electoral process is completely hollow."

"But you said in your Labor Day speech . . ."

Jack laughed. "This government runs on one thing, Sophie. Influence. It always has, always will. In public, I may appear to be a highly principled, ideological man. In private, I am as cynical a pragmatist as you will ever find. If I succeed at convincing the electorate that I'm Jimmy Stewart headed to Washington to restore The Dream, good for me. If I have to pay lip service to all the going superstitions of the day—right now they're called *family values*—I'll do that, too. In this nation, even to look outside our *cage* is an immoral act. We must dearly love the sight of our own prison bars, they're so comforting. I don't believe in the fairy tales our kids learn in high school history. I think it would be better to tell them the truth, but that's not one of our current values. However, I do believe in the power of the single, truly elegant idea. No matter what problems I've had in my past, I'm going to get elected, Sophie. And I'm going to be a good—no, make that a great—senator."

She felt the intensity behind his bright eyes. And she couldn't help but believe him. The only question that still bothered her was where did the real man leave off and the image begin? "I'd never do anything to prevent that dream, Jack. Surely you know that."

He picked up the dagger-shaped letter opener and began playing with it. "Thank you. I'm going to take you at your word. You deserved an explanation. It's not a period in my life that others can understand, so I don't generally talk about it. I've taken a risk telling you all this. Don't let me down." Abruptly, he stood.

"One question," said Sophie.

"Yes?"

"I just need to hear you say it. You didn't have anything to do with these murders, did you?"

Jack shook his head. "You know, I've always found it strange, this manly American preoccupation with physical courage. The only real courage that matters in life is moral. No. I didn't murder my father or Ryan or Sydney."

"Do you believe in God, Jack?"

He smiled. "Mark Twain thought that if there was a God, he was evil. No, Sophie. I don't. But don't go telling that to *The Washington Post*."

30

Late that same afternoon, Sophie drove her car into the dirt parking lot at Castle Rock Tavern. She'd survived tea with Amanda earlier in the day and was now ready for a good, relaxing meal. Amanda had been understanding when she'd explained why she and Bram were taking a room in town. She'd even encouraged it. Still, Sophie felt a certain guilt about leaving at a time like this. Over the long afternoon, that feeling had turned into a permanent queasiness in the pit of her stomach. Even though her mind anticipated a wonderful, juicy steak, she knew her digestion was on the verge of rebellion.

On the front deck she spotted Bram leaning against one of the wood pillars, watching several children collect driftwood from the beach. "Hi," she shouted, sliding out of the car seat. "I found three hotels."

He turned when he heard her voice. "We only need one."

"Don't be cute. I thought we could discuss them and then call for a reservation." She stepped up on the deck and gave him a kiss. "You smell like a carp."

"Thank you."

"Were you waiting for me long?"

"Actually, I just said goodbye to Amanda. She left a few minutes ago."

"That's funny. I didn't see her car."

Bram pulled open the heavy door. "You came on the expressway. She took the scenic drive." He led her to a table in the back.

"Where are your fishing buddies?"

"Steve drove into town to get his wife. Ted decided to go

along for the ride. They should be back any minute." He sat down and handed Sophie a menu.

"What was Amanda doing here?"

"When we arrived, she was sitting at the bar, drinking. She came over to the table, but said she couldn't stay. She seemed pretty agitated. Said she needed to get up to Two Harbors to see Claire right away."

"Then why didn't she take the expressway?"

Bram shook his head. "Yeah, I thought about that, too. Maybe she had to stop by the house first. You just came from there, right? I assume you brought our suitcases. By the way, is Luther back yet?"

"He was released a few hours ago. Amanda brought him home and he went straight to bed. He looked completely worn out."

"That was quick. Someone must have gotten a judge to charge him and post bail right away. That's no small feat." He waved at a waitress.

"Amanda said she had a good lawyer, but I know it was Jack's doing. He's got a lot of friends in this town."

"Lucky Luther."

Sophie wasn't so sure. She felt ill-at-ease about leaving him there all alone. But Alice would be back soon. "This may sound kind of strange, but I think he may have been safer if he'd stayed in jail."

Bram nodded at the menu. "Let's order an appetizer. I'm starving."

"All I want is coffee."

The waitress arrived with two glasses of water.

"I'd like a large draft beer and an order of your famous homemade onion rings. My wife here, the ascetic, would like a cup of coffee. Black. And something to flog herself with. An old rope would be fine."

The waitress cocked her head. "Yes, sir." She walked off, muttering something under her breath.

"I've been doing a lot of thinking today," said Sophie, watching the waitress disappear into the bar.

"Listen, sweetheart, the police don't go arresting people unless they have a pretty good reason. I know Luther is one of your dearest friends, but have you considered that he might actually be guilty? You can bet we don't have all the facts."

"I realize that."

"But what? Something's still bothering you. What is it?"

"Well, I had a long talk with Jack this morning. I asked him point-blank if he had anything to do with the murders."

"And?"

"He pleaded not guilty. Said he didn't murder his father, Sydney, or Ryan."

"And you don't believe him?"

"No, that's just it. I do. But don't you find it strange that he left out Lars Olson?"

"I don't know. No, not really."

"But think about it for a minute. Every one of these murders could easily have been committed by a woman—with the exception of Olson's. I know Wardlaw said it was possible that a woman could have done that, too, but she'd have to be pretty strong and agile to get up on that bridge. It wouldn't have been easy."

"You think the murderer was a man, then?"

"I think the person who murdered Olson was a man, yes. I'm not so sure about the rest."

"Two murderers? Let me get this straight. You think Jack might have murdered Olson, but not the other three?"

"I think it's a definite *maybe*." She leaned back as the waitress set her coffee down in front of her.

Bram took a long sip of beer. "Kind of farfetched. Where'd you come up with this?"

Sophie scratched her head. "Well, as I think about it, it must be something Luther said. When we talked last night, he mentioned that he was pretty sure he knew who was behind everything. It was one of his family or friends. He said he hoped this person wouldn't get caught because he understood the motivation. Even sympathized. The thing is, he said he'd be a willing scapegoat if the police arrested him. I know Luther isn't your typical, run-of-the-mill fellow, but that's completely out of character. Unless?"

"Unless what?"

"Unless the murderer was Amanda. Or his daughter, Chelsea. Those are the only two people he would willingly give up his freedom for. When he threw in the words family and *friends*, it was just a way to muddy the waters. He didn't want me to guess who he really suspected."

"You think Jack was working with one of them?"

"I guess I do."

Bram whistled. "Which?"

"That's just it. I don't know."

The waitress arrived with a large platter of onion rings. "Would either of you like ketchup?"

"No," said Bram, lifting a handful onto a small plate. "It's against my wife's religion. We'll wait to order dinner until our friends arrive."

The waitress stared at him for a moment. "Of course." She nodded, and then left.

"That's quite a theory, Sophie. I don't know how you're going to prove it."

"I don't either." She popped an onion ring into her mouth and looked gloomy.

Bram sipped his beer, his eyes straying to the front door. "Here they are," he said, standing up and waving two men and a woman over to the table. "Sophie, I'd like you to meet Ted Johnson. You already know Steve and Carol."

Sophie stood and smiled. As they all took their seats, she caught Bram's eye and motioned him aside. "Listen, honey, you'll probably think this is crazy, but I want to drive back to Brule House for a few minutes. It won't take me long."

"But Sophie—"

"Really. I just want to check on Luther. Make sure he's okay. He was asleep when I left. I'll be back in ten minutes."

Bram's face sank as he watched the onion rings rapidly disappear. "Maybe I should come with you."

"Absolutely not. You better get in there and fight for your food. I'll be back before you finish your beer."

"All right. But if I don't see that smiling face of yours in fifteen minutes, I'm coming after you."

"Fine." She grabbed her purse and disappeared out the tavern door.

Amanda pulled a thick file of papers out of a drawer in the living room desk. Limply, she carried it over and dumped it on the coffee table. Sitting down in one of the wing chairs, she lit a cigarette and watched the smoke rise into the darkened room. Claire had been smoking too much lately. She said stress weakened her resolve. Well, two could use that excuse. Out of the corner of her eye, she caught a flutter of movement. "Who's there?" she called, turning her head. Someone had hesitated and then stopped in the shadowy archway.

"It's only me," said Luther, stepping into the dim light. He was holding a bottle of Scotch in one hand and a nearly empty glass in the other. "I didn't expect to see you back here so early."

Amanda studied the glowing tip of her cigarette. "I forgot some papers I needed."

"Is that right? Well, I suppose since you're here, I should tell you the big news."

"What are you talking about? What news?"

He sat down opposite her. "Nothing terribly important. It's only that I've discovered who's responsible for all these murders."

Amanda's body stiffened. "Don't joke about something so important."

"I'm not joking."

She watched him sip his drink. "All right. I'll bite. What's your theory?"

"It's not theory. I've known for quite some time, but I haven't said anything. It didn't seem pertinent. Now it does."

"Who? How?"

"Why, darling, I've rarely seen you grow monosyllabic so early in the evening. It usually takes two or three brandies before you lose your wonderful way with words."

"Stop it. I hate it when you drink too much. Just tell me what you think you know."

He tossed back the remainder of the glass. "Still the disbeliever." He clicked his tongue.

"Don't play with me, Luther."

"No? Perhaps you're right. The direct approach is always best. All right: envelope please." He whipped a piece of typing paper out of his pocket. "And the winner is?" With great flourish he stood, flapping the paper in front of him. "Jack Grendel."

Amanda's wariness turned instantly to anger. "Jack? What kind of game is this? You actually think you can get away with accusing my brother? I won't stand for it, do you hear me? What's that piece of paper you're holding?"

"This?" he said, dangling it enticingly. "It was pushed under my bedroom door while I was taking my nap. You don't recognize it by any chance, do you?"

Amanda grabbed for it but Luther quickly stuffed it back into his pocket.

"Bastard!"

"Sticks and stones. No need to get huffy. I'll even tell you what it says. The note was addressed to me. It said, and I quote: *If you want to know who's behind the pig murders, meet me at the lighthouse at seven-thirty. Come alone.*"

"And was it signed?"

"No. It was not."

"Then how do you know it's from Jack?"

"Trust me. I know. You see, I imagine I'm going to be the last little piggy. This is his clever way of getting me down there alone. Perhaps I should tell you something I failed to mention to the police. The day of the barbecue, I saw him come out of my study a few minutes before Sid's body was found. He, of course, didn't see me. At least I don't think he did. Earlier in the day I'd seen him grab that rat poison from under the kitchen sink. All week I've been watching him play out his little game. He's guilty, all right. The only question is, does he have an accomplice?"

Amanda's eyes followed him as he dropped down on the couch. "Have you told anyone about your suspicions?"

"I'm no snitch," he said petulantly. He poured himself

another inch of Scotch. "But I find this all terribly fascinating."

The grandfather clock in the foyer struck seven.

"Oh, deary me. It's almost the witching hour. By any chance would you care to join me?"

"Me? But the note said to come alone."

"Oh, come on, sweetie. I'm not walking alone into a trap. You know I never follow rules I don't like. If the study of philosophy has taught me anything, it's taught me how to rationalize brilliantly. I'll meet him there, all right, but you'll be waiting outside. What do you say?"

Amanda seemed to be thinking. "All right. That sounds like a good plan." Her voice grew more confident. "But I should take some protection. Maybe I should bring along a gun."

"A gun? Excellent idea. I'll get one for you." He jumped up and hurried back to his study, returning a few moments later. "Here." He handed it to her. "It's completely loaded. You can check it if you want."

"No need."

"Splendid. It warms my heart to see how much you trust me." He downed the last bit of Scotch. "You can wait in the woods and watch to see who comes into the lighthouse. If you think I'm in any danger, come up right away. I'm *dying* to know what Jack has to say for himself, aren't you?" He giggled. "No pun intended."

"Hello?" called Sophie, stepping quietly into the front foyer. "Anybody here?" She could hear the radio on in the kitchen.

"Oh, it's you," said Alice, walking briskly out of the dining room carrying a vase of fresh-cut zinnias. "I thought you'd gone out."

"I did. Where's Luther?" She attempted to sound as casual as possible.

Alice set the vase down on a Louis XVI table and stood back admiringly. "Why, I think he and Mrs. Jorensen left about fifteen minutes ago."

"Do you know where they went?"

"Well," said Alice, a slight hesitation in her voice, "I wasn't eavesdropping or anything, but I did hear Mr. Jorensen say something about the lighthouse."

The lighthouse? thought Sophie. "Were they going for a walk together?"

Alice wiped her hands carefully on her apron. "I don't know. But something did kind of scare me. I probably shouldn't be saying anything, but with everything that's been happening . . . "

"What?" said Sophie. "Tell me!"

"Well, I'm pretty sure it's too late in the day for the shooting range in Knife River to be open. It'll be dark soon. See, the thing is, Mrs. Jorensen had a gun."

"A gun?" The significance of her words took a moment to sink in. "Listen carefully, Alice. Call the police. Tell them to come to the lighthouse right away. Then call Castle Rock Tavern. Ask to speak to my husband. Tell him what you just told me and that I've gone after them."

"But what should I say to the police?"

"I don't know. I don't care. Tell them you heard a gunshot. Anything. Just get them out here!"

Alice rushed off, shaking her head.

Without stopping to consider the potential consequences, Sophie flew out of the house and down the front lawn. It was the quickest, if not the easiest way. She didn't want to admit it, but deep in her gut, she knew Luther was in danger.

31

Luther rested uncomfortably on a long wooden bench in a small room at the top of the lighthouse. Absently, he brushed a fly away from his face. Amanda had assured him she would wait at least half an hour. If no one showed, she'd come up and together they would decide what to do next. Perfect, thought Luther. Absolutely perfect.

As the minutes ticked by, his back began to ache. He got up and leaned out one of the deep windows overlooking the bay. Even in the growing dusk, he could clearly see the treacherous rocks that spread around the base of the lighthouse like a web. For a moment he was mesmerized by the lovely patterns emerging from the water. Shifting his gaze to the woods, he spied a dark figure approaching through the tall grass. He fumbled in his pocket for his glasses, but before he could get them on, the figure moved into the clearing and disappeared. "Damn," he muttered to himself. Rotten luck.

Sitting back down, he rubbed his sore eyes. Suddenly, his ears picked up the sound of footsteps on the stairs. He waited, his heart racing, as the footsteps reached the top and the door creaked slowly open.

"Sophie!" he cried, jumping to his feet. "What are you doing here?" He pulled her further into the room and shut the door. "Shhh." He put his finger to his lips. "Please. You've got to be quiet. I think I hear someone else coming."

Sophie was surprised by the hard edge of annoyance in his voice. She moved behind him. A few seconds later, the door opened again. Out of the darkness stepped Amanda, a gun in her hand. Quickly, Sophie reacted. "Put the gun down, Amanda. Don't drop it. Just lay it on the floor."

Amanda seemed confused. "Sophie? Is that you? I saw someone come in but I couldn't make out who it was. What are you doing here?"

Calmly, Sophie repeated, "Please. Just put the gun down. Everything's going to be okay."

Amanda laid the gun on the floor and backed up a step. "All right. Sure. I just had it for protection. But what's going on?"

Luther leaned down and grabbed it, stuffing it into his

sweater pocket. "I fear, dear Amanda, that Sophie has discovered the truth."

"What are you talking about?" She inched further backward, her eyes growing wide.

Luther sighed, his expression a curious mixture of sadness and elation. "Unfortunately, I believe she knows who's really been behind all these murders. I knew she'd put it together eventually. You shouldn't have underestimated her, my dear. You should have taken my advice and sent her packing days ago."

"I don't know what you're talking about. If you mean Jack, he's completely innocent."

"Jack?" laughed Luther. "Come on now. We're all friends here. You can drop the act."

"But Luther!"

"Save it for the police." He turned his full attention on Sophie. "Would you like to see something interesting? Look at this." He pulled the piece of typing paper out of his pocket. "Read it."

Sophie stepped closer to the window. The deep violet evening light was just bright enough to allow her to make out the words: *This little piggy went wee wee wee all the way home.* "My God," she said, looking up. "How did you get this?"

Luther scowled. "I felt Amanda slip it into my pocket on our way through the woods. You didn't know that, did you dear? I'm sure you were planning to put a bullet right between my eyes. Or were you going to threaten to kill me if I didn't jump to my death? What was the plan, dear wife? Either way my body would have been found broken on the rocks." He glanced again at Sophie. "It would've been difficult for her to leave her usual calling card unless she put it into my pocket before the murder."

"Sophie," said Amanda, her voice rising in panic, "none of this is true! You've got to believe me."

"It's no use," said Luther. "No one believes you anymore. I'm sick of covering for you. Sick to death of your lies. It's time to pay the piper."

Sophie was sure she heard more footsteps on the stairs.

Luther, obviously hearing the same sounds, abruptly pulled the gun out of his pocket. "Step away from the door," he whispered. "Hurry!"

A bright beam of light struck the windows behind them, illuminating the dim room with an eerie, stark luminescence.

A second later, the door burst open and Detective Wardlaw and another policeman moved in, guns drawn. "Put the gun down, Mr. Jorensen."

Luther seemed momentarily startled. "Why, of course. But you don't understand."

Sophie watched in stunned silence as Luther pulled Amanda between two of the windows, putting his arm tightly around her waist.

"Please, Mr. Jorensen. Don't do anything stupid. You can't escape. We've got sharpshooters surrounding the lighthouse. Do the intelligent thing. Let your wife go and give yourself up."

"What makes you think I want to get away?" He squeezed Amanda more tightly. "For your information, I was already issued a death sentence months ago. Do you think I'm even the least bit frightened of anything you can do to me?" He laughed, his eyes locking on Sophie's.

"And you. You've been the wild card all along. I never expected you to come for the opening of the restaurant. I thought it was all settled. You and Bram were too busy. It was safe for me to begin my final work. And then, there you were, wonderful, kind, funny Sophie, sitting in the Gasthaus, smiling your warmth and love at me, and, selfish man that I am, I couldn't bear to send you away. You don't know how alone I've been. I didn't realize it myself until I saw you. Chekhov was right: if a person is afraid of loneliness, he should never marry." His eyes began to tear.

"Sophie, can you understand? I never should have involved you in this. I never should have sent you those notes, but I was afraid Bram was going to take you away. I couldn't be alone anymore. I just couldn't!" His voice cracked. "I simply couldn't . . . die alone." He fought to keep his grip, his concentration. "You became my ace in the hole. I was going to use you to destroy Amanda. I tried to give you enough information to lead you in the direction I wanted. If my plan had worked, you'd have helped me put her in prison." He shook his head violently.

"Don't look at me like that! You think I have no conscience, but you're wrong. After what happened in the sauna the other day, I could see that what I'd started could no longer be controlled. I don't know who locked you in there, but given enough time, I would've found out. And I would have made them pay. The bottom line was you were no longer safe. As much as I needed you, somehow I had to make you leave! That's why I wrote that last note. I wanted to frighten you. But you're still here! Why didn't you follow my advice? You could have ruined everything!" His eyes looked momentarily wild and angry. With great effort, he struggled to compose himself. "It doesn't matter now. Nothing matters."

Sophie couldn't believe what she was hearing. The truth of his words flashed inside her mind like a match being struck in the darkness. She felt soiled. Angry.

Luther continued a bit more calmly, "You despise me now, don't you? Don't bother answering, I can see it written in your face. It's all right. But will you at least grant me a few moments? For some reason I feel the uncharacteristic need of a last confession. Perhaps it's really absolution I'm seeking, in which case, I will rest my case with you." His voice softened. "All right, will everyone kindly give me their attention." He laughed at the inanity of his request. Clearing his throat, he began, "Every person I killed was a worthless and immensely loathsome human being. I realize no judge would consider those considerable qualifications grounds for execution. But may I suggest that, in the abyss we call philosophy, a case can be made. George Bernard Shaw suggested that when a man kills a beast he calls it sport, but when that same beast tries to kill the man, we call it ferocity. The distinction between crime and justice is no greater.

"The first pig, Lars Olson, made a habit of seducing every female employee under the age of fifty. He made life

miserable not just for *them*, but for each of us who happened to work with him at UMD. Those he didn't care to
seduce, he merely tortured. His specialty was professional
humiliation. God, how I despised the sight of him. When I
began my leave of absence last summer, I swore I'd make
him pay for all the years he spent trying to undermine me.
The night he died, I stood watching from my car. Perhaps
I should have said a little prayer for his immortal soul, but
all I did was grin like an idiot." Angrily he kicked the
bench away from the wall. "You see, I think of myself as
a kind of cosmic vacuum cleaner. I'm not crazy, so don't
feel you need to feign sadness for a brilliant mind gone
bad. If I were insane, it might be easier for you to understand. Forgive the inveterate nature of a philosophy professor, but Nietzsche was right when he wrote: *'Many people
wait throughout their whole lives for the chance to be good
in their own fashion.'* I'd simply waited long enough. If I
could rid the world of a few vermin before I went, good for
me." Still holding a terrified Amanda tightly in his grip, he
wiped the sweat from his forehead.

"And Herman Grendel?" prodded Wardlaw.

Luther twisted his lips into a smile. "Yes, I suppose you
do have an interest in this confession, don't you? Well,
you'll be glad to hear, I've told you the truth all along. I
guess that was a mistake, because, somehow, you knew.
God knows how, but you did." He shook his head in a kind
of respectful amazement. "All right, where were we? Ah
yes. Herman Grendel." He cleared his throat and resumed
his professorial tone. "Kierkegaard said we need ask only
two questions. Is it possible? And can I do it? Herm was an
execrable human being, totally devoid of natural human
emotion. Never, in the twenty-some years I was married to
his daughter, did he ever let me forget that I wasn't good
enough for her. I never made enough money—which, for
Herm, was the bottom line. The air smelled sweeter to me
the instant his soul left his putrefying body. I hated him
more than any other human being I've ever met and I hope
to God I sent him straight to hell. And Sydney." He spoke
softly into Amanda's ear. "That was a bonus. At first I had

someone else in mind for the third little piggy, but when Sydney appeared, it seemed only natural to turn my attention to him. Did you know he raped our daughter when she was only twelve?"

Amanda struggled to look at him. Her eyes grew wide with horror.

"I kept it from you because I thought it would only cause you pain. I tried for years to get Chelsea to see a therapist, but she refused. All I could do was force him to leave town. In the end, that simply wasn't enough. When he came back here all puffed up because he had enough dirt on your brother to blackmail him for the rest of his fucking political life, I saw my chance. I would have preferred to peel his skin slowly off his body, roast him over an open fire, but with time constraints being what they were, I felt rat poison was a reasonable alternative. You'll be glad to know he died in acute pain. I only wish it could have taken longer. As he lay dying on the floor, for some reason I thought of that old Portuguese proverb. You know the one. *Visits always give such pleasure—if not the arrival, then the departure.*"

Amanda made a move to break away from him. Angrily, Luther clutched her arm and drew her back hard against his chest. "No you don't, darling. You have to listen to this."

Amanda's eyes pleaded with Sophie for her to do something! Wardlaw quickly caught her attention and nodded for her to remain quiet.

"And then, we mustn't forget Ryan," continued Luther. "The little piggy who had none. I believe I first conceived this while sitting in the bathtub one night eating a ham sandwich. Ryan would, of course, have disapproved. Such a self-righteous, basically priggish little weasel. At the barbecue, Sydney gorged himself on roast pork. Thusly, he became the piggy who ate roast pork. A bit broad perhaps, but then there it is. Ryan, in contrast, being an abstemious vegetarian, had none. Did you know, any of you, how much I despised Woodthorpe on general principle? He embodied everything I hate in my own gender. Too facilely charming. A liar. An athletic body that he used to his own sexual ad-

vantage. Outwardly, he appeared to be the sensitive, liber-
ated, *new man*, but it was all cerebration. Nothing internal.
Whatever ideals he thought he held, he was going to fuck
Jenny over the same way men have fucked women over for
centuries. And who was going to be his next victim? None
other than our daughter, dear wife." His voice began to
shake. "The idea of his touching Chelsea nauseated me.
This consummate, burbling, opinionated, self-righteous fun-
gus was going to leave the woman he had just impregnated
to destroy our daughter's life! His death was going to be
my last gift to her. God, how I loved the sound of the bullet
hitting his chest." His smile was almost serene.

"But the crowning glory," he waved the gun in the air,
"was going to be paying you back, my dear Amanda, for
all the years of silence and isolation you've given me. I
didn't get married to live my life alone!" He tightened his
grip around her waist and brought the gun down close to
the side of her face. "I thought the piggy poem was a nice
touch. God, I mean I've had to listen to that cretin, Claire
Van Dorn, wax eloquent for months on the raptures of children's poetry. It was only fitting to show her what an un-
sullied *adult* imagination could do. I also thought it would
directly implicate a feminist. I mean, don't women call men
chauvinist *pigs* anymore? Did I miss a jargon change somewhere? But then I suppose one must never be surprised at
the police department's lack of sociological understanding.
Well, no matter. You'll pay now, my dear, for all the years
you *tolerated* my presence. You think I didn't know about
your little love tryst with that pathetic cow?" His voice fell
to a whisper. "At first I was simply jealous of the time you
spent with her. But shortly after Sydney arrived, he told me
what was really going on. You remember how good he was
at ferreting out secrets? Listening at doors has never been
my style. I don't mind telling you, old Sid had a good
laugh at my expense. I'm surprised he didn't take out a
full-page ad in the local newspaper." Luther pulled her back
hard against the wall. "How could you do that to me, darling? I gave you my love. I gave you my intelligence. I

brought my need to you like a little boy with a precious gift."

"I did love you!" pleaded Amanda, finally breaking her silence. "But you never understood that. Nothing was ever enough! You wanted someone to worship, Luther. All these years and you could never forgive me for being human! Don't you see? You can only worship something that can't talk back!"

Luther pushed the gun further into the soft part of her neck. *"Oh most pernicious woman. Smiling damned villain!"*

"But that's the truth," she cried. "My truth. Luther, surely you must see we couldn't go on living together. I tried to talk to you about it. Remember, last year? We spoke about a separation. We were poisoning each other. We have been for years."

Tears began to stream down his cheeks. He batted at them with the hand holding the gun. "I see nothing of the kind. But it doesn't matter anymore. Hate and revenge have been the only things keeping me alive. Now we're almost done with it. I think I should tell you, dear Amanda, what I had planned for you. I knew that once you saw no one was coming up here tonight, you'd come up yourself. I'd decided to jump to my death with that note safely tucked away in my pocket. Did you realize Alice saw us leave together? She couldn't miss the gun in your hand. My death would have sealed your own destruction. Eventually, I'm confident, you would have been charged with all the murders. Sophie here would have seen to that. And"—he laughed—"you even played right into my hands with that swindle you managed from your Association. That was another little secret Sydney told me about. It almost made me think I should start listening at keyholes myself. Lucky for me, it gave you the perfect motive. Anyone who stood in the way of Jack's election became your target. You couldn't afford to have him lose because he'd take you down with him. Since I knew the truth about his breakdown, I was to become your final murder victim. By the way, I felt it was my obligation to inform the police about what was going

on. Anonymously, of course. Knowing your fate, I could
have gone to my grave a happy man!"

"Luther," she said softly, "have I caused you such pain?
Have I hurt you so badly?" Her voice was filled with aston-
ishment.

"Those people I killed, they weren't even human. But
you, *you* knew what you were doing. You betrayed me!"

"I would never have left you!"

Luther gasped. "But you left me *years* ago!" He pointed
the gun at Wardlaw, tears beginning to impair his vision.
"Now," he said, his mouth close to Amanda's ear, "climb
out that window. There's a metal ledge out there. You
won't fall. Do it!"

Amanda glared. "I can't!"

Luther pointed the gun directly at her. "Of course you
can. As I see it, you have two choices. Do what I say or
I'll shoot you right here."

Amanda backed up, calculating her options. "All right,"
she said, swallowing hard. Carefully, she hoisted herself
through the opening.

Luther crawled after her shouting, "Wardlaw, tell your
men not to fire. They might hit an innocent person—if they
can tell the difference."

The floodlight followed in the darkness as Luther edged
toward her.

"What are you going to do?"

"I'm going to cause you some pain, Amanda dear." He
grabbed her ankle.

"Luther," she called. "Think what you're doing! If I'm
going to die, I can't change that. But will you listen for one
second?"

He stopped, balancing on his knees, his face black
against the beam of light behind him.

Amanda spoke slowly. "I haven't always been a good
wife. I know that. I know now I've hurt your terribly. If
you want us both to die on those rocks down there, I can't
stop you. But the truth is, I've never stopped loving you.
The form may have altered—"

"No!" he cried, closing his eyes. "I won't listen to this."

"I'm not lying!" she shouted. "I'm so sorry. We've spoken such different languages. We've each had such different needs. I didn't understand." Her eyes blurred with tears.

"God," cried Luther, looking up at the sky, "why have you always been so silent?" With his whole body convulsing, his eyes seemed to turn inward. "No more," he whispered. Releasing his grip on her ankle, he fell forward, dropping into the abyss.

Amanda grasped at the spot where a second before he had knelt. With her fists clenched, she pounded the cold metal, her guttural cries barely recognizable.

Sophie watched quietly as Wardlaw and the other policeman helped Amanda back inside. Gently, they led her through the door and down the steep steps to the bottom. Sophie leaned out one of the windows, noticing that the beam of light had finally been switched off. The beach seemed a vast, bleached wasteland in the weak moonlight. Carefully, she climbed through the opening and crawled out onto the ledge herself. She could just make out the form of Luther's body broken on the rocks below. Men were climbing out to him. How could this man, a man she'd loved and trusted, have ended up down there? How could he have been responsible for four murders? He'd lied. Manipulated. And yet, even now, she couldn't think of him that way. She shivered on the ledge as she watched the police lead Amanda away through the tall grass. Looking helplessly up at the moon, Sophie drew her arms around herself and cried.

32

"I thought I might find you in here," said Bram, unzipping his leather bombardier jacket. He held a mug of coffee in one hand, the remnants of a sandwich stuffed into his side pocket.

Sophie sat hunched over Luther's desk, staring out the window at the bright, cloudless day. She would have felt more comfortable if the weather had at least attempted to replicate her mood. "How was Amanda?"

"I picked her up at the police station and took her to Jack's house. She said she simply couldn't come back here. Not after last night."

Sophie nodded. "I keep thinking this is all a bad dream and I'm going to wake up."

Bram sat down in a chair, wrapping his fingers around the warm mug. "I'm so sorry about all this, honey. I haven't known these people as long as you have, but—"

"All my life," said Sophie, shaking her head in disbelief. "I've known Amanda and Jack all my life. And Luther? I loved him, Bram. Like a brother." She turned her face away.

"You know," he said, his voice gentle, "Jack stopped me in the drive after Amanda had gone into the house. He was on his way to see Chelsea."

"I wonder how she's taking all this."

"Jack said she was pretty shook up. Both about her father *and* Ryan. Anyway, what he wanted to tell me was that it seems Nora was responsible for locking us in that sauna. She thought we were getting a little too snoopy and wanted to scare us off. According to her, she was on her way back to let us out when she got waylaid by some guy who insisted she talk to him about a political fund-raiser she's supposed to attend next week. Remember, Jack had a staff meeting that morning? Well, by the time she did make it back, she saw Luther carrying you out of the smoke and laying you on the ground. She got so freaked, she simply left. Never said a word to anyone. But apparently, last night she got pretty drunk. Told Jack the whole story. She also admitted to switching off the light in the attic the other evening. Jack's more than a little worried. If we say anything about the sauna incident to the police, she could be charged with attempted murder."

Again, Sophie let her gaze drift out the window. "I don't want that. As far as I'm concerned, I'd like to let the whole incident drop."

Bram nodded his agreement. "Me too. Oh, and Claire drove up as I was carrying in Amanda's overnight case. It seemed like they wanted to be alone so I didn't stay." He paused. "I can't help but wonder . . ."

"Wonder what?"

"Did Luther know about them? Was that why he hated Amanda so much?"

Sophie gave a deep sigh. "He knew, but only since last Monday. What pushed him over the edge was much more complex than simple jealousy." She picked up a picture she'd taken of Luther and Amanda many years before. Luther was sitting on the deck of a large sailboat, holding a bottle of beer. Amanda was standing behind him, pretending to feed him a hot dog. It had been a glorious time. Full of high spirits. They'd spent the entire day together out on the lake. Why had Luther saved it all these years? He must have been looking at it very recently. For some reason it made Sophie think of what Virginia Woolf had once written. *The beauty of the world has two edges, one of laughter, one of anguish, cutting the heart asunder.*

Bram waited as she studied the photo.

"The difference between love and need is sometimes a fine line. I think Luther knew if it wasn't for his illness,

Amanda would leave him. He couldn't stand being pitied, and yet, he needed her help."

"Her help?"

Sophie nodded. "He needed her help to die."

Bram shuddered. "God, that's awful."

She put the picture back inside the drawer. "But you know, knowing Luther as I did, I think the worst thing for him was that, in some part of himself, he still loved her. In the end, that love humiliated him."

Bram shook his head. "I wonder what's going to happen to Claire and Amanda now? Wardlaw said they'd illegally appropriated Association funds to help Jack's campaign."

Sophie closed her eyes and leaned back against the chair. Where was all of this going to end? "I suppose if Jack's elected, they'll be able to repay it."

"With the storm that's brewing over the year he spent at the Saltzman Clinic, it looks pretty doubtful. Not to mention what's come out about Grendel Shipping's involvement in the illegal dumping of chemicals in Lake Superior. Jack was executive vice president the year it happened. People don't believe he didn't know."

"Terrific. Just terrific. What I don't get is how did the press find out about Jack in the first place? I mean, surely Amanda and Chelsea wouldn't say anything."

"I asked Jack about that. Seems Ryan Woodthorpe had mailed a bunch of secret documents to a friend in Clouquet with specific instructions that if anything ever happened to him, the friend would hustle it posthaste to the nearest reporter. It's a damn shame, too, if you ask me. Jack would have been a great senator. But he's a realist. I think he knows his political days are numbered. He was even talking about taking a teaching position at some college out West. He mentioned that he wants Chelsea to come live with him. He said he's never been one to push her, but he feels she needs to face the world with more than a high school diploma. From the way he talked, Chelsea was ready to leave as soon as she could appoint a new CEO for the company."

The phone began to ring.

"Do you want me to answer that?" asked Bram.

"No, it's okay." She picked it up. "Hello? Well, hi! No, you're not interrupting anything." She held her hand over the mouthpiece. "It's your daughter," she mouthed. "Sure, I understand. What? When?" She looked up. "He said that?" Her eyes slowly widened. "Did you get the flight number? No, we'll be back tomorrow afternoon. We're leaving first thing in the morning and driving straight home. Right. What? Say that again? Margie, have you thought about this? I see. All right then. Sure, I'll tell him. Thanks. See you soon, kiddo." She hung up.

"Didn't she want to talk to me?" asked Bram. He sounded a little hurt.

"She was in a hurry." Sophie's expression was so odd, Bram rose and leaned across the desk, grabbing her hand. "What's wrong? Are you all right?"

"I don't know. I'm not sure."

"Is it Margie? Is she—"

"She's fine."

"Then what? Tell me!"

"It's Rudy. He called our house last night. I guess he tried to call here, but there wasn't any answer. Margie talked to him."

"That's great! What did he say?"

She swallowed hard. "He's coming to Minneapolis. Flying in tomorrow night. He's enrolled at the University of Minnesota this fall and wanted to know if he could stay with us."

"You're kidding? That's incredible! See, what'd I tell you?" He narrowed one eye. "I thought you said he'd be going to that Bible college?"

"I guess not."

"Norm is letting him come?"

"So it would seem."

Bram scratched his chin. "Did you get a flight number?"

"Honey, there's something else."

"What do you mean?"

She took a deep breath. "Margie told him he could have her room."

"Huh? I don't understand. Why would she say that?"

"She's moving out. She and that new boyfriend of hers are going to live together. In St. Cloud."

"Over my dead body!"

"They signed an apartment lease yesterday morning."

Bram sank down in his chair. "I'll hire a lawyer."

For a moment they both stared blankly at the wall.

"Looks like this is going to be an interesting year," said Sophie, her voice too stunned to register emotion.

"What's that new boyfriend's name?"

"Lancelot."

"You're kidding?" He groaned. "Forget the lawyer. I'm buying a shotgun."

The Jane Lawless series by

ELLEN HART

Published by Ballantine Books.
Available in your local bookstore.